THE TR

MASQUERADE

CAROLE STRACHAN

INDEPENDENT INNOVATIVE INTERNATIONAL

Published by Cinnamon Press
Meirion House
Tanygrisiau
Blaenau Ffestiniog
Gwynedd LL41 3SU
www.cinnamonpress.com

ISBN 978-1-910836-25-5
British Library Cataloguing in Publication Data. A CIP record for this book can be obtained from the British Library.
Designed and typeset in Garamond by Cinnamon Press. Cover design by Adam Craig © Adam Craig.
Cinnamon Press is represented by Inpress and by the Welsh Books Council in Wales.
Printed in Poland
The publisher gratefully acknowledges the support of the Welsh Books Council

Acknowledgements

The Turn of the Screw Opus 54 (Myfanwy Piper/Benjamin Britten) © Copyright 1955 by Hawkes & Son (London) Ltd. Reproduced by permission of Boosey & Hawkes Music Publishers Ltd.

Eugene Onegin Opus 24 [English] (Alexsandr Pushkin/Pyotr Tchaikovsky/David Lloyd-Jones) © Copyright 1971 by Schauer & May Ltd. Reproduced by permission of Boosey & Hawkes Music Publishers Ltd.

Sea Fever by John Masefield Reproduced by permission of The Society of Authors as the Literary Representative of the Estate of John Masefield.

And, after all, what is a lie? 'T is but
The truth in masquerade; and I defy
Historians, heroes, lawyers, priests, to put
A fact without some leaven of a lie.

Lord Byron, Don Juan

Dedicated to my brother, Andrew

1958-1984

THE TRUTH IN MASQUERADE

Prologue: January 2006

It was a wretched end to a gripping story. Later, Anna came to believe it was the turning point after which her life with Edwyn was never the same.

The barge had disappeared into the darkness, moving slowly towards the Thames estuary, its strange cargo settled on a makeshift mattress for the long journey back to sea. Though the river was still alive with the lights of rescue crafts and camera crews, there was little to see now. She huddled against him, hoping his closeness would warm her after the chilling hours of watching and waiting, hoping for good news. Feeling no reciprocal squeeze on her arm, and aware he'd been quiet for some time, she looked up to see his head bowed, his face tired and worn.

He felt disheartened. Despite his efforts, the unyielding past would not give up its secrets. He'd hoped that witnessing the communal effort to save London's whale would lift his morale, but was subdued by a nagging unease over how it would turn out. The winching of the frightened, disorientated creature from the pontoon onto the barge had been a pitiful sight and he feared the trauma of the rescue would be fatal.

He felt Anna shudder alongside him and saw her long fair hair fluttering in the wintry breeze. He knew that after his bitter rebuke the night before he should offer her some sign of reconciliation.

'Come on,' he said. 'They're doing the best they can for her—let's go into the warm and get a drink.'

They picked their way through the dispersing crowds and headed towards the Lamplighter. The pub was filling up with other shivering whale-watchers and the usual Saturday night drinkers. Anna hoped that the upbeat weekend atmosphere would prove a tonic for them both. She was saddened by the plight of the whale and still smarting from Edwyn's uncharacteristic outburst.

She found a small table in the corner near a window from where she could watch him ordering their drinks at the bar. He looked well, his striking silver hair just beginning to thin, but he'd lost weight these last few months and she realised with a pang that he'd aged. She thought he'd feel her eyes on his back and would look round, but he stayed resolutely staring into the large gilded mirror behind the counter on which he leant.

She loved this pub, its walls lit by oversized dressing room light bulbs, covered in photographs of well-known opera singers and posters from long past productions. Sammy, the landlord, had spent thirty years as a barman at the Royal Opera House, and five years earlier had opened the pub after which he'd always hankered. He was there tonight in one of his signature silk waistcoats, chatting to regulars, telling the scurrilous stories for which he was notorious.

Edwyn brought over their drinks and sat beside her. Looking drained and distant, he avoided her gaze and looked distractedly across the room. She searched his face for clues of what was wrong, but found only disconcerting blankness.

He'd been fine the previous day when he set off to pursue a new lead for his research, though he'd been vague about where he was going.

Some dusty archive or other, she'd assumed.

But on his return, his hostile reaction to her eye-catching display in the hallway had shocked her.

'He was always squirrelling stuff away in his damn boxes and God knows what might be in there.'

She'd loved her father-in-law and mourned his death. The boxes, carved from birch wood and poplar and painted

8

with Jim's distinctive designs, were so much part of who he had been, she felt it right to show them off as a tribute to him. Briar roses, daffodils, forget-me-nots, sunflowers, peacock feathers, butterflies—gathered together and arranged on shelves in the narrow alcove in their hallway, she thought the effect was pleasing, so Edwyn's irritation was bewildering.

His father had died before Christmas and he'd shown no inclination to begin sorting through the old family home, so that day, Anna had decided to make a start herself. Many of the boxes were empty but some were a jumble of the detritus collected over a long life and she'd assumed that one day, when he felt ready, Edwyn would want to explore them, might treasure their contents.

They rarely argued—this was unfamiliar territory—but she knew it would fall to her to mend the fault line between them.

'I've got my first music call on Monday,' she said.

Edwyn looked up with surprise: 'You're starting early.'

'Yes,' she replied. 'The music's tricky so I want to be sure I've got it sung in to my voice before we start rehearsals in July. I'm aiming to be off the book by the time I get to Myddleton.'

'Are you looking forward to it?' he asked, taking a sip of wine and studying her closely for the first time.

'I am,' she said cautiously. 'I love Britten's music and *The Turn of the Screw* is such a wonderful ghost story—together they make a terrifically spooky opera.'

'And you're to be its unreliable heroine.'

'Yes', she said, with a smile. 'The Governess.'

Edwyn gazed into the ruby red wine in front of him and considered the journey that Anna and the Governess would take, a venture beginning in hope and anticipation and ending in dread and despair. The thought made him wince; a mixture of pity and remorse he didn't fully understand.

He became aware of activity and shouts outside the window. The door of the pub opened and a group of people came in, led by a large man whose jacket bore the distinctive badge of the British Divers Marine Life Rescue. His dark hair was wet and matted and he was visibly exhausted.

'We've lost her,' he said. 'She's gone.'

There was a gasp of collective disappointment.

'It was always touch and go,' he said, 'though she seemed to be doing well, but then she went downhill fast and...'

His voice trailed into a silence eventually broken by a low murmur as conversations resumed in muted tones.

'She lost her way,' Edwyn said after a while, twiddling the stem of his glass. 'Separated from her family. She must have been terribly scared.'

Anna nodded and blinked, and he could see from the tears shining in her pale blue eyes that she was upset, but he could find no words of comfort, the whale's sad end only compounding his own desolation.

The unexpected ringing of the pub bell made him look over to the bar where Sammy was calling for quiet, his puffy face more flushed than usual.

'Let's have a moment's hush for the whale,' he said, and Edwyn saw him reach down to the CD player he kept behind the counter. Straining to listen as the bar gradually fell quiet, he heard the low notes of a piano chord and saw instant recognition in Anna's face.

'*Sea Fever*, John Ireland,' she whispered, sitting back to enjoy the muscular baritone voice filling the room with the haunting ballad.

"I must go down to the seas again, to the lonely sea and the sky,
And all I ask is a tall ship and a star to steer her by;
And the wheel's kick and the wind's song and the white sail's
shaking,
And a grey mist on the sea's face, and a grey dawn breaking,"

From the first sonorous chord it drew him in, the music sometimes robust, at other times gentle, moving from anxious tenderness to pressing urgency. The steady rhythm of the piano accompaniment conjured the swell of the sea, while the voice part began tentatively, but gained confidence as the call of the ocean impressed itself on the singer.

"I must go down to the seas again, for the call of the running tide
Is a wild call and a clear call that may not be denied;
And all I ask is a windy day with the white clouds flying,
And the flung spray and the blown spume, and the sea-gulls
crying."

Edwyn sensed the melancholy, too; the reality that anyone 'going down to the sea' is inevitably leaving family and friends and native land.

And this singer could tell a story that was almost visual: from the barest pause it was clear that he had heard 'the seagulls crying' as he pondered the voyage of life.

"I must go down to the seas again, to the vagrant gypsy life,
To the gull's way and the whale's way where the wind's like a
whetted knife;
And all I ask is a merry yarn from a laughing fellow-rover,
And quiet sleep and a sweet dream when the long trick's over."

Anna loved the setting and the singer, admired his rich, subtle voice and his willingness to express the sentimental core of the song. She knew what skill it required to make something sound so effortless.

Sammy had judged perfectly the wistful mood of the room and the drinkers listened in rapt silence. The man from the rescue crew was unashamedly wiping his eyes, while the woman he'd sat with was patting his back, just as earlier he had patted and consoled the struggling whale.

Anna longed for Edwyn to reassure her that all was well, but though he was still there, sitting beside her, it was as if he had gone missing.

Her stomach lurched and she felt a sudden, strange fear that he no longer had need of her.

Chapter 1

Edwyn had said that Myddleton was a classic setting for a ghost story: a Victorian country house, set in sweeping grounds of park and woodland.

Anna had hoped to arrive in welcoming sunshine, not under darkening skies and with the threat of an impending storm. But the summer day's brightness had faded and apprehension overtook the mood of determined confidence in which she'd set off. She had never before made this journey alone without Edwyn waiting at the end of it, and as she drew closer to Oxford, the familiar route assumed an almost alien unfamiliarity.

She approached the house from the main entrance up a long, tree-lined drive, just wide enough to allow cars to pass in both directions. As the drive swung round to the right, Anna caught her first glimpse of the house and in her astonishment at what she saw, found herself braking abruptly. By lowering her head and peering through the windscreen, she could take in the whole of its extraordinary frontage: it was as if Keble College had been transported from the centre of Oxford and dropped in the countryside as an extravaganza of Rogue Gothic. Its red brick, patterned with banding of white and blue, and its pointed arches and plate glass, made it an ebullient combination of medievalism and Victorian modernity.

The drive curved up to the front of the house, where a circular area of neatly raked pale yellow gravel led to a handsome main entrance with a teak bench placed to the left of the door. Her agent had told her that the stage area was to be along the right-hand side of the house where there was a large paved terrace from which lawns, gardens and parkland fell away into the distance.

Further to the right, she could make out the shimmering waters of the lake and knew that it was there that she would find the Forester's cottage that would be home for the next few weeks. She needed to take a fork off the main drive and make her way round to the far side of the lake, but realised that she'd gone too far and had to reverse the short distance back to the turning she could see in her mirror. Once she'd turned into the lane, she stopped the car and got out, intending to pause a while and take in the surroundings, hoping to feel the same *"summer sweetness"* that Henry James's unnamed heroine described on her arrival at Bly.

In summers past she would not have been here.

For almost half her life, she'd had a base with Edwyn in Oxford whenever she needed it, and in early summer, when he was busy with exams and marking, she had normally spent any free weekends there, too. Now, she'd had to find a place for herself, on her own; somewhere she could live in privacy and reasonable comfort for over a month. She was still self-conscious about what had happened, fearing that even strangers could tell at a glance that she had only recently clambered out of the chasm which had opened in her life. She'd been glad to learn there was a cottage available for rent in the grounds of Myddleton, where she could bury herself in the countryside, away from the connections which would be painful in the nearby city.

Even now, six months on, she felt the brutal, shocking suddenness of it. Remembering the call from her agent that had brought her to Myddleton, Anna winced at the life changes so short a time had brought. On that cold, grey Saturday in December, Edwyn had been excited at the prospect of her appearing at Myddleton. At their home in Richmond, over coffee and croissants in their tiny conservatory, he'd described it to her with all the vivid detail and enthusiasm which characterised his academic work.

The house, he said, had been built in 1860 by a wealthy industrialist from the Welsh valleys; a man who'd always longed to retire to the gentle, rolling countryside of the Cotswolds. In 1878 it was bought by an Italian nobleman whose considerable wealth allowed him to create a luxurious retreat for his opera-singer wife, where they could entertain lavishly and she could recharge herself after exhausting tours.

In 1883, the Count embarked on a major development of the site, using the original architect, William Butterfield, and adding wings to the north and south, a clock tower, orangery and a small private theatre that was modelled on the Theatre Royal in Drury Lane. The names of famous composers were inscribed in its ornate mouldings, with Mozart holding pride of place over the centre of the stage.

Following Madame's death in 1900, the grieving widower retired to his family home in Sicily and the estate endured a sad succession of unsuitable owners, each one increasingly ill-equipped to maintain it. During the Second World War, it was requisitioned as a hospital, and then for over thirty years it was a shabby but respectable retirement home, until it was closed when fire gutted the first floor and caused the deaths of three elderly residents.

Thereafter, it remained shut up and cheerless until good fortune produced a saviour determined to restore Myddleton to at least some of its former glory and to make its charms accessible to anyone who shared his love of music.

Daniel Ennis had studied at New College and Edwyn had met him on a number of occasions when he'd returned for reunions. He'd made his fortune in the early years of the mobile phone revolution and had indulged his passion for opera by providing financial support for a couple of productions at Glyndebourne. When his company was bought out, he was wealthy enough to fulfil his dream of developing a small summer festival near his childhood home in Oxford.

When he first saw Myddleton, it had been empty and for sale for so long that even the agents who were marketing it had despaired of ever finding a buyer. They feared it was the wrong house in the wrong place: close to northern cities of industry and invention, like Leeds or Manchester, its Victorian ostentation might have found approval. Within sight of Oxford's dreaming spires, most house-hunters searching for country residences were looking for genteel properties of pleasing proportions built in the mellow hues of Cotswold stone.

So Daniel was able to negotiate a price far more favourable than he'd expected to pay for a property and estate that met his requirements so perfectly. The north wing now housed a mixture of small companies: graphic designers, media agencies, a literary agent, and a firm of architects, while the entire south wing was taken over by an independent film company which specialised in scientific and nature films. A grant from the Heritage Lottery Fund enabled him to restore the orangery and the theatre, and in August 2005 the first Myddleton Festival took place.

Held over a fortnight, the festival was a miscellany of classical music performances, most held in the theatre, some outside. For the first week the main focus was an out–door opera, the design of which could make full use of the ornate exterior of the house, the wooded grounds and the ornamental lake.

Despite the serene surroundings, Anna felt overwhelmed by the challenge ahead. She felt the hot colour creep up her neck into her face, and not for the first time, she asked herself whether they only wanted her as the Governess because they believed she would appear convincingly unhinged. Did they plan to play on her state of mind to suggest that the innocents were corrupt and that ghosts walked abroad at Bly even in the brightest sunlight?

No, she reassured herself: the offer had come several weeks before that shattering decision at the end of January.

She sighed and got back into the car.

The lane was narrower than the main drive and she made her way cautiously, praying she wouldn't meet anyone coming towards her. By now, the lake was on her left and ahead of her were three detached cottages, built as homes for bailiff, gardener and forester, but now let as holiday properties. The backs of the cottages looked out over the lake and each had a small front garden bordered with a picket fence and a gate on which a brass plate bore the relevant name. The Bailiff had been granted the largest and grandest of the three, while the other two looked identical, though Gardener's had a terracotta colour front door and paint work, while Forester's had green.

The road came to a dead end beyond the cottages, but widened enough to form a turning and parking area. Two battered Volvos and a yellow soft-top indicated that Anna had neighbours, and as she manoeuvred her silver grey hatchback alongside them, she could smell the acrid fumes of a barbecue that was struggling to catch light.

Chapter 2

He had seized the best of the weather in which to take his regular Sunday walk along the coastal path. The day had looked set to be one of endless grey skies and miserable drizzle, but as the afternoon drifted into early evening it had brightened into an unexpected blaze of blue and yellow.

Because it was late when he left home, he drove further east than usual to pick up the Llyn path and walk towards Criccieth. He parked his car at the Feathers pub directly opposite the boyhood home of Lloyd George and made his way down the long farm track that led to the point where the river Dwyfor curled round to join the sea. The sun was in his eyes as he turned left and made his way along the uneven track with the sea on his right and farm fields on his left. He peered through the dazzle of sunlight, waiting for the bulk of the time-worn castle that dominated the coastline to come into view.

The path was quiet—he passed no one—and he was alone with the swarms of tiny white butterflies that danced ahead of him along the path like handfuls of confetti suspended just out of reach. He had never seen them in such abundance before and guessed this must be their time to thrive in an all too brief lifespan. He wondered if Jim had these white butterflies in mind when he splashed them over the jewellery box he'd made for Anna to mark their engagement and which she kept on her dressing table.

He bent to retie the loosening laces on his boots and looked up with a jolt as a man's voice ahead of him called out 'get along there!' He smiled as he realised the command was not directed at him. Making their rolling way towards him was a small herd of cows, the sight of them incongruous in this beach-side setting. He stepped off the path on to the sandy beach so that he would not have to encounter them head-on and settled his back against a small dune to wait for them to pass.

He was glad of the excuse to stop and take in the scene. He sat with his knees hunched awkwardly under his chin and gazed out to sea. The image of Anna's jewellery box had not only conjured troubling thoughts of her, but also of another box, painted with lilies, once prized by another woman. He pictured it now, sitting on his desk alongside a fading wedding photograph in a tarnished silver frame.

He watched a man playing in the shallows with a wriggling toddler who was screeching in delight as the water swirled and frothed around his chubby sunburned legs. He wondered what it would have been like, what pleasure it might have been to see a child grow up to adulthood; imagined grandchildren, too, with some likeness of him or Anna.

He knew Anna regretted their childlessness, not realising that he was relieved to be spared the risk of failure, the fear that he would recreate the prickly, uncommunicative family in which he'd grown up.

Behind him he heard the farmer call again. 'That's it, my lovely. Up you go,' and he turned to see the last of the cows disappearing up a path away from the sea, helped on her way by a friendly pat on the haunch from the farmer.

Tranquillity returned to the path but as he resumed his walk, he felt a stab of melancholy, his conscience unsettled by thoughts of Anna. He shook himself and picked up his speed, following the path round to the left and towards the promenade above the West Beach. Here, there were more people around, several families walking on the sand, inspecting rock pools and collecting shells. He passed a couple sitting on one of the benches on the stretch of headland that led into Marine Parade. The man was reading a local paper while his wife dozed, her head on her chest, and both hands clutching the handbag on her lap.

In the mellowing sunshine, the tall Victorian villas in their assortment of pastel colours had an old-fashioned charm, the eye forgiving the juxtaposition of aspiring gentrification and shabby decline. He walked to the far end of the terrace towards the hulking castle with its broken walls and one remaining gatehouse. Along Marine Terrace the houses were a mix of private homes, guest houses and holiday flats and whatever their state of repair they commanded the same spectacular views over Cardigan Bay, with Harlech in the distance and the mountains of Snowdonia beyond.

He stopped as he always did outside one of the few houses without a name, a plain number 9 on its royal blue door. The refurbishment was coming on well and behind the scaffolding he could see a tasteful frontage re-emerging out of the flaking paint and ugly staring windows that had so disappointed him when he first saw the house many years before.

He wondered if he would ever feel able to knock on the ornate cast iron door-knocker and impose himself on the goodwill of the couple who lived there. He turned away from the house and looked out to sea. A few people further along the esplanade were peering through binoculars, perhaps hoping to catch sight—as Edwyn never had—of the harbour porpoises and bottlenose dolphins said to regularly visit Criccieth's beaches. As he began to walk back the way he'd come, he made a pact with himself: if ever he spotted one of these friendly creatures at play in the waters visible from number 9, he would regard it as a sign that he should pay a call.

When he returned to the headland, the wind was getting up and all the benches were deserted. The elderly couple had gone, leaving the newspaper behind, its pages blown open by the breeze and threatening to scatter. Thinking to deposit the paper in the waste bin he could see ahead, Edwyn gathered up the pages and was about to fold them together when a striking photograph caught his eye. The large handsome manor house must once have been splendid, but it was clear that after years of neglect, nature had moved in and taken over. The headline told him that it was to be redeveloped as a health spa and hotel and, after years of planning disputes, the builders were about to begin work. Nothing remarkable or unusual in that, but the caption to the photograph made him suck in his breath—this was Cadwallader Hall, a place he had searched for and never found.

Chapter 3

Her immediate impression was of uncluttered, comfortable charm and as she stood in the doorway, Anna felt her taut shoulders soften with relief.

'Yes,' she thought. 'I can live here for a while.'

The front door opened straight onto the open-plan downstairs living area, with a kitchen at the front and a lounge-dining room at the back, overlooking a small patio and, beyond that, an expanse of lawn that ran to the water's edge.

She put down the box of groceries she'd brought in from the car and ran her hand along the cream work surfaces which served to separate the kitchen and living areas. The kitchen was new and a quick look in the pine cupboards reassured her that it was well-equipped and clean. There were a couple of homely touches—a copy of the Radio Times and the local paper on a long coffee table in front of the sofa—and on each of the two windowsills in the kitchen, there stood a squat glass vase overflowing with pink and lilac sweet peas.

Anna leaned across the sink and sniffed. Their delicate fragrance, she realised, made little impact on the distinctive smell of the place—a mix of toxic air-freshener on top of liberal use of bleach and disinfectant. She spotted the air-freshener on the draining board and tipped it into the pedal bin, making a mental note to burn some toast the next morning to diffuse these odours and impose herself on her new home.

Throughout the downstairs, the predominant colours were cream and a muted bottle green, with touches of dusky pink. There was a two-seater sofa and matching chair, a flat screen television, a music centre and against the left hand wall, a small pine dining table with three chairs. Double doors opened onto a flagged patio, on which there was a small wrought iron table with two matching green chairs.

Anna opened the doors to let in air and to check how much privacy she would have from her neighbours. She could hear no signs of the people immediately next door, so she stepped to the end of the patio and looked to her left towards the other two cottages. All three were detached and had paths which ran down both sides into their gardens, partially screened from each other by low hedges. She could see that the patio doors of the Gardener's cottage were open, but there was nobody around and all she could hear from inside was the muted rise and fall of a cricket-match commentary.

Beyond that was the much larger garden of the Bailiff's cottage, which she guessed had three bedrooms rather than the one she would find upstairs in Forester's. The barbecue was still spluttering and she could hear women's shrill voices from inside the cottage calling to the two men who were ostensibly in charge of it, but who were standing by the lake, sharing a joke. From the clatter of crockery, Anna feared that a party was in preparation and she wondered with dread just how many people the two Volvos had borne to Bailiff's Cottage. The smoke was drifting towards her and when she felt her eyes smart, she hurried inside, closing the doors behind her.

'Oh God,' she groaned.

She was feeling neither sociable nor in the mood for neighbours whose noise and cooking would intrude on what she had hoped would be a peaceful evening. She recognised the onset of irrational disgruntlement and as she went out to the car to get her bags, she felt the beginnings of a headache tightening around her forehead.

She carried her heavy cases upstairs one at a time. A pine staircase directly ahead of the front door led to a narrow landing off which there was an airing cupboard, a large double bedroom overlooking the lake, and an immaculate white bathroom above the kitchen. Up here, dusky pink became the principal colour, with splashes of green to add depth. Above the bed there was a shelf full of books and she remembered noticing a small low bookcase in the lounge. The books calmed her, as if they had been put there to be her companions over the coming weeks.

She sat on the bed and studied the row of creased and faded spines. They were mainly shabby paperbacks of well-known classics and she guessed some might have come from the big house, though previous guests could have left the more recent bestsellers. Her eye was caught by a book, which had toppled over towards the edge of the shelf and against which the weight of the other books was pressing. She righted the books that were leaning over and lifted the one that had fallen onto its side, a cheap and dog-eared edition of Thomas Hardy's *Far From the Madding Crowd*, with an unattractive front cover photograph of an over-made-up woman standing at a tall window, holding a Japanese fan to her chin.

'Like a rustic Madame Butterfly,' she mused with surprise.

She turned it over and studied the publisher's text on the back cover, mouthing the words silently, as a child might.

"Tracing the life of the beautiful Bathsheba Everdene, this is one of Hardy's greatest love stories. Sergeant Troy, the dashing but faithless soldier, and Mr Boldwood, the lonely bachelor of repressed and violent passions, both court the independent young heiress, deflecting her life from its intended course of rustic happiness with the most devoted of her suitors, Gabriel Oak."

She tipped the book towards her so that it briefly touched her chest.

'Gabriel Oak,' she murmured. 'Where are you now then?'

For a few moments she sat still, her lids closed against the encroaching headache, her mind's eye looking back on a younger self, standing under the Armistice Magnolia tree in the gardens of St Hugh's College. She tilted her head, testing the intensity of the pain, then opened the book and flicked through it until she found the last pages of Chapter 4.

The Mistake

In the copy that had once been hers, the words had been underlined in red ink.

She closed the book and placed it carefully at the end of the shelf, propping against it a smooth mottled stone she found on the dressing table alongside the bed.

She felt an urgent need to busy herself by unpacking and settling herself into her temporary home. Two sleek pine wardrobes with drawers and hanging space provided plenty of room for her clothes and in the bathroom there was a deep window seat on which she laid out her toiletries and makeup. She enjoyed the sense of nesting and for a short while she forgot both her irritation and her headache.

Downstairs, and feeling hungry, she unpacked her groceries and made herself a ham sandwich and a cup of tea. She placed them on the coffee table and sat back on the sofa to enjoy the view of the lake.

The small side window in the kitchen was open a fraction and the aroma of barbecuing burgers was unmistakable. She balanced her plate on her lap and picked up the *Oxford Times*, glancing at the date to check that it was the current edition. She scanned the front page and leafed through the paper, taking in the impression it had always given her of a town more notable for its crime and lawlessness than as an ancient seat of learning and culture. She had just found the arts pages when the party at Bailiff's Cottage got into full swing. Clearly the whole household was now in the garden making merry to the jangling accompaniment of what sounded like Johnny Cash.

'Not for long,' she hoped uncharitably.

She looked through the double doors at the sky that was darkening perceptibly and thought they would soon be driven indoors by rain. She pushed the paper away and finished her sandwich, though she had lost her taste for it, the tranquillity shattered, as she had feared.

As she sipped her tea and gazed ahead, an advertisement in the listings section caught her eye and she picked up the paper once more.

It was for a concert that evening at New College Chapel to be given by the New Oxford Chamber Choir. Though it was fifteen years since she had last sung with NOCC, she still thought of it as *her* choir.

Her heart raced and for a moment, she wavered. She had planned a solitary evening preparing for the next day, and it felt foolhardy to risk the ghosts she might meet beneath the Bridge of Sighs and down New College Lane. But the noise of the barbecue had unsettled her and she was tempted by the soothing diversion that an evening of choral music might provide.

She looked at her watch.

Chapter 4

Though she guessed that cross country there would be a more direct way into Oxford, Anna decided to retrace the route she had taken earlier through Marcham and rejoin the dual carriageway at the Abingdon/Witney interchange. As she made her way along the quiet country roads, the sky ahead shifted and changed in harmony with her fluctuating moods.

As she headed north on the busy dual carriageway, the skies lightened as if Oxford was beckoning to her. She knew that once she came off the A34 at Hinksey Hill, she would have missed her last easy chance to turn back. The traffic lights at the top of the exit slip road turned green as she approached them and she took this as a sign she should go on.

'Right then.'

Now, however, she was faced with how best to negotiate the city's one-way system so as to arrive in time.

She waited at the traffic lights on the Abingdon Road in order to turn right onto Donnington Bridge.

'Come on!' she exhorted the lights in frustration, mentally counting how many more sets lay ahead along her chosen route.

Green at last.

From there, she made steady progress and relaxed a little, pleased that she had summoned the energy and courage to go on with this unexpected venture.

'Keep going,' she exhorted the timid learner driver a few cars ahead of her.

As she made her way over Magdalen Bridge she pushed away the thought of punts jostling for space on the river below and turned right into Longwall, where she could see that it had already rained, and though it must have been only a light shower, the sky ahead looked an ominous shade

27

of charcoal. She made her way past university departments and college sports grounds, intending to turn left into the wide expanse of Mansfield Road and park at the far end as close as possible to Holywell Street and the entrance to New College.

She jumped with surprise as enormous raindrops clattered with force against the roof and windscreen, obscuring her view until she turned on the wipers which, because she had jabbed at them in haste, came on at their most frenetic speed. As she adjusted them and the windscreen cleared, she saw that the turning into Mansfield Road was blocked by two fire engines and was unpassable.

'Damn!'

She glanced at the clock on the dashboard.

'Let's hope there's a space round here then,' she muttered, continuing past the Pitt Rivers Museum up to the traffic lights, and increasing her speed as she saw them about to change to amber. As she turned left, the rain stopped as suddenly as it had started. She saw that there were only a few cars parked in the bays outside Wadham College. She took the first space she came to and fumbled in her purse to find coins with which to feed the meter.

The air was full of the smell of rain on dust and seeing that the sky still threatened, she grabbed a small umbrella off the back seat and stuffed it into the side of her bag. She hurried past the college and hesitated at the corner outside the King's Arms, where the wooden tables and benches were wet and empty, the recent rainstorm having driven the drinkers inside.

'Where now then?' she asked herself, pondering which way she should go.

If the entrance in New College Lane was open, that would be the quickest option, but despite being the front gate of the College, Anna knew it was often closed. However, she had a knack for finding it open.

She lifted her head heavenwards and silently implored the porter.

The streets were almost deserted and in the thickening light they looked cold and unwelcoming. Anna waited as a cyclist idled through the green light and then she hurried across the road onto Catte Street and towards the Bridge of Sighs that linked two buildings of Hertford College.

She started to run now, her footsteps echoing down the secluded alley which led to one of the two entrances to New College, and which, if it was open, would bring her out into the Front Quadrangle near the entrance to the Chapel. Her breathing quickened as she ran faster. She turned the bend into the long straight stretch between the walls of the cloister and Warden's Barn and could see the three-storey Gate Tower ahead of her.

'Why do I do this?' she berated herself. 'I hate being late!'

The gate was closed and forbidding.

She stopped and clutched her side, where she'd felt the sharp, stabbing pain of a stitch. As her breathing steadied and the cramp receded, she looked up at the top storey of the Tower with its welcoming figures of the Virgin, an angel and the founder of the College, kneeling as if in homage to those who passed through the gate. From past experience, she knew that it was worth continuing up the alley and testing whether the door was really locked or not.

She pushed against it and relaxed as its heavy weight gave way to her.

She blessed the unknown porter and made her way through into the Quad, where she saw that people were still straggling into the Chapel, some stopping in the antechapel, as she did, to buy a ticket and collect a programme from a curly-haired girl seated behind a rickety table. She tip-toed round the ancient brasses set into the flag-stoned floor and as she stepped into the Chapel itself, she shivered in its cool air, remembering that the temperature remained chilly, even in summer.

She stood for a moment to take in the familiar building, founded by William of Wykeham, Bishop of Winchester, at the end of the fourteenth century. He wanted worship to be at the heart of College life and so the Chapel was designed to be the most inspiring of the College buildings.

The choir were filing in through a door on the left-hand side of the Chapel that led through to the vestry and beyond it to the Song Room, where they would have rehearsed and lined up. She found a seat towards the back, sitting alone on the end of a row, alongside the central aisle, from where she hoped she would have a good view.

The singers stood in two lines in front of the altar, with the decorated panel of highly intricate tracery behind them, ten men in the rear and fifteen women in front of them. The side door opened and the conductor made his way through to stand in front of his choristers, facing the audience who were clapping with enthusiastic anticipation.

The young man opened his arms wide and took a step forward, waiting for the applause to peter out. When it did, he moved closer to the audience, standing in the aisle among the first few rows.

'Thank you, ladies and gentlemen, thank you,' he said in a genial Yorkshire accent. 'It's very good to see so many of you here with us at New College. Tonight's concert is something of a homecoming for us—and an end.'

He cupped his hands as if he was holding something fragile.

'For the last ten days, we've been on a tour of what we called Wessex and tonight is the final performance of this programme of glorious English music before we go our separate ways for the summer.'

'Wessex,' Anna thought. 'How romantic.'

She watched him and smiled. He was still talking— about the music, why he had chosen it and how most of it would be sung *a capella*—and in his animation he frequently gestured with his arms or ran a hand through his increasingly untidy hair.

He reminded her of Gerry, who had conducted NOCC during her second and third years: though Gerry's broad accent was that of the Belfast outskirts, both men were short and slightly tubby, with thin fly-away dark hair, large, old-fashioned glasses and passionate enthusiasm for their music.

She glanced down at the programme and nodded with recognition and pleasure. Vaughan Williams, Howells, Stanford, Delius and Britten: she had once sung all these pieces with a youthful delight in the beauty and skill of the settings.

The conductor turned to face his singers, waiting with his head bowed until the audience had settled and the last few coughs had died away. Then, with a quick and purposeful movement, he lifted his arms and launched into a set of folk songs by Vaughan Williams.

Anna peered at the rows of choristers—the men in dark suits, the women in what Gerry had always called "long coloured" which tended then, as now, to create an impression of a riotously coloured garden run wild.

She tried with difficulty to make out individual faces. Light streamed through the magnificent transformed windows, but inside the Chapel it became a half-light, which created an unreal, twilit world in which the faces she saw in front of her blurred with those she had known so well sixteen years before.

From the back row, came the glint of glasses reflecting in the light.

'Why do men in choirs always wear glasses?' she wondered.

Where a couple of angled spotlights fell on them, the women's faces looked bleached, their features naked, making them appear implausibly young. One girl caught her eye, as she shifted and swayed every time they sang the cheerful refrain *"Just as the tide was flowing."*

The sound was full of energy and vigour with a beguiling freshness that only the very young can produce. Every item they sang in an ambitiously planned programme was polished and professional.

'Were we this good?' Anna asked herself as they rose to the harmonic challenges of some particularly dissonant pieces by Peter Warlock and some rich and expressive part songs by Finzi that called for unforgivingly long-breathed lines. They were exuberant and confident—fearless even— and she guessed that this final performance, coming at the end of an intense tour, would be special for all of them, particularly those leaving Oxford for the last time.

After the Finzi, the tallest and most gangly man in the choir stepped forward and the conductor moved to the side and sat at a piano, which Anna noticed for the first time. Referring to her programme, she felt a fleeting ache. Benjamin Britten's plaintive setting of a poem by Thomas Hardy called *The Choirmaster's Burial* was Mark's song—a piece that time and time again his fellow choristers insisted be included in programmes of secular music, whatever the season; a haunting tale of a kindly man whose last wish for a musical send-off was denied by the slothful vicar but granted instead by celestial musicians undeterred by frosts and cold weather.

Though he looked nervous, the young tenor soloist was good and his ill-fitting suit with its over-large jacket somehow added a convincing innocence to his spirited performance. After the first spare, melismatic lines, Anna shut her eyes and there before her was Mark, fair-haired and slightly freckled, his unfailing good nature shining through an honest face, his sweet-voiced tenor singing out in heartfelt support for the loyal Choirmaster.

Noisy applause brought her abruptly back to the present and, after the briefest of bows, the smiling soloist slipped into the ranks of the back row, making way for two girls who stepped forward from the centre of the front row to take solo parts in Herbert Howells's choral setting of *The Summer is Coming.*

Under the sympathetic guidance of the conductor, the breathy, fluttery voice of the diminutive soprano and the fruitier tones of the more mature alto enhanced the lyrical, English music. This was the last item in the first half and when it was over, the conductor leant towards his soloists and gave each in turn a brotherly peck on the cheek.

Anna guessed that his female choristers would love him for the gentleness and warmth that was apparent even from this distance, while he would love them for their prettiness and their vivacity and would be destined to find friendship and willing companionship—but probably not love amongst them.

'Better that way,' she thought, slipping out through the antechapel and into the Quad to be on her own during the brief interval. The air felt heavy and close, warmer here than in the Chapel, and for the moment there was no sign of rain. She walked down the side of the Chapel and turned left through an archway, which led past the Song Room into another huge Quad that opened off the Holywell entrance. A short way to her right, there was a bench, which looked dry enough to sit on.

'Well, better for them, I suppose, if not for *him.*'

She winced at the memory of her almost disastrous first year in the choir, when by falling for the Chorus Master in her second term, she followed a long line of other blonde, blue-eyed sopranos who had endured the same ultimate humiliation.

'Just like Sergeant Troy,' Mark had been quick to point out. 'Dashing but faithless.'

Mark's friendship had been one of the reasons she had decided to stay on in the choir and when Gerry took over at the start of the next academic year, she felt her blotted copybook had been wiped clean.

She had known, though, that Mark's affection for her was growing. Even then he saw himself as Gabriel Oak to her Bathsheba Everdene.

The light in the chapel was murkier as she took her seat for the second half. She opened the programme to remind herself what was coming: Britten's *Flower Songs*, *The Bluebird* by Stanford and more Vaughan Williams, but it was the opening item, as soon as the first humming notes emerged, which stirred the most powerful emotions.

Delius's entirely wordless piece *To be sung of a summer night on the water* was one of the most melancholy and atmospheric Anna had ever heard or sung. Gerry had introduced it to the choir at the start of his first summer term and somehow it had inspired the suggestion that when everyone was done with exams, they should take punts and picnics on the river and sing under the city's bridges, allowing passers-by to gather and listen.

The audience in New College was still, perhaps transported to water by the stunningly evocative mood music. All around her, Anna was aware of captivated faces, all eyes focused on the source of magical images.

Yet the only face she saw was Edwyn's—leaning over the parapet of Folly Bridge and aiming with surprising precision, a white carnation into her lap. She knew that she had blushed in a confusion of embarrassment and pride, her pleasure marred by the cloud that had settled on Mark's equable features; the accusing expression that said:

'So you've met your Mr Boldwood.'

It was at the start of their second year that Mark had started calling her Bathsheba. It was said playfully, but behind the banter lay infatuation, tinged with the sadness of being unrequited.

'Why? Because... despite all the tragic twists and turns, it just seems so fresh and hopeful,' he had said, when she asked him why *Far From the Madding Crowd* was his favourite book.

'I suppose I'm intrigued by fate; I like the idea of second chances—third chances even—true love being found, unrequited love being requited in the end.'

They had been sitting on one of the more private lawns in the gardens of Trinity College and head down, he was plucking absent-mindedly at the close-cropped grass.

'So,' she'd asked, nudging his arm, 'you see yourself as Gabriel Oak, do you?'

'Maybe,' he'd said, tossing away a handful of torn grass ends and looking at her sideways.

He pushed her gently.

'Well, at least we've got Sergeant Troy out of the way.'

Anna had shifted uncomfortably then, keen to steer the conversation away from becoming personal, but unsure what to say. Before she'd thought of something, he'd continued in mock-gloomy tones.

'Mr Boldwood next, though.'

For the remainder of the concert, Anna found it hard to focus on the present, the singers standing in front of her merging in her mind's eye with those she had sung with. The music evoked so many memories that for periods in the second half she was one of those fresh-faced soprano choristers, Mark standing behind her, and Edwyn visible at the end of a row a short way down the chapel.

She then had been the soloist in *The Bluebird*, not the fragile-looking girl here with her child-like treble. Stanford's setting of Mary Coleridge's poem of the blue hues of a bird and the sky, and the reflection of both in a lake, was a showpiece for a soprano soloist. Though Anna had known that her clear, pure voice could effortlessly negotiate its high-lying legato lines, she was tense and dry-mouthed as she came to the front. As she moistened her parched lips, she remembered a trick from her school days when, at end of term concerts, she would scan the faces of those at the front of the audience and find and focus on a stranger whose expression looked interested and friendly.

So had she first met Edwyn's steady gaze, and his kindly, handsome face had encouraged her to sing at her best, soaring with the bird high over the hills above the waters of the lake. When it was over and she was receiving the applause, she saw that his face was flushed and his appreciation enthusiastic.

Later, in the crush and noise of the King's Arms, he had sought her out and introduced himself as Edwyn Maxwell, Fellow in History at New College.

Now, in the fading light of the chapel, as she grieved for the life that was gone, she imagined him sitting near the front, bestowing smiles, and felt utterly alone.

The concert had lost its appeal; any semblance of quietude hijacked by too many ghosts. Oblivious now to the singers and their songs, she sat still and numb, as if in a trance. Music had been her consolation, but not for the first time, she recognised its powerful capacity to induce sadness as well.

She knew that the programme was to end with another group of folksongs by Vaughan Williams, the second of which, *The Turtle Dove*, had always been a favourite of hers. She remembered Gerry telling them that because of its mournful voice and the fact that it is commonly thought to mate for life, the turtledove features in several songs about love and loss.

Though his voice was thin and uneven, Gerry was a sensitive musician and he could sing in tune, and at the rehearsal in the Song Room at which they had sung through the setting for the first time, and before he'd decided who should take the solo baritone part, Gerry had crooned it himself above the quiet, humming accompaniment provided by the choir. His light, sweet rendering of the simple, sad melody had been remarkably affecting and had moved the whole group, their surprise registered by a shivering silence.

As she had then all those years ago, Anna found herself swallowing hard in an effort to rid her throat of the lump that threatened unwanted tears. She had not forgotten the text and, as she sat with her eyes tight shut, the words and music played their way insistently through her mind.

Fare you well, my dear, I must be gone,
And leave you for a while;
If I roam away I'll come back again,
Though I roam ten thousand miles, my dear,
Though I roam ten thousand miles.

So fair thou art, my bonny lass,
So deep in love am I;
But I never will prove false to the bonny lass I love,
Till the stars fall from the sky, my dear,
Till the stars fall from the sky.

The sea will never run dry, my dear,
Nor the rocks melt with the sun,
But I never will prove false to the bonny lass I love,
Till all these things be done, my dear,
Till all these things be done.

O yonder doth sit that little turtle dove,
He doth sit on yonder high tree,
A-making a moan for the loss of his love,
As I will do for thee, my dear,
As I will do for thee.

Now a young man stepped forward to sing the solo, and she sensed she should leave, and stood up, aware of the heads that turned to look at her. She moved quickly into the antechapel and for a moment she hovered there, undecided whether to stay and listen, but after only the first few notes she knew that the turtledove's tale of lost love was more than she could bear.

As she headed back towards her car and left choir and concert behind, she had a sense she was leaving Edwyn there, too, and longed to go back and claim him.

She hurried past the King's Arms with only a fleeting glance into the hot, bright, crowded bars and the melee of drinkers that thronged the entranceway.

She slowed to rummage in her bag for her car keys, and when she looked up she saw she was standing directly opposite the closed wrought iron gates of Trinity College. Though it was dusk now and the light was fading fast, she could make out the pristine lawns and the gravelled walkway that led up to the buildings where Mark had once lived.

She crossed the road and gazed through the gates at the silent, deserted gardens, at the lights beginning to cast their faint glow in the encroaching darkness, and knew that she had not left the ghosts behind her in New College.

Chapter 5

Back at Myddleton, the air was cooler than in the city, and as she parked alongside the brightly coloured sports car, Anna noted with some relief that there was now just one Volvo outside Bailiff's cottage, suggesting that the rain had caused the party to disperse early. Lights glowed from some of the windows, creating a welcoming sense of community that she was glad of as she prepared to spend her first night in a place that did not yet feel like home.

Once inside, she turned on the upstairs landing light and moved quickly round the living room to turn on the television and a couple of table lamps in an effort to drive away the shadows and haul herself back into the present. She drew the curtains and switched on the concealed lighting in the kitchen beneath the wall cupboards. She liked the effect created by the muted colours of the décor in the soft lighting and immediately relaxed.

She took the concert programme out of her handbag and glanced at it briefly before dropping it into the cane wastepaper basket near the television.

She sighed, 'well, it got me out, I suppose, and filled an empty evening.'

She switched on the kettle and tipped a sachet of Horlicks into a pale green mug. On the television, the late evening news had just finished and the weather forecaster was predicting a fine and sunny start to the week.

'That's good,' she thought, pouring boiling water over the pale coloured powder, and wondering what to wear to the first day's rehearsal. She moved over to the sofa and with mug in one hand, she flicked through the channels with the remote control, soon deciding she needed quiet to prepare for the next day.

Her brown leather music bag was propped against the leg of the coffee table where she'd dumped it when she first arrived. It was a sturdy handsome piece of craftsmanship, bought in the Khan in Cairo and taken on all her work engagements; big enough to hold her music and all the study paraphernalia she accumulated when preparing a role. She unpacked it on to the low table, relieved to see that she had not forgotten anything vital like her score, an aberration that would once have been unheard of, but recently was less unlikely.

She took a sip of the malty drink and put the mug to one side while she sorted the contents of the bag: vocal score, separate libretto plus analysis, Henry James's novella and study notes, old opera programmes, several DVDs, CDs and a notebook, bearing a label which read *The Turn of the Screw Myddleton Festival July–August 2006.*

She had prepared hard—as she did for all her work—but Britten's brittle, complex music posed great challenges, while the role of the Governess demanded that she immerse herself in a highly-strung character with whom she could all too closely relate—a woman bewildered and afraid but trying to do the best she could in testing circumstances.

As she finished her drink, she flicked through her notebook, an amalgam of jottings and ideas she had recorded while researching the opera, designed to help her create a convincing character.

She wondered how Jonathan Wyatt, the director, would deal with the mysterious menace which threatens the children in the Governess's care. He was known for his intelligent, intellectual productions and she was looking forward to working with him on a piece which allowed a director so much artistic leeway. Do the children 'see' the ghosts, she pondered, or are they the product of the Governess's overwrought imagination? Are Miles and Flora preyed on by corrupt ghosts—or by the Governess? Or, would he fudge it and ask the audience to decide for themselves.

She shivered and thought it might be time to go to bed, though musing on a macabre ghost story was not the best preparation for a deep and untroubled sleep.

'I need something to read,' she said to herself, realising that she'd forgotten to bring the Wilkie Collins novel she'd started the previous weekend. She walked over to the sink with her mug and rinsed it under the tap, leaving an inch of hot water to soak off the residue that had stuck to the bottom.

She leant against the sink and looked across the work surfaces into the lounge, pleased that with her books and papers and music scattered across the table, it looked and felt increasingly like home. She was worried, though, about sleeping. In the last few months, when the combination of light reading and the radio on at low volume had failed to soothe her to sleep, she had sometimes resorted to a sleeping tablet.

She turned off the kitchen lights and went over to the bookcase in the lounge.

She knelt on the floor and read out the names of some of the possible authors as she scanned the books from left to right: Jean Plaidy, Winston Graham, AJ Cronin, Daphne du Maurier.

She opened *My Cousin Rachel*, but the spine had cracked and the pages had come away in chunks so that the middle of the book was missing.

She put it back and picked up its neighbour.

The Birds and Other Stories.

'Well, I don't want to read *that* just before I put the lights off,' she thought, opening the book at the contents page to read the other titles: *Monte Verita, The Apple Tree, The Little Photographer, Kiss Me Again, Stranger, The Old Man.*

'These sound more hopeful,' she said, getting to her feet and turning off the lights, before going upstairs.

*

Fifteen minutes later, she was propped up in bed and ready to wind down towards sleep. Outside, it was the sort of dark night you forgot existed when you lived in a city, and all was silent, apart from the occasional call of an owl. The restful colours and the soft lighting created a mellow effect and she snuggled lower down the bed, opening the book at *Monte Verita*. It was a long story about two friends who had loved the same woman and whose lives took different paths. She was soon transfixed by the chilling tale of a mountain paradise promising immortality at a terrible price. Undeterred by the strange subject matter, she read on until half way through she came to the following passage:

"It was not chance that brought us together again. I am sure of that. These things are predestined. I have a theory that each man's life is like a pack of cards, and those we meet and sometimes love are shuffled with us. We find ourselves in the same suit, held by the hand of Fate."

She turned the book face down on the duvet and closed her eyes. She did not believe in the supernatural, but she did believe in destiny, and over the last few months she had looked for signs of how things might work out for her and Edwyn, of what the future held in store.

Sometimes, she allowed herself to hope that Edwyn would realise that he could not simply walk away from something as indestructible as she had believed their marriage to be. At other times, she feared that even if he came to regret his decision, there was no going back and she would have to face a life without him.

But this passage offered some hope that the ties that had bound them had not been entirely severed.

Chapter 6

'Don't go inland cross country,' the postman had said, 'or you'll never find it. Take the coast road and head towards Criccieth, that's the easiest route.'

Edwyn had done as instructed but the traffic, stretching miles ahead, had been stationary for almost quarter of an hour. He tapped against the driving wheel in frustration.

The day was hot and sunny, with no sign of the forecast rain. A car door in front was thrust open as a woman passenger snatched a crumpled child from the back seat and held him over the grass verge to spew up. Edwyn looked away and sighed. In the distance, he thought he could see signs of slow movement and the driver in front beeped his horn to signal to his passengers that they should get a move on. The woman wiped a handkerchief across the child's scrunched up face and scrambled with him into the backseat.

Edwyn eased the car into first gear and inched forward, relieved the traffic ahead was flowing more freely. He glanced down at the notes he'd made from the postman's directions: take the B4411 just before Criccieth and head towards Rhoslan. Go straight through the village and at the Crown pub, take the left turn down an unmarked track.

He took the left turn off the main road to Rhoslan and after about three miles, slowed as he got into the village. There were no pubs in the centre so he kept going into open countryside, glad he had the landmark of the Crown to look out for. After another mile or so, he came to a crossroads where the Crown Inn stood on the corner. He slowed and indicated left, but his way was blocked by a dusty black Discovery stopped at an angle across the road, its driver conducting a shouted conversation with some teenagers sitting on the wall, brandishing beer glasses as they spoke. One of the group, a girl with limp brown hair and a grubby-looking vest-top, caught his eye and fixed him with a contemptuous look. Feeling old and tired and anxious to get away from the girl's stare, he edged to the right and around the Discovery.

The noise of the car's air-conditioning had become irritating and he switched it off before winding down his window to breathe in fresh air. As he did so, he saw on the right-hand side of the track that a temporary sign had been erected: Construction traffic only. He guessed that he was now only a short distance away and he would not be deterred this time. He pressed on down the track that had been newly tarmacked, no doubt to accommodate the trucks and heavy lifting machinery.

Jim had never been there and had only the vaguest idea where it was. 'A few miles north of Criccieth, in the direction of Caernarfon,' was the best he could do and despite a detailed local map, Edwyn had never been able to find it on previous attempts. Huw the postman, however, had grown up on a farm near Rhoslan, and stories of the Hall were part of his childhood. He knew all about the plans to transform the place into a luxury retreat and said he was glad it would bring visitors with money into the area.

'It's no use to anyone sitting ruined like that,' he said to Edwyn that morning. 'It'll be good to get some new life back into it at last.'

The house had been designed by Mark Soane, commissioned in 1785 by George Cadwallader, a local manufacturer who'd wanted to live out his later years in luxury and seclusion. It overlooked parkland and woodland, with views of the sea from its upper windows but it stayed in the family only a short while after George's premature death. Several fortunes were spent expanding and renovating it before it became a convent, but the nuns' tenure was ended by the onset of the Second World War and the house was briefly home to Polish refugees.

In 1944 a descendent of George Cadwallader reclaimed the house for his family but used part of it as a nursing home and refuge for unmarried mothers. He had been a missionary in Africa who'd returned home with a wealthy American wife. The Hall was run by a succession of nurses-cum-managers until it was sold to a couple of London bankers who hoped to convert it into a hotel. Lengthy battles over planning permission meant that a house once heralded as a neoclassical masterpiece had been abandoned and largely forgotten.

Edwyn made his way cautiously down the track until he came to a wide gravelled area on the left hand side where a dozen or so vehicles were parked. He pulled up next to a battered jeep and got out to see how close he could get to the house he guessed was out of sight at the end of a drive that snaked away into the distance.

The rusting iron gates lying flat on the ground on either side of the drive must once have been elegant, and though some of the vertical stiles were missing and the remainder were mostly bent and misshapen, a few were intact and still surmounted with their fleur de lys finials. The driveway was broken and uneven, its edges covered in debris from rotten branches fallen from dying trees that would have formed a proud guard of honour along the avenue.

As he picked his way over the rutted moss-covered surface, Edwyn tried to picture this entrance sixty years earlier, imagining the troubled and frightened women making their way through the arched gates and up the tree-lined drive, clutching only what possessions they could carry and perhaps uncertain of the reception that awaited.

After a few minutes, the drive curled round to the right and the house at last came into view.

It was a dismal sight.

Already in a poor state when it was sold to the developers, it had been neglected and stripped, gradually decaying to the ruinous condition that met Edwyn as he gazed at it from outside the steel fencing that had been erected by the contractors. The house was covered with scaffolding behind which he could see pale discoloured stonework peeping through blankets of rampant green foliage, windows blank and gaping and a vast expanse of roof that had partially caved in and worn away.

Somewhere out of sight came the muted thunder of pneumatic drills, and the dozens of birds lined up on what branches remained intact suggested that a process of evicting the resident wildlife had begun.

"Keep out," said the sign tied onto the steel barrier.

Men in high visibility yellow jackets were inspecting some derelict outbuildings, but no one took any notice of him peering through the fencing.

He thought about the women who had lived hidden lives here—the silent nuns wanting only kinship with Jesus, the women and girls seeking shelter for themselves and their babies, grateful to avoid, if only temporarily, the judgement of disappointed families and a disapproving world.

Jim had told him that the staff were kind, the spacious accommodation made reassuringly homely. The women, he said, viewed Edwin Cadwallader and his spirited, unconventional wife as angels of mercy—disappointment and disapproval exchanged for understanding and acceptance.

That was some comfort.

Though the estate was in a sorry condition and no doubt bore little resemblance to Cadwallader's handsomely restored Hall, he was glad he'd come. Despite the pervading aura of decay, he felt its strong sense of *place*. The woods and parkland were badly overgrown, the footpaths almost invisible, the buildings ramshackle but this was once somewhere people had come in search of refuge and solace, and he took heart from the belief that Cadwallader Hall would have provided this and more to some of those travellers.

As he turned back onto the main road, he could see that the pub terrace was deserted, six empty beer glasses lined up on the wall the only visible evidence of the young people who'd sat there earlier. He decided to stop for a drink and a sandwich before heading home and back to his writing.

The pub was quiet, the shabby, darkly lit interior gloomy, so he sat outside at one of the tables on the terrace with a half pint of bitter and a cheese roll. As he settled himself and stuffed the £5 note change into his wallet, something dislodged from another pocket of the wallet and a small square photograph fluttered onto his lap. He picked it up and studied it: one of his favourites—Anna with head turned, facing the camera, flushed with the exertion of an arduous walk up a huge Cornish sand dune and smiling. She still looked girlish and young for her thirty-seven years and the faint lines under her eyes and her pale unmade-up skin gave her the appearance of vulnerability.

She was lovely; there was no getting away from it.

He sipped his beer and munched half-heartedly at the stale powdery roll. He felt his spirits dip as if the shadow of something unwelcome had descended on him. He missed her still, and felt remorse at the manner of their parting, but told himself that self-pity was a pointless indulgence. After all, it had been his decision, but he wished he could have carried on as she had wanted to, that being on his own had not seemed like the only option.

With a start of guilt he remembered that her rehearsals began today and knew she would be anxious. He pictured her making her way to Myddleton, imagined her re-enacting the Governess's journey to Bly, and having made this pilgrimage to Cadwallader Hall, he felt somehow connected to her.

His instinct was to send her a text wishing her good luck, but he hesitated, fearing that whatever he said, she might misconstrue. He took his phone out of his pocket, but the sun was behind him, rendering the screen invisible. He laid the phone down on the table and pushed the plate away. The beer at least was good.

He wished her well and was sad that it was no longer his right to hear how this first day had gone. The light was changing and he looked up to see rain clouds fast encroaching on the blue sky overhead. As his table fell into shadow, he picked up the phone again and began to pick away at the keypad.

Chapter 7

Sunlight streamed through the tall windows of the Orangery and doors had been left open on two sides of the long narrow room to allow air to circulate and cool the hothouse interior. At one end, on a linoleum acting area, which had been marked out with black gaffer-tape, a number of rehearsal props—a chair, a table, a bed and a piano—had been placed in what looked like random positions, while at the other end, a series of trestle tables had been pushed together to produce a large rectangular surface, around which the cast and some of the crew of *The Turn of the Screw* were gathering for the first rehearsal.

Anna chewed on the inside of her lower lip and plucked at the delicate string of pale green glass beads round her neck. She dreaded this part of the production process when initially, in the presence of people she always assumed to be more talented and confident, insecurity conspired to unnerve and discomfort her. She had taken her seat early, directly opposite where Jonathan Wyatt had left his score and in between Grace and Harri, two people she knew well and was pleased to see again. Grace had got up to talk to a bushy-haired man with a straggly beard while Harri was turning out his music case in the hope of finding his mislaid glasses.

Only a few people had already sat down; the others were helping themselves to tea and coffee from flasks laid out on a separate table in the corner. Anna sipped from a bottle of water and looked anxiously around her, relieved to spot some familiar faces among those creating the hubbub of laughter and animated reunions. She watched with interest the two children who were to play Miles and Flora and who looked remarkably composed and at ease. They were sitting together and talking quietly with Toby, the repetiteur, who she guessed would have coached them in their roles and had seen it as part of his job to look after them today.

'Got them! Come here you little buggers.'

With a flourish, Harri produced his glasses from the bottom of his ancient music case and squinted through their scratched and smeared lenses before giving them a vigorous wipe with a crumpled paisley handkerchief.

'That's better.'

He perched the glasses on the edge of his nose and held his score about a foot away from his face.

'What's this then? *Turn of the Screw*. Never 'eard of it.'

Anna laughed and he dropped it on the table and turned to look at her.

'How are you then, lovely girl?'

'Oh... You know, fine.'

He put his arm round her shoulder.

'I heard—I'm really sorry.'

Anna relaxed, remembering what a decent, kindly man he was and what fun to work with—especially when things weren't going well and all around him were losing their cool. She'd been surprised to learn he'd been cast as the sinister Quint, and looking now at his tanned and homely face, she thought how clever the makeup would have to be to transform it into something menacing. When they had last worked together in *Rigoletto*, he had played a jovial, rakish Duke of Mantua and wooed her Gilda with good-humoured enthusiasm and no trace of caddish callousness. She knew, though, that his ringing tenor voice would easily negotiate the music and sensed that he would win the confidence and friendship of the boy who was to be in his thrall.

'Daft bugger, leaving a lovely girl like you. What's the matter with the man?'

Anna laughed again, enjoying his solid, reassuring presence.

'Have you done this before?' she asked.

'I just told you—never seen it. Good bit of sight-reading this'll be.'

Anna's eyes narrowed.

'Come on. You have done it, haven't you?'

'Oh alright then, I confess. Guilty as charged.'

He leant towards her to speak in a stage whisper, his thick Welsh accent becoming increasingly more pronounced as he warmed to the story.

'I keep quiet about it because it got the sort of reviews you have to hide from your mam or she'll tell you to stop messing about and get a proper job.'

Anna laughed as he rolled his eyes in mock horror.

'It was awful. Every time the ghosts appeared, the audience fell about—wetting themselves they were by the end. The first night party was like a wake. And then we had to go on tour with the damn thing—two months, two shows a week.'

'I'm surprised you've agreed to do it again.'

'Wife and two daughters to feed and clothe, mun! A man's life's not his own!'

Grace was sitting down again and with a scratching of chairs on the flag-stoned floor, the whole company took their seats as Jonathan tapped the side of his mug with a pen to signal that the rehearsal was due to begin.

'We'll have a chat later,' Grace whispered. 'I want to know how you are.'

'Great.' Anna squeezed Grace's hand. 'I've missed you.'

As Jonathan bowed his head to indicate that he was waiting, the room gradually became silent, though the hum of lawnmowers could be heard in the distance. Jonathan raised his head and looked round, his smile taking in the whole group.

'Welcome everybody. I'm Jonathan Wyatt. Good to see you all. '

Though he was still only in his early thirties, he was acquiring a reputation for original, thought-provoking work and had just completed a successful first year as Artistic Director of a regional theatre. Anna had worked with him once, about a year before, in a semi-staged performance of one of Bach's *Passions* and had found it stimulating and enjoyable. She was looking forward to working with him on something more substantial, but knew she had not been his first choice for the lead role, (the original singer having discovered she was pregnant), and hoped that in her fragile state of mind, she could live up to his expectations.

He held up his score and flicked through the pages.

'We've a lot of hard work to do between now and the 12th of August,' he said with a deep intake of breath to emphasise the challenge they faced. 'It's a complex, disturbing piece, so though this afternoon we'll focus on the music and sing through some of the key passages, I want to spend this morning just talking round the opera. Giving everyone a sense of its richness and ambiguities.'

His voice was clear and upbeat, his manner assured and authoritative. Anna saw that the whole company was listening closely. He spoke with fluency and fervour, fired with the passion that drove him.

'Rebecca West described the story as 'the best ghost story in the world' and it's true, this is a ghost story which can undoubtedly terrify, but it's one in which the existence of the ghosts is debatable to say the least.'

Several people nodded their heads in agreement.

'Henry James's tale is, in fact, two tales in one,' he went on, 'and it's consistently and irresolvably ambiguous, permitting two interpretations and refusing to let the reader settle for either.'

'I hate that,' Harri whispered to Anna. 'I like to know what's going on, me.'

She smiled sideways at him and then looked back at Jonathan. He was a striking looking man, with a mass of loose dark curls and black framed glasses which gave him an owlish, erudite look, but having seen some of his publicity photos, Anna knew that without the statement eye-wear he had the arresting good looks people associate with the Romantic poets.

'Before we get into that discussion, though, perhaps we can go round the table, giving everyone the chance to introduce themselves and tell us whether they have any previous experience of the work.'

'I've definitely got previous,' Harri quipped.

'Ah, yes,' murmured the man sitting next to Jonathan with a smile, and a number of people in the know laughed, while others looked intrigued.

'Why don't you start then Paul?' asked Jonathan.

'Right you are. I'm Paul Everett,' he said in a tight, clipped voice. 'I'm Musical Director of the Festival and I'll be conducting.'

Anna sensed some of the company tensing a little, their attitudes to musical directors perhaps coloured by experience of working with maestros who were difficult, demanding and autocratic. She knew that Paul Everett was neither difficult nor autocratic, but he was demanding and meticulous. He was a tall, lean man with a long aquiline face and a courteous, slightly old-fashioned manner.

'Jonathan and I have known each other since Cambridge and we've worked together several times since then, but for both of us, this is our first Britten opera, so we're on a journey.'

Jonathan nodded.

'Looking forward to it,' Paul smiled, before turning to the person on his left, the hairy man with whom Grace had been talking.

'Cheers guys. I'm Graham—lighting designer.'

That was all they were getting from him and the group turned their attention to the man on his left.

'Hi there,' he said in an accent that suggested Antipodean origins. 'I'm Patrick Gardiner and I've designed the production.'

Anna prepared to listen with interest, knowing from experience the profound importance of the design concept and how it related to the director's ideas.

'I have to confess,' he said, 'this is the first time I've designed for an outdoor production and I didn't accept Jonathan's invitation until I'd come to Myddleton and seen what fantastic scope it offers, especially for a ghost story.'

'Patrick,' Jonathan interrupted, 'would you like to say something about your ideas now and then we can have a look at the model and the costume designs when we've gone round the table.'

'Sure thing.'

Anna watched as he rustled through the pile of sketches and other papers in front of him, his fingers stubby and sturdy and stained by several different coloured inks, his face worn but alert. He pulled out a page of what looked like handwritten notes and while he peered at them as if trying to make sense of them, she wondered how good he would be at describing his visual ideas in words.

'We'll be using the terrace here,' he said, pointing through the windows, 'as the acting area, but the house itself will be suggested by only a few basic items of furniture. There'll be no obvious divisions between inside and out, no walls or barriers—everything will be fluid and ambiguous.'

He pointed in the direction of the set model and said, 'You'll see that the stage will be set up with the orchestra to the left hand side in a sort of Victorian bandstand, which will appear to be part of the design.'

He turned to look at Graham and said, 'That poses challenges, I realise, because we'll need to give the players enough light but I hope that for the acting area, the lighting can create a misty, half-light so that even an inanimate object like a piano seems to have a life of its own.'

Graham shrugged, raised an eyebrow and nodded and then made a note in a dog-eared exercise book.

'I want to create a world,' said Patrick, 'where you never know if what you saw was a ghost or simply the wind moving a curtain or light casting ghostly apparitions behind the reflecting glass of these windows.'

He seemed to have finished, but then added, 'the outdoor setting will be great for the ghosts, too—they can materialise from the thicket of trees to the right of the terrace and behind the seating area which will be erected on the grass in front of the terrace. That should work really well.'

'Thanks Patrick,' said Jonathan. 'I suppose the other thing to say is that we plan to start the performances at 8.30pm, when it will still be light for the Governess's arrival at Bly, but it will be getting progressively darker as the sense of evil intensifies. With a short interval, the show should come down at about 10.45pm.'

'Not much time for a drink, then,' Harri muttered in Anna's ear.

The introductions continued, with members of the technical crew giving just their name and job title, and as they did so, Anna sketched out a hurried diagram for herself, scrawling the names against crosses she marked round a rectangle.

She looked up when there was a slight pause to see who was next.

'Louise Gregory—Miss Jessel. Apologies for looking so pale and ghostly—I didn't mean to get straight into character—but I only got back from Vancouver on Saturday and I'm still feeling a bit groggy from the jet lag.'

Everyone looked at her sympathetically and laughed. Anna, however, noticed with interest that behind the tired and wan expression she looked vulnerable, too, and she found herself pondering this woman's story.

It was Harri's turn next and she guessed he'd take the opportunity to play the clown.

'Hiya everyone. Harri Gwilym—Quint. Now look, Jonathan, I may be a bit of a comedian, but it's my firm belief that this here opera is not a comedy, right? I don't want to be a laughing stock—again, OK?'

Everyone laughed.

'And,' he went on, looking at Patrick, 'this business of materialising from out of the trees, it's all right for you to say it should work well, but have you sorted out the weather? Otherwise, you could have a pair of very soggy ghosts, eh Louise?'

The whole company was still giggling when Anna knew it was her turn to speak.

'Hello,' she said, aware that her cheeks were burning and that there was a lazy wasp hovering worryingly close, 'I'm Anna Maxwell. I'll be singing the Governess—for the first time.'

She was always painfully nervous on these occasions and, though she would like to have spoken as easily as Harri and others did, she knew that she would say little until she felt less self-conscious. She had at least managed to say it with a smile and now it was Grace's turn and the eyes of the company shifted.

'Hello everyone. I'm Grace,' she said. 'I'm the Company Stage Manager. If you like, you can think of me as a gentle sergeant-major.' Several people round the table cheered at that and Grace nodded and smiled at the wide-eyed youngsters. 'However nervous you are, I'll look after you and get you on stage.'

'With a firm shove, if necessary!' Anna thought with a wry smile and wished she felt bold enough to say it out loud.

Everyone who knew Grace loved her, especially singers, because she had the ability to reassure and relax them. Always quietly spoken, she maintained a calm authority throughout the hurly-burly of rehearsals and performance. And as a friend she was a rock: loyal, warm, and positive, and despite the disparity in their ages, she and Anna were close and could pick up effortlessly even after the long periods of separation which were the norm in their nomadic business.

The grey-haired woman on Grace's left hesitated before speaking until a couple of gardeners arguing outside the open windows had walked past out of earshot.

'This feels a bit like University Challenge,' she said at last, in a deep, mellow rather plummy voice. 'Elspeth Dean, singing Mrs Grose, the Housekeeper, for the umpteenth time but looking forward to it.'

Next to her was the girl who would be Flora. Anna noticed that amidst the clutter of papers and scores, coffee cups and water bottles that had taken over the surface of the table once everyone had sat down, she had established her own ordered space. In front of her, in two neat piles, she had placed her score, and neatly aligned alongside it a notebook on which she had put a sparkly pink pencil case.

'Hello,' she said. 'I'm Charlotte and I'm seventeen and this is the first professional production I've ever been in, and I'm a bit nervous, so I hope I'll be OK.'

The company gave her an encouraging round of applause, which caused her to blush and hide her pretty, babyish face in her shoulder-length fair hair. Anna thought she was small for her age—perfect for playing a girl of about fourteen—but despite the shyness when she spoke, there was a grown-up composure about her that suggested she would cope with the demands of the production.

'Hello, everyone, I'm Toby,' said the prematurely bald young man sitting next to her. 'I'm the rehearsal pianist, and including a production at college, this is the third time I've worked on *Turn of the Screw.*'

'So you can play it then,' quipped Paul and Toby laughed and pulled a face.

Anna smiled over at him. He spoke modestly but she'd had some coaching sessions with him a few weeks earlier and knew he was not only a superb pianist, but had a wicked, dry humour. She already felt better, sensing this would be a good company and that the work, though challenging, would offer the distraction and companionship she needed.

Next to Toby, and on Jonathan's right, sat a visibly excited little boy who announced himself as Michael Manning.

Anna studied the boy with keen interest, knowing that the relationship and the dynamic between she and him would be critical to the success of the production.

He would be the enigma at the heart of the piece.

Poor orphaned Miles—isolated and haunted.

Genuinely innocent or calculating and devious?

The boy, too, was small for his age, and with a neatly cut head of brown hair and expressive eyes that were almost too big for his open, elfin face, she suspected he might make a disturbingly angelic Miles. As he spoke, he laid his hands on the table and even from her seat across from him, Anna could see how badly bitten his nails were.

'I'm twelve years and three quarters and I'm going to be Miles,' he said, in a light, bright voice and with an energy and lack of self-consciousness that suggested he might chatter away at length. 'I've sung in lots of concerts and things but I've never done opera before. I think this music is quite hard but Toby's been teaching me and I think I know most of it now.'

He turned to grin at Toby and then back to the assembled company who were listening with amusement as he spoke with such bright-eyed lack of inhibition.

'I've read the story and I've seen the film about it called *The Innocents*—I don't understand it all—but I think I get most of it.'

'Well done,' said Jonathan as the company laughed and banged the table.

Michael waited a moment for the noise to die away before he completed his introduction: 'I had to audition for Paul and Jonathan to get the part and my music teacher at school told me that the boy in the original production sang *Where ere you walk* by Handel, so that's what I sang, too. I learnt it specially,' he smiled, before adding, with a squeak, 'I just hope my voice doesn't break now!'

The company laughed again and he flushed.

'Patrick,' said Jonathan, 'I can see you've put the set model on a table over there but shall we look at the costume designs first?'

'Sure thing,' Patrick replied, preparing to talk through the designs while his sketches were passed around the table for everyone to see them.

'They're beautiful,' said Louise, handling each one gently, before passing them on.

'I've worked with a limited palette of colours,' Anna heard Patrick saying, as Harri passed her the pile of watercolour drawings.

She did not know Patrick's work, but she could tell at a glance that he was an artist as well as a designer. Never before had she seen such care to create not just a look and a period, but a character; a gallery of real people took shape. With the tilt of a chin, the position of a hand, the shape of a mouth, Patrick was able to suggest so much.

There was Miss Jessel—lost and pathetic and just as Henry James described her: *"dark as midnight in her black dress, her haggard beauty and her unutterable woe"*; Mrs Grose—steadfast, but full of foreboding; Flora—smiling and playing with her doll, but a doll who had lost her head; Quint—sleazy and seductive; Miles—small and frail but with an expression which bore an unflinching gaze; and the Governess—determined but deranged, wringing her hands on the brink of breakdown.

'I want Quint's appearance to change,' Patrick was saying now, as the designs arrived back in a pile in front of him, 'so that at first he's quite appealing and unthreatening, but gradually, thanks partly to makeup, he needs to become menacing, so that when he's seen listening to the children sing "Tom, Tom the piper's son" I want him to look genuinely insane.

'I won't need makeup by then, boy,' said Harri, pulling a ghoulish face.

'The way you look now, Harri,' said Jonathan, 'we're going to have to whiten you up a bit. Where did you get that colour?'

Everyone looked at Harri's ruddy complexion and nodded, no doubt thinking, as Anna had, that transforming him into something corrupt and evil-looking would take some doing.

'Golf course in Newport,' he replied with a grin and Jonathan shook his head and smiled.

'These designs are terrific, Patrick. Splendid. Really,' said Paul, who had flicked through them again during this exchange and looked at Patrick with genuine admiration. The company murmured its own collective approval.

'So, going back to the story,' Jonathan continued, 'as I said earlier, it's all about ambiguity—you don't know if the Governess is mad and imagining the supernatural events and therefore projecting her own delusions onto innocent children, or if a trustworthy governess is in fact relating a barely imaginable tale of malign revenants and of children depraved beyond description.'

Throughout the morning, Anna looked at Michael and wondered what he was making of his first rehearsal. She had watched him earlier as he studied the sketch of Miles and she'd seen him purse his lips as if to say, "I can be this boy." He was listening carefully to the discussion, all of which so far had been devoted to an appraisal of the novel and differing interpretations of the opera. Some of the talk had touched on the subjects of child abuse and homosexuality and several times already, Anna had hoped that Jonathan would temper what he said, given that Michael was only twelve years old. She wondered if the boy's parents realised that he was to be at the centre of such a troubling story about the corruption of innocence. The thought worried her and she found herself feeling increasingly protective of this child who was to be in her charge.

She gazed towards the open doors through which there came the sweet, strong smell of newly-cut grass. A breeze from outside sent a sudden fierce draught across the table, disturbing the pile of costume designs, leaving them fluttering until Patrick put out a hand to secure them and the gust died away.

'In our production,' Jonathan went on, 'I want to restore the ambiguity of James's original story so that at the end, we are left wondering whether Quint and Miss Jessel are "real" ghosts or merely figments of the Governess's vivid imagination. We need to suggest that something wicked has gone on here, and though we need to personify the ghosts —and of course, unlike in the novel, where they remain silent, in the opera they sing some extraordinary text—I want to send people away unsure about what they have witnessed.'

Paul had been listening closely to director and designer and added, 'I like that.' He nodded at Jonathan then turned back to the company. 'And later on you know, at the death of Miles, the Governess sings *"What have we done between us?"* in recognition of the fact that in trying to pull Miles back from Quint she has in fact pulled him emotionally apart.' He paused momentarily, as if hearing the scene in his head. 'And when she insists that Miles denounces Quint, the boy's final words *"You devil!"* can as easily be heard as referring to the Governess as to Quint. Indeed, I remember reading that Britten said he believed Miles's last words unmasked the Governess's true nature as the person whose mania had caused his death.'

'Mm—interesting,' said Jonathan, looking round the table to see whether others agreed.

Anna, too, took a moment to observe the group and assess their reaction to the discussion. From experience she knew how important these first talk-throughs were and how a director could lose a cast and crew right at the beginning if his ideas provoked scepticism, even ridicule. Looking at the engaged faces around the table there seemed little chance of this, and though Graham still wore the deadpan expression with which he had started, she guessed that appearing inscrutable was part of his persona.

'Jonathan?' said a piping voice, and the company turned to Michael, who looked as if he was bursting to speak.

'Yes Michael? Go on.'

'I think Miles misses Quint—perhaps he wants him back.'

Another gust of wind caused one of the open doors to slam shut.

'After all,' the boy went on unperturbed, 'the children have lost their parents and their uncle doesn't want them.'

'That's right, Michael. Absolutely,' said Jonathan. 'And now they've also lost their surrogate parents, Miss Jessel, the former Governess, and the valet, Quint.'

The company was silent, their attention caught by the boy's unexpected insight.

'I think the ghosts are their lost loved ones.'

His words hung in the air as people considered them.

This is a boy, thought Anna, whose mental age far outstrips his physical, but she sensed, too, that behind the intelligence and the childish ingenuousness, there was something unsettlingly sad about him.

She realised she was not the only person in the room who had sadness to subdue or demons to battle.

Chapter 8

'God—men! Don't you just love them? When they get scared, they either cling like babies or run like rabbits... What?.... OK, I know that's harsh and yes, it may be stereotyping, but still... oh come on, you're the psychotherapist—haven't you ever noticed a pattern?'

Clutching an unwieldy brown paper bag containing ingredients for a salad, Anna came round the side of the old Bothy in the Kitchen Garden to discover Louise sitting on a nearby bench in agitated conversation on her mobile phone. Their eyes met and both women flushed with embarrassment before Anna raised her bag of vegetables in awkward but friendly acknowledgement and tried to walk past as if she'd heard nothing. Louise waved in return and gave a watery smile, before lowering her voice to resume her call.

Anna hurried away towards a circular path that took her on to open parkland dotted with thick clusters of trees and led at last to the turning area outside the cottages. The late afternoon sun was still high in the sky and the air was warm, with just an occasional hint of the earlier breeze. As she made her way through a shadowy glade, Anna wondered about her new colleague, sensing she was someone for whom life was currently difficult, who might appreciate support. She stopped, thinking she might invite Louise to join her and Grace for supper, but decided it would be better to wait. Tonight she was looking forward to catching up with her old friend and wise sounding board.

She wondered who Louise had been talking to—surely she wouldn't talk to her own therapist in that exasperated, almost peevish tone?

'*Do* men cling like babies or run like rabbits when they get scared?' Anna asked herself. 'Was Edwyn scared? Is that why he ran away?'

The thought perplexed her.

Emerging back into the sunshine, she remembered that she'd not checked her phone for messages since lunchtime and she rummaged in her bag for her mobile.

No voice messages, but one new text.

"Good luck. Thinking of you. Hope you're OK. Lots of love Edwyn."

After weeks of silence, the apparently innocuous message took her by surprise. She picked up her speed and by the time she arrived back at Forester's, she was hot and flushed.

She dumped her bags on the sofa and threw open the patio doors. Stepping into the garden, she forced herself to focus on breathing deeply and listening to the calming sounds of nature. From the direction of the main driveway, she heard the distant rattle of a hedge-cutter, while all around her birds chirruped and twittered in carefree song-making.

She walked slowly down to the water's edge, feeling her shoulders drop and her eyes fill with tears that were never far away. She looked across the lake to the House and saw sunlight bouncing off the expanse of glass that was the Orangery. The day had gone well—she'd enjoyed it—but her mind was once again full of questions that chased away hard-won equilibrium.

What did he mean? Was he missing her? Did he regret his decision, but not know how to reverse it?

She knew she would analyse the message over and over again, but it would give her no answers. The only person who could do that was Edwyn and he had shown a determination not to explain what lay behind his decision to leave.

Her brother had urged her to write to him, suggesting that a man at home with words might find it easier to answer her questions in writing. Anna had resisted, feeling it unnatural to write to her own husband and fearing she would sound stilted or histrionic.

She looked at her watch—it was only quarter to six, plenty of time to compose something before starting to prepare supper. She watched the waters of the lake rippling and glistening below her feet and tried to ignore niggling worries about how she would sound to her erudite husband.

She went inside to collect a note-pad as well as some elegant Myddleton writing-paper she'd found in a drawer in the bedroom.

Seated at the table on the patio with pen poised, she looked down at the blank page, rubbed the top of the pen against her chin and tried to summon the right words, but all that swam before her mind's eye was the memory of sitting at another table, writing a different letter: a hot summer's evening in a stuffy theatre deep within the walls of the Barbican and her younger self playing one of opera's most touching heroines, Tatyana, writing her brave but impetuous letter, in which she lays her life and her love before the enigmatic Eugene Onegin.

Anna first sang the role in the summer she graduated from the Guildhall, just months before she and Edwyn were married. She was enchanted by the shy, unworldly country girl whose ideas of love come entirely from romantic novels, and had understood the turmoil Tatyana feels after meeting Onegin for the first time. A scene of feverish intensity demanded a display of mutating emotions, doubt giving way to ecstasy, excitement mixing with fear.

Anna closed her eyes, hearing the moment when Tchaikovsky balances his music on a knife-edge as Tatyana asks a series of plaintive, fateful questions:

"Are you an angel sent to guard me?
Or will you tempt and then discard me?

Resolve these doubts I can't dispel.
Could all my dreams be self-delusion?
Am I too innocent to tell?
Has fate prepared its own conclusion?"

For Anna—then—there was no such uncertainty or doubt. Now, like Tatyana, she had been rejected and humiliated.

The thought spurred her to write with the same feverish passion with which she'd enacted that scene all those years ago. The words came in a torrent, her handwriting increasingly scrawled, whole phrases abbreviated, as her hand struggled to keep pace with her racing thoughts.

Reading it back when she had no more to say, she found some of it hard to decipher. The draft became even messier as she edited and tempered passages that were too jagged and ugly to leave.

With care, she copied the letter onto the smooth, cream notepaper, the cottage address embossed in green in the top right-hand corner.

Dear Edwyn,
Thanks for your text. It was good to hear from you. The first day went well and the cottage is lovely, but it feels so strange to be here without you, still trying to make sense of why you left. Time seems to have run at a different speed since then and these last few months have been the most difficult and wretched I've ever known. I've begun this letter not knowing whether or not I will send it to you; I hoped it might help me if I put some of my feelings in writing.

It had helped, she thought, already feeling cleansed, lighter —even if in the end she did not send it.

I'm still reeling from the brutal shock of your decision to end so precipitately what had been such a loving and happy relationship. I had absolute faith that our marriage would endure to the end, till death did us part, no matter what challenges fate threw in our paths. I

66

believed you to be an honourable man, so it's doubly hurtful that you made a life-changing decision with reference only to your own needs, and seemingly with no regard for my happiness. It has felt as if you discarded our marriage as carelessly as you might rid yourself of unwanted rubbish.

Strong, accusatory words she knew, but she felt she could allow herself to vent some of her anger and frustration on the page.

You may argue that you had been thinking about your decision for some time and that it was neither sudden nor unconsidered as far as you were concerned. That may be so, but you guarded your feelings of anxiety and unhappiness and denied me any insights into them. For me, your decision was a body blow out of the blue and remains bewildering.

You have said that you had to get away from Oxford and the ivory tower existence, that you could not contemplate retirement in London, that you feel you will be better off living the rest of your days in Wales. But what about me? Do you have any sense of how bereft I feel? Do I not have a say in any of this? You gave us no opportunity to explore ways in which we could make adjustments to our lifestyle and face the future together. You even presumed to present your decision as if it was in my best interests! Were you trying to spare me the upheaval and inconvenience of moving to Wales? It just doesn't make sense, because you say you've never stopped loving me.

Her eyes filled up as she copied the words, and she put down her pen and blew her nose. As she breathed hard to recover her composure, she realised how peaceful it was. The hedge-cutter had done its work and was silent and all she could hear was the sound of humming insects and chattering birds.

I fear you may be ill—that you may have had some sort of breakdown and be embarrassed to acknowledge it or seek help. Is that why you won't see me? How else to explain such irrational behaviour? It's hard to think of you facing illness or unhappiness and not be with you to support you through whatever this is—this crisis you've gone through.

My future feels full of uncertainty, not least about where I will live. The house in Richmond has been home for so long, and right now, it offers some important stability. I'd like to go on living there if at all possible.

But if I'm to move on with my life, I need some honest answers about why you ended our marriage—answers which will put a stop, once and for all, to this endless speculation, which is torturing me. I need to know what went wrong between us, what I did or didn't do that caused you to leave me.

Please know that I wish you health and happiness for the rest of your life. I will always be grateful for the experiences we shared together. There are so many special memories to treasure and which I'm sure will never fade.

She wanted to say that she would never forgive him for having such a love and throwing it away, but she held back from committing to paper anything for which she might later reproach herself. While she entertained hopes of reconciliation, she dare not talk of never forgiving.

It was done, and with a sigh she signed the letter with all her love.

Chapter 9

'It's not your fault, you know.'

'What do you mean?'

Anna turned round from the sink to look at her friend. Grace made it sound like a self-evident fact, but Anna was struggling to understand the role she had played in the breakdown of her marriage.

'I mean it's not your fault that in Edwyn you chose someone with a hidden side, a side that remained in shadow, only to appear when a personal problem emerged he couldn't share with you.'

Anna had finished washing the dinner plates and walked back to join Grace at the table. They had moved the dining table in front of the open patio doors so that they could look out on the now darkening garden. Inside, the table lamps cast a soft, warm glow which framed Grace's almost white hair like a halo, giving her the appearance of a kindly sage.

Over a simple supper of pasta and salad they had chatted—about Grace's recent trip to Australia to visit her sister, about the prospect of lodging for the next few weeks with her scatter-brained niece—and gossiped about mutual friends and acquaintances. Inevitably, the conversation had turned to Anna's marriage.

Grace looked thoughtful as she swirled the remains of her wine around her glass.

'Maybe it's something to do with the stereotype you overheard Louise talking about—or maybe it's to do with—I don't know—deeply buried, unresolved problems.'

Anna shivered as the cooling air momentarily made the hairs on her arms tingle and shook her head at the unfathomableness of it all. She nibbled one of the purple grapes which Grace had brought and, with her index finger, moved some crumbs of cheese around her plate while she considered her friend's last comment.

'It's just mystifying to me that he would contemplate old age alone after the loving relationship we had for so long.'

Her voice quivered and broke and she bowed her head, focusing hard on the remains of her cheese. Something about Grace's calm, steady gaze unnerved her, as if her friend could see truths that she could not.

'Maybe he looked into the future and did a bit of a reality check?'

Grace, too, had lowered her head in an attempt to catch Anna's eye.

'Am I being too blunt?' she asked, squeezing Anna's hand until she at last looked up.

'No—not at all. I really appreciate hearing what you make of it. Go on, please.'

They stayed for a moment with hands clasped, until Grace withdrew hers to put her arms into the sleeves of the pale blue cardigan she had draped around her shoulders. As Anna watched her, she marvelled at how unlined her skin was and how clear her eyes, despite the fact she was only a few years younger than Edwyn.

'I don't know him very well,' Grace went on, 'but I'll be honest, Anna, I sometimes wondered about all those overseas lecture tours, the sabbaticals, the solitary walking holidays in Wales. You've been together a long time, I grant you, but with your work as well, you know, you've never lived together properly, day-in, day-out, and maybe—with retirement pending—he realised that *would* mean living together fulltime in one place—that you would expect it— and he couldn't do it.'

Anna opened her mouth to protest—'but we got on so well!'—but stopped, as the insight behind Grace's words began to make sense. She got up to close the doors and draw the pale green curtains, and hesitated there, wondering whether to confide something she had kept to herself.

'When he first went to Wales,' she said at last, 'I asked him whether he missed me and he said of course he did, but he also said he feels safer now and more relaxed on his own.'

She stood still for a moment, remembering how the words had stung her and how she had challenged his use of the word "safer."

Grace touched her arm as she came back to the table to sit again.

'Oh Anna, that must have seemed so cruel—but you know, I don't think love or devotion are the issue. I think, though, that commitment might be.'

She paused.

'It just didn't look that way to you because he always seemed so devoted, so pleased and happy to be with you.'

Anna nodded, and as she fiddled with the long stem of her wine glass, she recalled the first time she had drunk wine with Edwyn over dinner at a restaurant in Turl Street, directly overlooking the lodge of Exeter College. It was March, just a few days after the concert at which he had first heard her sing, and it was snowing outside. From the warmth of their table in the window, they had watched people scurrying and skidding past in the yellowy street lighting like characters in a Victorian Christmas card, and Edwyn had told her about himself. How he had had several girlfriends, but never married, how he joked that no one would take him on, how his late mother had feared he would never settle and lead a normal life with a family.

He had seemed so candid and open as, with warnings and self-deprecation, he laid himself before her, but she wondered whether he was unwittingly flagging up the problems which beset them now, having remained, as Grace said, in shadow for so long.

Grace was watching her closely, as if debating how much more to say.

'You often said how dedicated and committed he was to his teaching and his research, how hard he worked, even when you were on holiday,' she said. 'Perhaps, even before he met you, he had got into the habit of making work an alibi.'

Anna recalled with a pang how often it had been she who put herself out in order to win them time together, especially at weekends, frequently travelling long distances late at night after performances so that they would wake up together.

'Perhaps that's why he was still single in his forties,' Grace went on. 'I mean he was—is—a good-looking man. You must have meant something special for him to have tried to make that commitment.'

Anna shrugged.

Somewhere across the lake a dog barked and then fell silent.

'You sound as if you're speaking from experience?' Anna said at last, knowing that Grace's marriage had ended over fifteen years ago.

'No... not really from my own experience, but I have seen it quite a lot in this business.'

'What went wrong for you and your husband?' Anna asked, glad to turn the focus from herself and conscious that Grace rarely spoke about her personal life, other than as it related to her family, to whom she was close.

Grace tilted her head to one side and narrowed her eyes.

'I think I always assumed I could combine work and marriage, but Jack felt excluded and threatened—by the intensity of it, by the type of people I worked with, people he couldn't relate to.'

She sighed.

'He married again, soon after we parted. Another teacher.'

Anna sensed that even from this distance, there was a residue of pain and regret.

'Do you still think about him?' she asked.

'Sometimes.'

Grace stopped as if to steady herself.

'Sometimes something will remind me of him and I'll feel sad for a while, but really, those feelings are just echoes now.'

Her words struck Anna as sad and yet encouraging; perhaps the intensity of pain and longing would not last.

'So many things remind me of Edwyn,' she said. 'He's always on the edge of my thinking, however deeply engrossed in something else I think I am. Little things will set me off. I can't look at bacon in supermarkets—let alone smell it cooking—without remembering Sunday mornings with bacon sandwiches and coffee and the Sunday newspapers spread all around us. I read things or hear things and think, "I must tell Edwyn that" and then I remember, and all the feelings of loss and emptiness come flooding back.'

She put her hands to her face to cover her mouth, knowing she was close to tears.

'How do I get over this Grace?'

'Oh, Anna, it's such early days yet. Don't expect too much of yourself.'

Grace waited while Anna shook her head and sniffed back the tears.

'I don't think you do get over it—it's more a question of accepting it and getting through it.'

Anna nodded, knowing what an important step forward it would be for her if she could only accept it.

'This may sound harsh, Anna, but perhaps you need to acknowledge that if the relationship really had been as right as rain, it's likely you would still be together.'

Anna looked at her friend with eyes blurred by tears which welled but did not fall.

'I felt so utterly confident that what we were to each other was indestructible.'

Grace cut herself a slice of Brie and buttered a small, broken piece of Ryvita.

'Do you think you may have tended to rather idealise the marriage?' she asked, before biting into the cheese and biscuit. 'I'm not saying you did, ' she said, flicking crumbs from her fingers onto the plate. 'I'm just wondering, because I think that might make a person feel under pressure.'

Was there a difference, Anna asked herself, between being confident about a relationship and idealising it? Had she been impervious to or ignored things that should have been addressed?

Yes, perhaps she had.

She remembered calling unannounced at Edwyn's teaching room at New College when she'd arrived in Oxford earlier than expected, just before Christmas. Though at the time she had suppressed her anxiety, even now, she could feel the unease she'd experienced when she saw that Edwyn had moved her photograph from its prominent position on an orderly bookshelf to one where it was lost among the clutter and muddle of a table in the corner. In its place on the bookshelf stood a photograph she had never seen before of Jim and Brenda on their wedding day gazing blankly away from the camera and a young woman—a bridesmaid she assumed—clutching Brenda's arm and smiling out at the photographer. When she'd asked Edwyn why he'd moved her picture, he'd only added to her disquiet by saying he thought "it was rather in your face where it had been," the very expression seeming bizarre and out-of-character.

Thinking about that now she wondered if he'd given the wedding photograph pride of place to make up for the disparaging way in which he had talked about his parents' marriage and because with Jim's recent death, he had lost them both.

'Would you like some coffee—or a glass of water?' she asked, going over to the sink. Grace shook her head as Anna let the water run cold before filling a glass for herself.

'You could be right,' she said, walking back to the table. 'Perhaps I did have an idealistic view of how things were. I suppose the reality is, that despite all the good things I thought we had, in the end, something compelled Edwyn to walk away from it. I know I have to accept that if I'm to move on, but it's hard.'

'Of course it is. It's a huge emotional adjustment and though you have work and plenty to distract you, right now there's a big hole at the centre of your being.'

Anna nodded in agreement.

'I'm sure you're doing as much as you can to help yourself move on, but you can't speed it up. As each month goes by, you'll feel better. Believe me.'

Anna gulped the last of the water and as she tried to smile before she had completely swallowed it, found herself wiping away dribble from her chin.

They both laughed and then Grace stood up and lifted her bag off the back of the chair.

'I should be going,' she said.

Anna put her arm round Grace's shoulders as they moved across the room together.

'Are you looking forward to this?' Grace asked as they stood by the door. 'I think it could be very good for you to be immersed in something so challenging.'

'I am actually—especially after today,' Anna replied, and even to her own ears, her voice sounded stronger and brighter. 'It seems like a really good bunch of people.'

She opened the front door and breathed in the strong, earthy air, while a couple of white moths fluttered past her and hurled themselves against the insides of the lamp-shades near the table.

She nodded towards them.

'Visitors.'

Grace shivered in the cool night air and did up some of the buttons on her fine cashmere cardigan.

'Don't get cold,' Anna urged. 'And thank you for tonight —for listening and for all your wisdom.'

Grace laughed and hugged her.

'Oh, I don't know about that.'

She pulled away a little, still holding Anna firmly by both arms.

'You'll be fine,' she said. 'I know you will, though perhaps you can't believe that right now.'

The birds had long done chorusing and the night was silent as Grace made her way towards her car. As she stopped to open the gate, she hesitated for a moment before turning back to whisper some final parting words.

'Try to look forward to seeing where life takes you next.'

Chapter 10

"It is a curious story. I have it written in faded ink—a woman's hand, governess to two children—long ago."

The piano struck up the sombre chords of the Prologue, and Anna watched as Harri assumed the part of an unknown man who introduces the new and nameless Governess and sets the scene for the events which will unfold in the opera. Though in performance, he would be wearing evening dress at this point, Harri was dressed for rehearsals in a pair of baggy black shorts, huge black sandals and a Welsh rugby shirt. He was standing at the side of the stage area reading from a tattered manuscript, while behind him Anna closed her eyes and prepared to assume her role.

Silently she began to enact the events he described.

She was to be Governess to two children in the country. Their only relative, a young man-about-town, had asked her to take complete charge of them—on condition that she never bother him about them, whatever the problems which might arise. Overcome by the gentleman's charm, the woman accepts the position and prepares for her journey.

The room was hotter than on the previous day and having 'narrated' the Prologue, Harri left Anna alone on the acting area and moved to the side where he sat, blowing air down the front of his shirt, his ruddy face glistening with beads of sweat. The music that followed evoked the motion of a coach as the Governess travelled to Bly, and Anna marvelled at the touch and skill with which Toby could conjure on the piano so many of the colours of the orchestra.

As was so often the case at the beginning of a rehearsal period when a role was entirely new to her, she was struggling to master the music. At the same time, she was trying to think her way into the disturbing world which

Jonathan was trying to create, one in which, from the start, the boundaries between the living and the dead were chillingly blurred.

Her long soliloquy in Scene 1 was a test both musically and dramatically as Anna strained to lay bare the Governess's inner state: her excitement and infatuation; her pride and determination; her fear and foreboding that in this grand mansion set in blissful rural isolation, all is not what it seemed when described in London by her handsome employer.

Anna turned to indicate that her journey was over and as Jonathan did not stop her, Toby continued with the next of the musical variations connecting each scene. Now Anna was plunged into the everyday world of Bly. She spun round as, from behind, Elspeth and the children came hurrying towards her—housekeeper and charges agog to meet their new governess.

"Will she be nice?.... Will she like us?"

As the children danced round Mrs Grose and bowed and curtseyed at her instruction, Anna heard their singing voices for the first time. Charlotte's was a sweet and pure soprano, but it had a warmth and bloom that belied her youth, whereas Michael's tinkled like a goat bell with just a hint of huskiness and fragility, which Anna guessed would later prove heart-rending.

Jonathan stopped them in order to choreograph the children's movements more precisely, encouraging Michael to play the fool, to mess up his newly smoothed hair and to fall over on his tummy when Mrs Grose tried to coach him on how to behave in front of his new governess.

'And now, Michael,' said Jonathan, 'seize Anna's hand with real urgency and pull her away, and you Charlotte—run after them and take her other hand. You want to show her everything, and we want to feel that she's enchanted and immediately bowled over by you both.'

The children's faces were flushed, their eyes glinting with excitement and purpose and Anna felt herself falling under their spell, loving them instantly, as did the innocent young woman she was endeavouring to portray.

They spent the rest of the morning working on the first two scenes, with Sarah, the Deputy Stage Manager, writing up Jonathan's stage directions in the prompt copy, and Paul making notes in the full score propped on a music stand in front of the high stool on which he perched at the side of the acting area.

When they broke for lunch, most of the company chose to go outside onto the terrace to eat the sandwiches provided, though a few leapt into a car to make a swift visit to the nearest pub. Jonathan, Paul, Patrick and Graham huddled together over a sheaf of notes while the others sat in small groups at the sturdy teak tables scattered around the terrace. Grace was sitting with Toby and Charlotte, and Elspeth—as she was in every spare moment—was intent on an intricate piece of embroidery. Louise sat alone to one side, nibbling half-heartedly at an apple, while scrolling through messages on her mobile phone. Anna could see no sign of Harri or Michael, though she could hear their voices somewhere close by.

Hesitating for a moment, she decided to join Louise. Though the woman had more colour in her cheeks today, her eyes still had a slightly glassy look as if she was some place a long way off—or wished she was.

'May I join you?' Anna asked, before sitting.

'Be my guest,' replied Louise, chucking her half-eaten apple onto the grass beyond them and reaching into her bag for her lipstick.

'How's the jet-lag today?' Anna asked. 'Still feeling groggy?'

'Yeah—pretty crap, really,' Louise replied, peering at herself in the small mirror of her powder-compact and pulling a face to suggest she was not impressed by what she saw. Then, as if fearing she had been rude or unfriendly, she turned to Anna and smiled.

'Thanks for asking,' she said. 'You're doing really well, by the way. It's a hell of a part. I'm just glad I can sit around recovering for a few days—I don't have much to do until Scene 8, apart from making the occasional ghostly appearance.'

She rolled her eyes and grimaced and Anna laughed.

'Yes, I wouldn't mind having slightly less to do. It's pretty relentless for the Governess.'

At that moment a football crashed onto the terrace, bouncing several times until it came to a halt under their table, its progress stopped by Anna's feet. Michael came flying around the corner of the house, with Harri doing his best to keep up with him, and both looking in vain for the missing ball.

Louise gestured to Anna to say nothing, but Michael spotted the intended subterfuge.

'Please Miss,' he chirruped to Anna, indicating at her feet. 'Please can I have my ball back?'

Both the women laughed and Louise leant forward and ruffled his hair.

"You see, I am bad, I am bad, aren't I?" he trilled, in exactly the way Miles does at the end of the first act when Quint and Miss Jessel have drawn the sleeping children into the night garden and the Governess and Mrs Grose discover them and send them back to bed.

Both the women laughed again and Anna felt herself entranced by this bright, endearing little boy.

'Ooh, someone knows his part!' said Louise.

Michael grinned at them and bent to retrieve the ball, by which time Harri had puffed his way on to the terrace and sat with a groan on the seat next to Louise.

'Duw, I'm too old for this,' he moaned. 'It'll be the knackers' yard for me, I can see it now.'

'Ah, come on Harri,' pleaded Michael. 'It's your turn to go in goal now. Come on.'

He held out a hand and Harri heaved himself to his feet and made great play of lumbering after the boy as if each step would be his last.

Anna watched them go. There was something about the easy companionship so quickly established between man and boy which made her spirits lift. Though so far she knew little about Michael, she sensed he was relishing this company for more than just the musical or theatrical experience it would offer him.

She became aware that Louise was watching her.

'Do you have children?' Louise asked.

'No,' Anna replied. 'I don't. Do you?'

Louise shook her head. 'Just as well really,' she said. 'They wouldn't have a father—well not for long anyway.'

She snapped her compact shut and got up to go, before explaining:

'I seem to make a habit of being left by the men I love.'

Chapter 11

The radio was on quietly in the background as Edwyn warmed up some soup for lunch, shivering slightly in the chill of the kitchen. The wet weather had hung around for several days and the temperature had dropped noticeably.

Music signalled the start of The Arts Show and he turned up the volume in time to hear the presenter say the first item would be a review of a show at the Royal Court by an Irish writer. A number of critics were gathered in the studio to share their views on a play about a dying woman confined to a crumpled bed and looking back over her life in a haze of morphine.

One of the speakers found the play static to the point of being stagnant and "too Irishy" for his liking, but the others were enthusiastic.

'It's not so much about dying as about how to live,' said a woman with a strong Irish accent. 'I laughed as much as I cried and I came away from the theatre feeling energised, not depressed, which is what I'd feared.'

'I agree,' said another woman, with tightly clipped vowels. 'I loved the way the woman said, "it's easy to be happy. It's a decision." It struck me this is a woman who's lived every second to the full, who's never let rancour or disappointment curdle her view on life.'

Edwyn stopped stirring the soup and listened, his interest captured, lunch temporarily on hold

'The performances were exquisite,' said the man, 'but I thought it cried out for editing. As a deathbed lament, by the end it just became too mawkish for my taste.'

The woman with the pinched pronunciation came back at him. 'Surely, it was too robust to be mawkish? I've found myself not being able to get it out of my mind.'

'Me, too', said the Irish woman. 'It seeps into your bones. It made me think that if we squander love, we squander the best part of ourselves.'

There was a pause and then for the first time in the discussion the presenter expressed his view. 'It left me wondering why do we so often choose unhappiness, when the only person we hurt is ourselves?'

Edwyn heard little of the debate that followed. Had he squandered the best part of himself in some perverse pursuit of unhappiness?

The sound of the soup sizzling and catching on the bottom of the pan brought him back to the present. He moved the pan off the heat and was stirring at the thickening liquid when the phone rang in his study.

It was Linda, the estate agent, calling with good news.

'That's soon!' Edwyn said in surprise. 'Do you think we can complete in time for them to move in then? It's only six weeks off.'

He listened as Linda explained that the couple were cash buyers and were anxious to move in before both started new jobs which required them to relocate to London.

'Yes, I can be ready,' he said. 'It will be good to have it sorted after all these months. Thanks.'

He sat at his desk, his lunch forgotten. It would be a relief to get the house off his hands—it was over six months since Jim died and the place had been empty ever since—but it was still the house in which he'd done most of his growing up, so parting with it would mark another severance of his ties with the past.

He remembered the excitement he'd felt when they'd moved there when he was six years old, the space of the new house a stark contrast to the cramped cottage in which he'd spent his first years. He glanced down at the wedding photograph and thought of his parents, living almost their entire married life there until Brenda had died sixteen years earlier.

When did it go wrong for them, he wondered? He thought of his mother, so bossy, never compromising—no wonder Jim used his carving and painting and gardening as excuses to stay out of the way.

He remembered an upsetting scene on a freezing beach somewhere in Norfolk: a long loaded silence, him busying himself with an elaborate sandcastle, and Brenda asking: "How do you put up with me being so awful all the time?" and Jim's response… "Well, it's just you isn't it?"

Even at that young age—he was ten at the time—he realised that was a turning point in his idea of what it must be like to be a grown up. If this was what was meant by being a family, he calculated, he didn't want any part of it. No frosty marriage or disappointed life for him, he decided, looking at the dejected faces of his parents.

Now, looking again at the photograph of that long distant wedding day, he shuddered to think what a bitter and corrosive thing lovelessness is and gave thanks for the love he had known with Anna.

It was her voice with which he had first fallen in love, though he was flattered that she had singled him out for attention as she gave that radiant performance of *The Bluebird*. Her lovely solo had captivated him and he had felt his shrunken heart open like a clenched fist relaxing to a loved one's gentle touch. He recalled how he had afterwards made his way through the usual throngs of students in the King's Arms hoping that, like most choirs, they would head to the nearest watering hole as soon as the concert was over.

And so he had pursued her, courted her, believed that with her youth and her guileless openness, she would save him, keep him whole, that he would, after all, survive.

He reached for his Filofax and looked up the number for the house clearers recommended by his solicitor. He would need to get things moving so that the sale could be completed in time for the deadline. Though he was sure he had taken all he wanted from the house, he realised with a sigh that he would need to make a final visit to collect anything he didn't want the house clearers to deal with.

He knew it made sense to combine the visit to west London with a visit to Richmond to pick up the few possessions he'd left there, in particular the research papers he'd forgotten and now needed. It would be easier to do this while Anna was away at Myddleton.

He picked up the phone and dialled.

Chapter 12

Michael didn't see her at first. As she studied his smooth, bright-eyed face engrossed in his book, she felt a surge of unexpected protectiveness and when he at last looked up and smiled, she was touched by his open expression.

'Hello,' he said shyly. 'Were you looking for me?'

'I thought I'd see if you'd found a nice spot to escape to.'

'Do you want to escape then?' he asked with a frown.

'Not really escape,' she laughed. 'Well, perhaps, just for a few minutes.'

The weather on that third day was again so glorious that when they broke for coffee, Anna decided to wander down the lawns which rolled away from the terrace and to sit for a few moments of quiet contemplation on the soft grass. She'd gone only a short distance when she spotted Michael sitting cross-legged with his back to her and his shoulders hunched forward. At first she'd feared he was upset and had hurried towards him, though as soon as he looked up, she saw that his face bore the look of rapt concentration of one who has been happily lost in another world.

'What are you reading?' she asked.

He held up the cover. It was a library copy of *The Little Sister* by Raymond Chandler.

'Oh,' she said, with surprise. 'I've not read that. What's it about?'

She sat beside him, wrapping her long pink skirt around her bare legs. The sun was in her eyes and she had to shield them with her hand in order to see his face.

'It's about a private eye called Philip Marlowe,' he said, 'who's been asked to find a woman's missing brother.'

Anna knew some of Chandler's work and thought his writing quite adult and uncompromising for a boy of Michael's age.

His next words perturbed her.

'I want to learn how to be a private detective so that when I grow up I can find my father.'

His gaze was clear and steady but Anna turned her head away to conceal her unease.

Why did Michael need to find his father, she wondered, squinting into the distance. Was he one of those people you read about who seem to mysteriously vanish or had he deliberately absented himself from his family, perhaps because he had gone away to start another one?

She became aware that Michael was watching her.

'I've never known my father,' he explained, laying the book down on the grass between them. 'I'm not allowed to talk about him. I don't even know who he is—my mother won't tell me.'

He blushed and hesitated a moment, and she wondered if he regretted saying so much, but then he shook his head and said, almost as if to himself: 'Perhaps she doesn't know.'

The remark shocked Anna. How much could a child of his age understand about the messiness of adult relationships?

'So, is it just you and your mother then?' she ventured.

'And my gran,' he replied, before adding: 'My mother's mother.'

He hung his head and plucked at his socks which were creased around his ankles.

'I don't know anything about my father's family—I've no aunts or uncles or cousins or anything.'

She looked sideways at him and noticed how slightly built he was. Below his baggy khaki shorts, his bare legs looked as spindly as those of a young gazelle. Yet he had an air of quiet resolve, as if the search for his missing father had become his own secret mission.

It was some moments before either of them spoke again.

'Who do you take after?' he asked at last, again taking her by surprise, so that at first she wasn't sure she understood the question.

'Your mother or your father?' he prompted. 'Which one of them are you most like?'

'Well,' she considered. 'I suppose I've got bits of both of them in me, but not just them. For example, I look like my mother's sister—same fair colouring, blue eyes and small bones, whereas my mum's dark and a much bigger build than me.'

'And are your parents musical?' he asked.

'They like music,' Anna said with emphasis, 'but my paternal grandfather had the good voice in the family.'

'Until you came along, that is,' Michael quipped, with a smile that Anna guessed would soon be melting the hearts of teenage girls.

She laughed and found herself blushing.

'I don't know where I get my voice from,' Michael said. 'Not my mum, for sure! She's tone deaf—can't even sing the National Anthem in tune.'

Anna laughed again.

'And football, that's another thing—no one in my house likes football, so I don't know where I get that from either.'

He stopped.

'It's very frustrating not knowing.'

'Yes,' she said, looking at his earnest, elfin-like face. 'I suppose it helps to know where we've come from, what made us.'

She thought about her upbringing in that lonely house on the windswept Fens.

'My parents taught me never to give up on something without giving it a fair chance,' she said. 'I'd probably have given up piano lessons before I was nine unless they'd drummed that into me.'

She had not known then that music would set her on her path in life; not until she was twelve when her piano teacher took her to Evensong at Ely Cathedral where she was enraptured by the sound of the choristers and resolved to see whether, she, too, had a voice that could thrill people like theirs had her.

'I play the clarinet,' said Michael with enthusiasm. 'If I don't get my voice back after it breaks, I'll concentrate on that instead.'

'Good plan,' she said. 'We're very lucky to have music in our lives—not everyone does.'

She glanced at her watch and began to stand up.

'Shall we walk back together?' she asked. 'We don't want to be late—and you've got to practise your *Lavender's blue* next.'

They were working through the opera chronologically, blocking scenes roughly so that by the end of the week, they would have covered the whole of the first act. At the start of the morning, they had run through the scene where the Governess receives a letter from Miles's school telling her that the boy has been expelled. Shocked, and disbelieving that Miles might be bad, she watches the children amusing themselves and is enchanted by their innocence.

Anna watched Michael and Charlotte playing together quietly, their pure voices blending sweetly in the traditional nursery rhyme, *Lavender's blue*. The conversation with Michael had intrigued her—and helped explain the boisterous friendship he'd established with Harri.

As they ventured deeper into the dark recesses of the opera, Anna found herself relating ever more closely to the role of the ambiguous Governess—able to suggest the agitation beneath the determinedly calm exterior of a woman who has heard a strange cry in the night and a footstep past her door.

Jonathan's rehearsal style—though relaxed in some ways —was in fact remarkably intense and Anna was finding the

89

process both stimulating and exhausting. Though he had come to the production with his ideas and concepts well developed, Jonathan expected the singers to contribute, too, and was constantly challenging them to make choices about the motivations and actions of their characters.

Just before the lunch break, they began work on Scene 4, when the Governess spies an unknown man staring at her from the top of a tower. At first, she hopes it might be her dashing employer, come to see how she is getting on, but soon she fears it's not him but some adventurer or intruder and flees back to the house.

'Throughout this piece,' Jonathan said to the whole cast, 'we're looking to characterise extremes of emotions, extremes of fear, extremes of obsession.'

'I want you,' he said, 'to create reined in sexual hysteria. But only just.'

Anna, standing alone in the acting area, felt unclothed and vulnerable. She heard the words reverberate around the silent, echoey room and observed the different ways in which each member of the cast reacted to them. Harri looked a little uncomfortable, Elspeth simply raised an eyebrow, while Louise tipped her head back and sighed.

'Think about what it's like in real life,' Jonathan suggested to Anna, 'when something unexpectedly awful happens, or something scares or disappoints you.'

Anna saw Grace look up quickly, her face full of concern. Yes, Anna thought, this was one of those moments when there was nowhere to hide. She cursed Edwyn for exposing her to such turmoil, though at the same time she sensed that working through this difficult process might in the end strengthen her.

'Can you try,' Jonathan urged her, 'to catch the conflicting pulls of duty and loyalty and terrified foreboding—which is what I think she's beginning to feel at this point. She loves her life at Bly—it's all been going so smoothly for her up until now, until the arrival of the letter and the appearance of the stranger.'

'And Anna,' Paul called from his high stool, as she moved back into position, ' I know it's hard but try to relax at the top of your voice.' He looked round so as to include all the other singers in his next statement: 'I think Britten maintains the extraordinarily high register of the voices in order to create musical tension which can match the dramatic tension of the story.'

To Anna, he said more particularly: 'Don't be scared of it. You've got the range.'

In the lunch break, Michael and Harri once again disappeared with a football, while Anna sat with Grace and Elspeth at a table in the shade. The settled summer days seemed unending, the bright sunny weather in sharp contrast to the unreal, twilit world they were constructing in the Orangery.

Anna put her hand to her throat and sighed.

'That was hard-going for you, wasn't it?' said Grace, looking at her closely. 'I hope Jonathan didn't push you too hard.'

Dear Grace, thought Anna, looking fondly at her friend —never far away from mother-hen mode.

Elspeth looked up from her embroidery and nodded in agreement.

'You're doing terrifically well,' she said.

'Thanks,' Anna replied. 'The children are good, too, aren't they? Jonathan seems to know exactly how to get what he wants from them.'

'And they're very quick and responsive,' Elspeth agreed.

'I'm glad to see Sarah and Emma taking Charlotte under their wing,' said Grace, nodding her head in the direction of the lawn, where the girl was lying sprawled alongside the two young women from stage management. 'Just as long as they don't sneak her off to the pub with them. I'm the official chaperone for the two kids so I feel I'm *in loco parentis* and that wouldn't do at all!'

The phrase made Anna think of Michael's mother and she wondered what the woman made of her young son's debut into opera—an opera so concerned with the fragility of childhood innocence, at the mercy of the adult world.

'Have you met Michael's mother?' she asked Grace.

'Yes, I have,' Grace replied. 'Lizzie. She drives him here from Abingdon and then comes to pick him up at the end of the day. You're sure to meet her sometime.'

As if on cue, Michael came round the side of the house, closely followed by a panting and red-faced Harri who slumped into the seat next to Anna's.

'That boy will be the death of me,' he said.

'Get away with you. You love it,' said Grace.

'Yeah, it's true—I always wanted a son. I love my girls to bits—even though they're hell bent on ruining me—but I always thought a boy would have been a good mate.' He laughed. 'Someone to share the pain when Wales lose.'

After a while, they all walked back to the Orangery together, where Jonathan and Paul were leaning over the piano talking to Toby and agreeing how much time they would spend blocking the remaining four scenes of the first act. Their schedule had been meticulously worked out and the singers knew exactly what was expected of them.

'I'm trying to avoid one act being over-rehearsed at the expense of the other,' Jonathan had explained on the first day.

For the rest of the day, they did more work on the Letter and the Tower scenes and touched on the long fifth scene, the tension building when the Governess sees an unknown man peering at her through the window and learns from Mrs Grose that the description matches that of Peter Quint, former valet to the children's uncle. Quint had been left in charge of the household and, according to the housekeeper, was "free" with everyone, including Miles.

The previous governess, Miss Jessel, had been forced to leave, and had subsequently died, while Quint was killed soon after in an accident. The horrified Governess fears Quint has returned for the children, and resolves to protect them.

They didn't get much further than the start of the scene where the children play noisily and sing another nursery rhyme, *Tom, Tom the piper's son*, encouraged by Jonathan to avoid jolliness and daintiness and find an underlying tinge of viciousness.

Both of them understood instantly what he wanted them to suggest—that children are not always sweet to one another, but can sometimes be hateful and horrid, and while Charlotte spat out her words and tugged annoyingly at Michael's clothes, Michael assumed a disconcerting air of knowing arrogance towards his 'little sister'. When they finished the song and ran out of the acting area, several of the watching cast and crew broke into spontaneous applause.

At the end of the session, the company dispersed quickly, with shouted arrangements from some about meeting later in the pub. Grace walked Charlotte and Michael round to the front of the house to wait for their lifts to arrive. Anna gathered her score and notebook together and was turning to make her way back to the cottage when Michael looked round over his shoulder to wave goodbye to her. His face looked small and pinched, as if the efforts of the day had tired him. Anna waved back and watched after him until he disappeared out of sight.

She wondered what Lizzie Manning was like, and in her mind's eye built an image of someone young and flighty who had mislaid the father of her son and thought little of it; someone liberal and free—bohemian even—who allowed her son to roam into complex adult worlds.

She wondered what Michael's father had done that was so bad that his mother had eradicated him from their lives, as if he had never existed. She bit her lip; despite his cheery, outgoing personality and his obvious confidence among adults, she guessed it was this yearning for a family he'd never had that occasionally gave Michael that air of loneliness.

As she set off across the park, Anna was struck that in casting Michael as Miles, Jonathan and Paul had chosen one troubled, fatherless child to play another.

Chapter 13

She felt weary, and as she strolled through the deserted gardens, she was overcome by a feeling of uncomfortable loneliness. Though she could not face the prospect of company, she felt daunted by the empty hours that lay ahead.

The neighbouring cottages were quiet when she opened the door to Forester's and breathed in the now familiar smell of the place. She dumped her bag on one of the work surfaces in the kitchen and reached for the kettle. The cold water came out of the tap with an unexpectedly fierce surge which made her jump and cry out as it splashed onto her hand and arm. Wiping herself dry with a tea towel, she leant against the sink and waited for the kettle to boil. She had no appetite for food so decided a cup of tea would sustain her until she could rid herself of her restlessness and relax into the evening.

A few minutes later, holding a mug in her left hand, she manoeuvred the double doors open and walked to the end of the garden. The grass was dry so she sat at the edge of the water, her eyes glassy and unfocused as she allowed the low spirits in which she'd walked home to take her over. She'd made the tea too strong, but was relieved that even at times like this she did not resort to large quantities of anything even stronger.

She recalled the moments back in February immediately after Edwyn had left, when alone and almost pole-axed by shock, she had thought she would simply open a bottle of wine and drink until she was completely anaesthetised from the pain. Something had stopped her—probably the saving realisation that drinking herself senseless would not bring Edwyn back.

Her self-absorption was broken by the squawk of a family of ducks, the smallest of which were making repeated and unsuccessful attempts to launch themselves out of the water and onto the bank of grass to her right. She hugged her legs together and watched them, admiring their seemingly futile determination—the water level was surely too low for such short and weak little legs—and inwardly cheered when one, then another, made the Herculean ascent and spun around in dizzying circles on the grass, until they tipped themselves back into the water to rejoin their agitated mother.

As the fluffy flotilla skid away from her view, she wondered how she'd kept herself together through all that had happened. She knew that taming the overwrought emotions while she was working was part of it, even though sadness sat solidly in her chest and fear lodged in her stomach much of the time. She knew, too, that she could draw on some of that raw suffering to create a credible and compelling heroine.

Exhausted after a day of inhabiting the world of another deeply troubled woman, Anna hankered for a straightforward job where she might distract the sadness and fear with simple tasks.

The lowering sun was gleaming off the glass walls of the Orangery across the water as Anna sat reflecting on her day's work. It had gone well, she thought; the necessity of re-examining herself following the end of her marriage somehow tapped into her creativity and resourcefulness. But there were times like this when the loss was so debilitating that she felt as if her body was splitting.

The tea was cold and bitter-tasting and she tipped what was left into the water, before easing herself to her feet. Her skirt felt slightly damp and she realised that while she'd sat, the evening dew had begun to settle. She made her way back to the cottage, feeling the need for warmth and comfort. She almost wished it was dark so that she could shut the curtains and cocoon herself in her tiny fortress. Though she loved this season best of all, and the performances they were working up to demanded long, dry, warm evenings, she was finding this summer hard, haunted by memories of late walks in Richmond park or lingering meals in a sheltered back garden.

She wondered what the others were doing. She guessed that Harri would be out on the golf course at Frilford Heath, relaxing effortlessly despite a day playing the devilish Quint, and later making new friends in the Clubhouse bar. Grace was going to the pictures with her niece; Elspeth would be quiet and content in the bed and breakfast she'd found in Cumnor village.

And Louise, also struggling with personal pain and disappointment, what would she be doing?

She felt too tired and dispirited to go for a walk, but it was not yet seven o'clock and she knew that if she was to avoid a miserable and wasted evening she must shake herself out of this torpor.

She recalled what Grace had said to her when they parted for the day as she was hurrying away to meet her niece in Oxford.

'Hang on in there, Anna. I know this is tough for you but I know from experience that delivering the goods at work is a lifeline in hard times. It will help you get through this.'

She went upstairs to change out of her creased and clammy skirt into something dry and comfortable and glanced at the row of books on the shelf above the bed. Though she had propped the small stone against it, the battered copy of *Far From the Madding Crowd* had once again fallen over onto its side.

In search for something that would shift her mood, she was inclined to see this as a signal, a sign that this book had something to say to her and would not be ignored.

But she hesitated.

She had sent Mark back the copy he had given her when they had their final encounter beneath the flowering magnolia. The section he had underlined in red had irritated her, an affront to her judgement and a betrayal of her impending marriage.

It was the spring of 1992. They had both graduated the previous year, but he had stayed on in Oxford to do a teacher training course while Anna had gone to the Guildhall School of Music and Drama to do postgraduate study in singing and performance. Their friend Gerry was leaving Oxford to take up a teaching post at the Yale School of Music and NOCC was holding a farewell concert and reunion party in his honour.

A concert at New College on the Saturday night had been followed by a lunch party the following day at St Hugh's, where Gerry had been a Lecturer. She was pleased to see Mark again, though her pleasure was clouded by the guilt she felt at having been so infrequently in touch with him during the preceding nine months, despite the fact that she and Edwyn often spent weekends in Oxford.

In truth, there had been unease between them ever since she and Edwyn had got together, but she had hoped the choir reunion would put them on a better footing. They had sat together in the pub after the concert and caught up with each other's news, but had been on different tables at lunch. She knew that something had changed between them; that the comradeship was not as it had been. He had been friendly, but somewhat distant, even guarded, but she had sought him out before she left, knowing that he was leaving for India a few months later, and anxious to part on good terms.

He was not with the crush of people drinking coffee in the Mordan Hall so she went downstairs to look for him there and noticed that the small door into the garden was slightly ajar, letting sharp but welcome fresh air into the overheated entrance hall. Stepping outside, she could see small groups of people—some students and their families in for Sunday lunch, some of the 'reunion-ites'—standing around braving the chill and enjoying the gardens. It was a bright and sunny day in early April and the gardens were carpeted with springtime flowers and alive with new growth. The brilliant sunshine dazzled her eyes but she spotted Mark standing alone near a glorious magnolia tree.

She had left her jacket in the Hall upstairs, but was worried that if she went back for it, she might miss him. She hurried towards him and when he looked up and saw her, he opened his arms in obvious pleasure.

'I thought you'd gone!'

'No, no, of course not—I couldn't find you. But I haven't much time—I promised Edwyn I'd meet him at the Randolph at four o'clock so we can have tea together before I get the train back to London.'

She was shivering and he rubbed her arms with his hands to warm her.

'You'll catch cold.'

She felt awkward, but laughed and shook her head.

'What were you looking at so hard?' she asked.

He pointed to a small plaque beneath the tree:

'Planted by the students of 1919 to honour all those who lost their lives in the Great War.'

'It's beautiful, isn't it?' she replied, touching one of the pale pink buds.

'The Armistice magnolia. It's flowered early—let's hope a late frost doesn't get it.'

'It's been so good to see you Mark—I know I've been a pretty poor friend lately. And you're going away soon aren't you?'

He looked at her with curiosity, perhaps hoping that she, too, cared that this meeting would be their last for another year at least. She looked away, feeling his eyes burning into her as he looked deep into her face. He moved towards her and before she knew what was happening, he had wrapped the generous fabric of his long overcoat around her and pulled her towards him. For one suspended moment, she allowed him to kiss her the way she knew he'd always longed to—tender, deliberate and lingering. She stepped back, flushed and agitated, and concerned to see his face alight with surprise and hope.

He kept hold of her hand and squeezed it gently.

'Bathsheba.'

His unexpected use of the old playful name was too much and she pulled away from him in embarrassment and guilt. He reached into one of the pockets of his capacious coat and brought out a copy of *Far from the madding crowd*.

'This is for you,' he said quietly.

She took it and nodded, not knowing what to say before she fled.

'Take care of yourself,' he'd called after her as she hurried towards the college.

At the door, she stopped to look back at him, but he was walking away, across the garden, coat flapping behind him, towards his Spartan student flat on Canterbury Road.

She had not seen him since.

She knew that a few years after he did his VSO in India, he went back there to teach long-term, but where he was now she had no idea.

She turned the book over in her hands. Must she at last return to a story she had shunned for so long? She feared that if she re-read it now there was the possibility that, like Mark had done all those years ago when they were fellow students of literature, she would come to view Edwyn as her Mr Boldwood.

That she would come to believe that her life had indeed been deflected from its intended course.

Chapter 14

Malo: I would rather be
Malo: in an apple-tree
Malo: than a naughty boy
Malo: in adversity.

The weather continued warm and sunny, Elspeth completed her embroidery and immediately began another, Harri and Michael spent spare moments either kicking a ball about together or poring over Michael's Arsenal scrapbook, and the production continued to make good progress.

Anna had still not decided whether to post the letter she had written to Edwyn. The mere act of writing, allowing her feelings to pour so freely, had been cathartic, but she was unsure whether sending it would make things any better—or, conversely, might create more of a barrier between her and Edwyn.

On Thursday they had moved from the window scene to that in the classroom where the Governess supervises the children at their lessons. Miles is practising his Latin declensions when he recites a mysterious mnemonic unfamiliar to the Governess.

The scene was a testing one for both children, with a lot to sing and the need to behave just strangely enough to give the Governess cause to feel less certain about them. Michael's plaintive rendition of the recurring '*Malo*' tune was particularly poignant and disturbing, the occasional fragility of his voice entirely appropriate for it.

He took to humming or crooning the mournful melody whenever he was alone or lost in thought, and something about his new obsession with it gave Anna a feeling of intense claustrophobia around the rehearsal room.

She was pleased when Louise suggested they have a meal with the others on Friday night. Louise had had little to do so far, other than note when Jonathan wanted her to make an occasional ghostly appearance from out of the trees, and even in the scene at the lake when the Governess believes she has seen Miss Jessel beckoning to Flora, she had no singing to do.

'I warn you—I've no idea what my voice will do when I do have to sing,' she had joked to Paul as they broke up for the day. 'There must be cobwebs in there by now.'

'Has it been frustrating for you this week,' Anna asked her later as they sat beside each other in the pub. 'All the hanging around and no singing, I mean?'

'Actually,' Louise replied, 'I've been quite glad to be so under-employed—it's given me the space I needed to try and process all the shit that's going on in my life.'

Anna remembered the snippet of phone call she had overheard on Monday afternoon and nodded in tacit acknowledgement.

The group was beginning to gather around three small tables which they had pushed together in the corner of the rapidly filling pub. Elspeth sat on Louise's left, while Grace was on Anna's right. Further along were Harri, Emma, Sarah and Jonathan. Harri was in high spirits—looking forward to going home the next day, but enjoying a bit of harmless flirtation with the two stage management girls.

The pub was not the closest one to Myddleton, but the singers had suggested it after they learned from Paul that it was no-smoking and served good food. Though the evening was still warm, they opted to sit indoors to avoid the gnats swarming in the garden, attracted by a stagnant-looking ornamental pond.

At the following morning's rehearsal they would be doing the night scene at the end of Act 1 and Louise would be required to sing for the first time, but tonight she was clearly intent on letting her hair down. The four women

102

had bought a bottle of wine to share, but Louise had already been back to the bar to get a second, before her companions had finished the large glasses she had poured for them.

'So,' she said, settling herself back at the table and looking round at them. 'How are we all? Well and truly spooked?'

Jonathan heard her and laughed.

'We haven't even started yet,' he said.

Louise lowered her voice to a stage whisper but made sure he could hear her.

'I'm worried he'll have me emerging out of the lake at some point like some poor demented drowned woman.'

'Don't encourage him, girl,' Harri quipped and for a while the group engaged in some light-hearted banter with their good-humoured director.

Their meals arrived before too long and while they ate, they talked more quietly to their neighbours rather than to the group.

'So,' said Louise grinding black pepper over her pasta and looking at Anna, 'it's not just me who's loved and lost then.'

Anna knew that Louise and Elspeth had heard about her broken marriage and as Louise was keen to turn the conversation to matters of the heart, Anna felt it would not be inappropriate to ask what had happened to her.

'Oh, the usual: met a new man, he moves in with me, everything's going swimmingly, even my mother likes him, I go to Vancouver to do a crap production of *Peter Grimes*, get back eight weeks later to find he's dumped me and moved out.'

She took a swig of wine and refilled her glass.

'Said he didn't want to get too serious.'

'Were you keen on him?' Anna asked tentatively, before winding her fork round some spaghetti.

Louise dropped her earlier bravado and nodded.

'Fraid so. Ever since my marriage broke up a few years ago, I've had a string of disastrous relationships, but I thought this one might be right. Might be "forever",' she said, using the index fingers of both hands to suggest the ironic inverted commas.

She paused.

'This one felt different.'

'So, have you been able to process it?' Anna asked.

Louise laughed and picked up her glass again.

'Yeah—simple. Women fake orgasms; men fake relationships.'

Elspeth put down her fork and let out a loud fruity laugh, which got the men at the far end of the table wanting to know the joke.

'You wouldn't understand,' Louise assured them.

'So what about you?' Louise asked Anna with genuine interest. 'Go on—tell us about it.'

Anna felt slightly awkward talking openly about her situation to a group of women, only one of whom she knew well. She also felt inhibited by the close presence of the others and feared they would overhear what she was saying. It was too early in the rehearsal process for her to feel ready for such disclosures of her pain.

'It came out of the blue,' she said at last, 'and it's still that suddenness that's one of the most shocking things to deal with.'

Louise was watching her expectantly and Anna knew that she would have to go on, even though she determined to do so with a certain amount of précising and understatement.

'We'd just spent Christmas and New Year together—I'd taken time off—and then a few weeks later, he said that he was going to take early retirement, that he needed to get away from Oxford, and wanted to go and live in North Wales.'

She stopped to take a gulp of wine, hoping it would help her to talk more freely.

'At first, I took it for granted that he wanted us both to base ourselves there, even though we might keep the house in London.'

She emptied her glass and was glad when Louise immediately refilled it.

'I spent a couple of weeks trying to talk to him about where we would live, looking at house prices, wondering what it might be like to live so far away from everywhere.'

She hesitated.

'At last, he spelt it out to me that he intended to go on his own—that I was not part of his future plans.'

She shuddered at the memory and flinched a little under Louise's unblinking gaze.

'We were so happy, so good with each other, I couldn't imagine what would ever come between us—and I still don't really understand what did come between us,' she said sadly, turning a pile of recalcitrant pasta round and round on her fork before giving up on it.

'Nothing really takes away the emptiness,' she said finally. 'I can be OK when I'm distracted like during rehearsals but when I'm left to my own thoughts, all the pain comes flooding back.'

Grace and Elspeth nodded, their faces softened by sympathy and concern.

Louise, toying with a piece of crinkly purple lettuce, looked sceptical.

'What?' said Anna.

'Well, you may not like this,' she said, 'but the way you talk about how wonderful it was, you don't think you were a bit like one of those celebrity couples, always proclaiming how blissful their marriage is, how they're permanently on honeymoon? Perhaps,' she said more gently, 'you weren't realistic in your assessment of how things really were.'

'Maybe,' Anna concurred, recalling the conversation she'd had with Grace a few nights earlier.

'It sounds as if Edwyn wasn't being honest with you for quite some time before he left,' offered Elspeth '– that you'd somehow stopped communicating about what was really important.'

Anna nodded, grateful for this chance to hear how other women interpreted a story that to her remained resolutely inexplicable.

Louise was clearly mulling over something.

'When I was in Vancouver,' she said, 'I went to see this really brilliant play about people who're physically present, but in fact have gone missing.' She paused, as if realising the potential impact of what she was about to say. 'I suppose it was about the pain of realising you've been living a lie....'

All four women fell quiet at that, but smiled when they realised that Harri had been watching them and was whispering the explanation "girl talk" to the group around him. Sarah and Emma looked at them with fleeting interest but then turned back to resume the animated conversation they were having with the men about their holiday plans in Corfu once the festival was over.

'I think one of my greatest disappointments,' said Louise once she was sure they were not being overheard, 'is finding out just how short "forever" can be.'

Elspeth sighed and shook her head.

'I don't envy you girls your heartache, I must say. It feels sad—but also a relief—to know all that's behind me.'

Anna knew that Elspeth had been widowed some years earlier after a long and happy marriage to another singer. Anna, too, felt sad at the prospect of not sharing her life with a man, but she could not imagine being with anyone who wasn't Edwyn, and was resigned as Elspeth—and perhaps Grace, too—appeared to be to a life of uneventful singleness.

'What's shocking for you Anna,' said Elspeth wiping her mouth on her napkin, 'is the lack of warning or discussion —the suddenness of the end.'

'It's as if he just held his nose and prepared to dive into very deep cold water,' said Louise, pushing her plate away and sharing out the last of the wine.

'But Anna you're not forty yet,' said Elspeth—'and maybe in time, you'll come to feel that this phase of your life was something you've done and now you're ready to try something else. After all, you were very young when you met Edwyn.'

She had got into her stride now.

'Like having regular holidays in one place and realising you need to stop going there and should explore other places.'

Anna laughed and pulled a face.

'I know that sounds a bit crass,' Elspeth said, looking momentarily flustered and pausing when a waitress leant across her to clear the plates away, 'but it reminds me of my brother and sister-in-law. For years, every summer they used to go sailing in the Aegean. They loved it and then one year, Bob said he thought they should have a change and do something completely different. Gilly agreed to go to France with a heavy heart, fully intending to drag him back to sea the following year, but now they're both complete Francophiles. I know they look back on the Greek holidays with very happy memories, but they're equally glad to have given themselves new ones.'

Anna mused on the unexpected analogy, not yet ready to embrace the sentiment.

Grace saw her look. 'I think you'll need to accept it if you're to move on,' she said, touching Anna's hand.

Louise put her hands through her wiry long hair and gave it a shake. 'If you don't mind me saying, you seem to have been rather passive about the whole thing,' she said to

Anna. 'Don't you feel angry with him? I'd want to tear him apart, limb from limb, if I were you.'

Anna was surprised by the description of herself as passive, but had to admit that she was not angry, just sad and bewildered.

'I need to process it, as you put it,' she said to Louise. 'Something must have happened to Edwyn, something must have triggered this and I think I'll only be able to understand what happened to us when I discover what that was.'

Chapter 15

The distinctive smell was still there. As soon as he opened the front door, the familiar pungent aroma of furniture wax and Old Spice conjured up memories of his parents, but for all that, the house had a dejected and empty feel about it. Brenda and Jim were long gone and little remained of their lives apart from a few pieces of furniture.

Edwyn could see that Linda was doing what she could to give the house a sense of still being cared for. A pile of circulars and free newspapers had been stacked tidily out of sight on the shelf underneath the hall table and the small patch of grass at the front was newly cut, the flower beds tidied. When he went through to the kitchen and stood by the double doors, he saw that the back garden looked surprisingly welcoming. The gardener had deadheaded the flowers that were going over and someone had made a simple potpourri of buddleia, roses and lavender and placed it in an old blue bowl that had always been kept on the kitchen table. The act of thoughtfulness touched him and he felt the unexpected prick of tears.

Linda no doubt.

She was a neighbour and had kept an eye on Jim in his last few years while he clung fiercely to his independence. When he succumbed unexpectedly to his final illness, she had visited him in hospital, taken him magazines and fruit. Edwyn was happy to entrust the sale of the house to her, guessing she would take a personal interest in it.

As he moved silently between the downstairs rooms he wondered what potential purchasers had made of the scraps of mismatched furniture dotted here and there. He had taken the best pieces to the cottage in north Wales, which though only rented, was likely to be his home until his financial affairs were resolved and he could buy somewhere permanent. The sparse furnishings revealed many of the carpets to be badly worn and the walls bore evidence of furniture once pressed up close to them, depths of colour preserved there in paint and wallpaper that had faded elsewhere.

He made his way upstairs, wary of the memories which might be awakened. The old double-bed in the main bedroom had been stripped and covered in a fine cotton cover he recognised as one that Anna had bought for Jim on a holiday in Egypt. He was surprised to see it there as Jim had kept it draped across the inside of the door of his workspace and he supposed Anna had found it and used it to cover the shabby, sagging mattress, its vibrant colours a striking contrast to the drabness of the room.

The smell of Old Spice was stronger here than anywhere else in the house and he wondered how many prospective buyers had been subconsciously put off by the sickly, old-fashioned perfume.

He sat on the edge of the bed, its springs squeaking and giving before they settled under his weight. He fingered the cover, remembering Anna's delight in the array of colours and patterns the stall-holder had unrolled for her consideration, and how she chose this one because she thought the striking blue, red and gold feathers might inspire a design for one of Jim's boxes. Edwyn decided he would take it with him and if Anna didn't want it, he would keep it himself.

There was little else in the way of personal possessions. Anna had sorted Jim's clothes, and the few books and bric-a-brac he and Brenda had accumulated had gone to charity shops. He was grateful to her for dealing with the intimate remnants of their lives, leaving him the far simpler task of choosing what pieces he wanted for his own domestic comfort in a new home. Selfish he knew, but it was all he could face doing at the time. The house clearers would come on Wednesday and take everything else away.

He folded the coverlet and went downstairs with it. He was thirsty and went into the kitchen to get a glass of water, but the wall-mounted cupboards that had once held glassware and crockery were empty. The tap spluttered with a cloudy spurt, splashing the stainless steel surround of the sink before it ran clear and cold and he could scoop a handful to his mouth. He wiped his hands on a tea towel hanging from a hook on the back of the door. The house was stuffy and needed airing. He took a small bunch of keys off the hook where they were kept, concealed by the floor length chintz curtains he'd always thought an odd choice for a kitchen. The doors were stiff and he opened them with difficulty. Once outside, he realised he should check out Jim's workroom in the sturdily built shed in the corner of the garden.

He fumbled for the right key to unlock the door, and when none fitted, gave it a firm shove and it opened with a rasping sound as it grated against the stone floor. He could see that the door had warped and no longer fitted properly into its frame. Jim's work bench was still there, but the floor and the surfaces had been swept clean of the wood shavings which Brenda complained Jim trailed into the house on his clothes and on the soles of his shoes. Though the shavings had gone the smell of wood lingered.

The shelves above the bench were bare and even the windows were clean and free of cobwebs. Linda—or perhaps her gardener—was taking care of this. Edwyn noticed a battered cupboard in the corner, on top of which Jim used to keep a kettle and mug and the means to make tea and coffee. He remembered that this was where Jim had stored back copies of gardening magazines that he hoarded until the small space was full and he was forced to have a clear-out.

The cupboard door was jammed shut but Edwyn remembered that the trick was to push against it before pulling at the handle. Once open, he could see that no one else had discovered the knack of releasing it because it was brim full of papers and magazines that slid to the floor at his feet. He lifted them onto the work bench where they spread across the surface in disorderly piles. He knew the house clearers would deal with them but felt he should at least try to stack them tidily. He sorted the glossy magazines into three large piles and put old copies of the local free paper together in another.

He knelt to check the cupboard was empty and spotted a folded piece of paper stuck at the back, caught on a protruding nail. Unlike the magazines and papers—which were just a couple of years' old—this paper was creased and fragile with age. At first he couldn't make out what it was, until he turned it over and saw a stamp saying 'The Wool Shop Ludlow' and realised with surprise that it was a knitting pattern for a child's toy—a woollen rabbit, shown in a faded black and white picture alongside a smiling boy with neatly parted hair and chunky fat legs.

His eye was caught by the words 'colour suggestion': knitting wool reference numbers were given first and then the colours—chocolate brown and cream. Someone had underlined the suggestion and put a tick by it. He gazed at the picture in confusion. Brenda had not been a knitter and despite his all-round skills as a handyman, neither was Jim. He looked again at the rabbit and knew that this was the pattern from which someone had crafted the much-loved toy of his childhood—Jack Rabbit, brown with cream spots and floppy ears lined with pale pink sateen.

He folded the pattern carefully, left the cupboard door ajar, and went out of the shed, dragging the door shut behind him. He walked back towards the house and sat on the wooden bench to the left of the double-doors looking down onto the lawn, the knitting pattern on his lap.

'Dear Jim,' he thought. 'An inveterate hoarder.'

But why, he wondered, had Jim kept this knitting pattern and who had it belonged to?

He closed his eyes and saw his six-year old self encountering this garden for the first time in the dusk of a cooling evening; remembered standing there in delight clutching Jim's hand, feeling full of energy despite the long fractious journey from Shropshire.

He opened his eyes and frowned, straining to remember why the journey had been so bad-tempered when to his childish mind it was an exciting adventure into a new world.

They had been late—that was it—late setting off and Brenda had been annoyed and grumpy for the rest of the day, chastising Jim for wasting valuable time that could have been spent getting settled for their first night somewhere new and unfamiliar.

He opened his eyes and squinted into the sunshine, the garden still full of the colourful array of different flowers and shrubs that thrived year on year, even as Jim grew older and less able to tend them as he once had.

A clump of yellow snapdragons caught his eye.

A bunch of yellow flowers—that's why they'd been late.

They had left Brenda packing up the last few kitchen things they would need when they arrived in London and he and Jim had gone off together in the car that was yet to be loaded for the long journey ahead. Jim had stopped in the village to buy flowers and had then driven out into the country. Edwyn remembered that he had taken his woolly rabbit with him, fearing it might be lost in all the chaos at home, and he was swinging it casually in his left hand as he and Jim walked up a long path and into what seemed to him to be a vast garden of stone. Jim led him on purposefully, seeming to know exactly where they were going, and finally stopped in front of a shiny black headstone. Edwyn recalled looking up at Jim in surprise as he leant to place the bunch of bright yellow daffodils across the base of the headstone. They stood together in silence before Jim took him by the hand and led him back to the car.

*

It was to be many years—almost a lifetime—before he visited that grave again. He thought of it now with more than a twinge of guilt, recalled only too vividly the neglect and abandonment he had found on his last visit.   He reproached himself for his negligence and knew he should do something to restore it to the pristine order in which Jim had left it over fifty years earlier.

There was now no one else who would.

Chapter 16

The next day the company broke up at lunch time, people going their separate ways until Monday. Harri was heading west to South Wales while others were going back to homes in London. Anna, too, toyed with the idea of returning to London and though she wondered how she would fill a weekend alone at Myddleton, she could summon little enthusiasm for the empty house in Richmond.

The rehearsal had been hard going—everyone was exhausted and looking forward to a break—but the night scene in the garden when the power of Quint and Miss Jessel has drawn the sleeping children from their beds was a crucial point and Jonathan had demanded full concentration so they could end the week having completed Act 1.

Anna listened half-heartedly to the plans being discussed by those who were staying around. A state of limbo beckoned, in which she could think of no appealing pastime other than the prospect of a soak in a hot scented bath followed by a long sleep.

When Grace rang her on Sunday morning to invite her to join her and her niece at a concert that night at the Sheldonian, she was grateful for the offer of company and for the focus it immediately gave to a day that otherwise might have drifted. She was happy to find ways to fill the day, knowing that come early evening, she would have something sociable to do.

Though the concert would take her once again into the heart of the city, she felt less apprehensive about this than she had the previous week. The traffic was light and she arrived twenty minutes early and decided to fill the time wandering beyond the Sheldonian, past the Bodleian and the Radcliffe Camera towards the University Church of St Mary the Virgin. The evening service had just finished and the congregation was straggling out into the hazy sunshine of Radcliffe Square, where the air felt as if a storm was building.

From deep inside the church she could hear the exuberant swell of the organ and leant against the railings to listen. Across the square, set into the wall of All Souls College, she saw the distinctive red casing of a post-box and, reaching into her bag, she pulled out a cream coloured envelope.

She'd intended to post it earlier while walking near Myddleton but had faltered and stuffed the letter back into her bag. Now, something about being so close to Edwyn's former rooms, drew her towards the post-box. She'd agonised over whether or not she should post this letter, but now it seemed the decision was beyond her control. She frowned at the unfamiliar address, hoping it was correct, as she'd had to write it from memory having mislaid her address book.

She slipped the envelope into the opening and turned away, knowing the letter was no longer hers. She made her way back to the Sheldonian where people were milling around the several entrances, many of them tourists attracted by the popular programme—or perhaps because the building's distinctive round shape marked it out from the surrounding architecture and intrigued them.

She waited at the foot of the steps on Broad Street, where the gorgon-like "Emperors' heads" on the wall gave the place an imposing air. Once or twice she was jostled by people anxious to get in and find their seats, and moving aside to avoid a gaggle of jabbering Italian teenagers, her eye was caught by a portly middle-aged man wearing a replica Wales rugby shirt and ducking into the low opening of the White Horse pub on the opposite side of the road. She smiled and thought of Harri: good, decent, funny Harri—as far away from her idea of Quint as it was possible to be, and though she'd appreciated his kindly support, she feared their relationship was too comfortable and sensed she would have to work hard to inject any semblance of threat or antagonism between them.

She frowned and sighed, knowing it would be difficult to achieve this on her own and that Harri, too, would need to play his part in establishing a more sinister dynamic. As she was pondering this, she heard her name being called. Looking round and expecting to see Grace, it was Louise she spotted first.

'I roped Louise in this afternoon,' Grace explained, 'when my hare-brained niece remembered she'd promised to baby-sit for some neighbours!'

The three women greeted each other warmly, all glad not to be at a loose end on a Sunday night in a place that wasn't home.

'So what have we got then?' Louise asked Grace as they made their way across the crowded courtyard towards an entrance on the left hand side of the building. 'Looking at this lot, I take it there'll be nothing too challenging.'

'No,' Grace laughed, 'it's billed as Music of the Baroque.'

'Oh, that's OK,' Louise said. 'Nothing to frighten the horses!'

Anna followed them into the auditorium and was relieved when Grace explained that she'd bought top price tickets so they could sit on proper chairs.

'I know we're a bit close to the band, but my back can't cope with sitting on those benches,' she said.

'Suits me,' said Louise as they sat a few rows from the front. 'We'll get a good view of the soloists from here.' She lowered her voice to a stage growl. 'I like to look into the whites of their eyes and smell the fear.'

Anna laughed.

'Remind me never to invite you to any concert I'm in.'

The three women sat in companionable good humour. Glancing at Louise, Anna thought she looked far less drawn and dishevelled than earlier in the week and that she'd recovered some of the feisty spirit she'd guessed had been there.

She studied the programme: though there were pieces by Purcell and Telemann, the concert centred on Handel, with one of his most popular concertos and the ceremonial fireworks music he wrote in honour of George 11, plus arias and duets sung by a soprano and a tenor.

'Nicholas Kirkby?' she said with surprise. 'Is he back on the scene again? I heard he'd been ill and was living in France.'

Louise looked quizzical.

'Don't ask me,' she shrugged. 'I don't know him. The soprano's good though—and quite a character by all accounts.'

Anna looked over to Grace who was sitting on the other side of Louise.

'You know him, do you?' she asked.

'A little—I worked with him a couple of times, quite a long time ago now. What about you?'

'No, but I've heard him several times and saw him at a party once after a show I was in—he seemed rather aloof and stand-offish.'

'Oh, I don't think it's that,' said Grace. 'He's always suffered with the most terrible nerves and insecurities— and yet he has—or at least he had—the voice of an angel.'

'There you are, my girl,' Louise joshed: 'don't judge a book by its cover.'

Anna laughed.

'No, you're right—I shouldn't judge him when I don't know him. There was just something inscrutable about him that I found slightly unnerving.'

The players in the period-instrument ensemble were making their way into the hall and there was a flurry of activity around the doors as ushers urged people to take their seats. Anna, looking round to see if she could spot anyone she knew, was pleased to see that the place was almost full, but wished that the auditorium was not so hot and stuffy.

In the *concerto grosso* with which the concert began, Anna marvelled at the sheer beauty of the writing for the strings and the stylish exuberance with which it was played by the small baroque group from Germany. Not only were they ravishing to listen to, but with their verve and energy they were a delight to watch as well, showing none of the uninvolved competence which marred the performances of many of the professional orchestras with whom she worked.

She felt impatient for the tenor to make his first contribution to the evening so that she could test whether Grace's assessment of his character was more accurate than hers. When his turn came, and the orchestra sat waiting for him, there was an uncomfortable hiatus and Anna wondered whether beyond the firmly closed doors he was doing battle with the demons of stage fright.

When he at last made his entrance to warm, encouraging applause, his posture appeared hesitant, his demeanour downbeat, until he stopped alongside the conductor and turned to face the audience with a flourish of his black tails and a determined straightening of his back.

He was tall and slender, his greying dark hair cropped into a fashionably scruffy cut, and with a light growth of designer stubble. His tentative smile suggested he would be grateful for support. His biography in the programme said he graduated from Oxford in 1990, and Anna calculated that like her, he was in his late thirties. His face, though, bore the marks of an older man, and heavy bags under his eyes gave him a haunted look.

As the orchestra launched into the introductory bars of *Enjoy the sweet Elysian grove*, Anna saw that Louise was smiling and realised to her surprise that she clearly found this man attractive. Anna had always found his sexuality hard to determine and she looked at him now with heightened interest. The voice was sinuous and alluring and nerves played no part in his rendering of any of the three arias he sang in his first group, though Anna felt that occasionally his light, quintessentially English tenor sounded perilously fragile and she feared for his ability to navigate and sustain Handel's fearsome coloratura writing. At the same time she sensed that it was this very quality of vulnerability and his pensive persona, especially in the aria where a heart-broken Jephthah prays for angels to guide his daughter's spirit to heaven, which gave his performance such poignancy.

In the interval, the three women escaped outside to the courtyard, hoping for respite from the airless atmosphere of the hall only to discover that it was as relentlessly close there as it was inside.

They moved away from the crush of the crowd.

Louise lit a cigarette and took a deep intake of nicotine.

'Well,' she said with emphasis, after tipping her head back to blow out a wispy ribbon of white smoke. 'Get a load of that!'

'I wouldn't have thought he was your sort,' Anna laughed.

'Oh yes,' Louise insisted, her eyes widening, 'I like them slightly frayed round the edges—and that voice—isn't it to die for? So seductive!'

She took another puff of her cigarette.

'How come I've never got to work with him? I'll have to have a word with my agent.'

'We'd better warn the poor man,' Grace teased. 'He wouldn't stand a chance.'

The interval bell was sounding and they hurried back inside for the second half, the ushers impatient to close the doors. The orchestra and the leader were already seated and when the doors opened again, a tiny, blonde-haired woman wearing a red strapless ball gown swept in followed by Nicholas Kirkby, looking more confident now, with the conductor hanging back to allow the soloists to have their moment centre stage.

The first item was one of Anna's favourites—*As steals the morn*—a rapturous duet, adapted from poems by Milton. The two singers stood side-by-side and though both sang out to the audience and fully engaged with the listeners, from time to time they leant in towards each other, exchanging glances and smiles and exuding a winning enjoyment of the music.

The young woman's soprano voice was pure but sumptuous and she performed her part with a mixture of sweet decorum and dangerous abandon, while Nicholas Kirkby appeared to enjoy playing along with her. Their voices entwined to delicious effect, hers full of honey mainly soaring above his; his full of velvet-toned tenderness, murmuring and whispering and occasionally striking out to sweep above hers.

Anna sensed that the listeners around her scarcely dared breathe for its entire duration and long after it had finished there was a deep silence before the whole audience broke into prolonged applause accompanied by whoops of approval.

Louise let out a loud whispered "Wow!" and fanned herself with her programme.

'How sexy was that?' she gasped to Anna. 'I reckon they must have done the business in the interval to have given a performance as outrageous as that.'

The thought had not occurred to Anna and it surprised and disturbed her, forcing her to acknowledge that she'd suppressed the part of herself that might have responded to such sensuous singing. She looked at her colleague, openly delighting in the sensual performance, and felt saddened at her own detachment.

At that moment, she seriously doubted her ability to convey the pent-up sexuality of a woman infatuated by a dashing young man whose approbation she hopes to win.

For the rest of the concert she was preoccupied by thoughts of the role with which she was grappling and realised that she could not allow her personal trauma to block the creative journey on which she and the rest of the company were embarked. She had a decision to make: was she prepared to use the harrowing experience of the last few months to find a resonance with the raw, obsessive behaviour of the naive young governess; to help her capture her hopes and desires and her implied sexual neuroses?

Even when the concert was over and she stood chatting with the others, Anna was distracted and a little agitated, when she realised she'd forgotten her cardigan.

She hurried inside to see if she could retrieve it before the ushers removed it. She need not have worried: the hall was deserted, the floor covered with the confetti of dropped ticket stubs and unwanted programmes, and her thin cotton cardigan was where she had left it draped on the back of her chair. She folded it over her arm and headed back towards the door, but her way through was blocked by two men standing outside and wrapped around each other in a warm embrace.

The man whose face she could see she didn't recognise; the man with his back to her in his smart black tails was unmistakably Nicholas Kirkby.

Chapter 17

For months Edwyn had shut his mind against the image of the pretty little house with its pale cream frontage and tiny garden, separated from the street by shiny black railings. With Anna away it felt easier to confront his feelings about returning to what had been their home.

He had little to collect as he'd taken most of what was his in February. One large archive box would be more than enough. As he looked down the quiet street towards the church at the far end, he had no desire to linger. He was tired after the long drive from North Wales and the visit to the family home, and he faced another journey when he was done here. He would take what he'd come for and leave.

As he turned his key in the lock, he caught sight of a woman watching him from a window of the house next door. He lifted his hand in acknowledgement, but hurried inside, not wanting to give her the opportunity to come out and quiz him.

Sunlight streamed into the hallway from the porthole window at the top of the stairs and particles of golden light shimmered in the air, illuminating the display of boxes in the alcove on the right-hand wall. He did not allow himself to dwell on these brightly painted boxes and the quarrel they had triggered. He had left them untouched, and he would leave them again today, undisturbed.

Most of what planned to take was in his study. As he made his way up the stairs, he glanced down to the left through the open door of Anna's music room, at the black upright piano with its shiny lid closed, the stool tucked neatly under the keyboard. From deep within the silent instrument came a tacit reproach and he felt her absence, longed to see her, but found the prospect difficult, knowing the hurt he had caused and the pain they both felt.

He carried on up and into the small spare bedroom which doubled as his study, the dark blue day bed acting as a sofa on which he could read in comfort when not needing to be at his computer. He opened one of the drawers to his desk and lifted out two bulging blue folders containing the research papers he'd forgotten in his haste to leave. He packed them into the storage box, along with a few reference books, and other bits and pieces he saw lying around.

He carried the box through to the main bedroom, slightly bigger than the other and dominated by a black iron bedstead covered with a delicately embroidered white eiderdown. He noticed how bare the dressing table looked, and supposed that Anna had taken her jewellery box and other paraphernalia with her. When he looked more closely he saw that she'd left her wedding and engagement rings in a tiny porcelain dish, the decorative gold wedding band and the finely-set emeralds and diamonds discarded and superfluous.

He turned away and saw that the table on his side of the bed was empty. On Anna's side he was surprised to see a book he recognised as his, left there as if she'd forgotten it or did not feel she should take it with her to Myddleton.

He picked it up: *No Name* by Wilkie Collins. He turned it over and read the publisher's copy on the back: *"Mr Vanstone's daughters are Nobody's Children"*. He sighed and laid the book back where Anna had left it and went downstairs. He had loved that book when he first read it as a student, but it troubled him to think of it now.

He didn't venture into the kitchen or the conservatory; he was keen to get away. As he balanced the archive box on his left arm in order to open the front door with his right, his elbow caught one of the boxes in the alcove and caused it to tip forward as if it would topple to the floor. He pushed it back into place with his free right hand, feeling its full weight, and then made to go, the front door now open, the car parked outside.

He stopped and glanced back at the display. The box he'd dislodged jutted out, revealing part of its intricately painted design—a riot of green hairy stems with narrow oval leaves topped by clusters of tiny azure flowers, their dainty petals pierced by a brilliant yellow eye—and he realised it was because this box was larger than the others that it didn't stack neatly. He hesitated, briefly intrigued, but he was weary and whatever it held would have to wait for another day.

Chapter 18

Somewhere in the distance a storm was building, its encroaching rumblings like a disgruntled giant being dragged groaning and grumbling towards Myddleton. Gone were the blue skies and bright sunshine of the previous week, and as the day wore on it was clear that the pale sun that had promised to burn through would fail to penetrate the sullen grey heavens.

The mood inside the Orangery was subdued, with Michael particularly forlorn. The news of Harri's accident had upset them all and though they were carrying on with rehearsals, they did so with heavy hearts.

Anna's shock was overlaid with guilt, her misgivings about Harri's dramatic abilities the day before seeming cruelly disloyal.

'Trust Harri,' Louise had said, though she, too, was visibly shaken by the announcement that had greeted them on Monday morning. 'Trust him to go and fall off a ladder.'

His leg was broken and he was badly concussed, Jonathan had said when he related the news at the start of the session.

'Obviously, the priority is to find another Quint,' he said, 'and Paul and I are auditioning a couple of people this afternoon, both of whom know the role and are Oxford-based. Crucially they're both available. Hopefully we'll make a decision there and then and he'll start immediately.'

Anna could tell that, like her, Michael was wondering who the new man would be and what he would be like. Judging by his glum expression, she guessed he feared the newcomer would be no match for the cheery fellow with whom he'd struck up such an easy friendship.

'What I suggest,' Jonathan said, 'is because we can't get on with Act 2 Scene 1, as we intended, that we spend the morning on Act 2 scene 2, get through that if we can, then

I propose that you all take the afternoon off, but if you're willing, I'd like us to reconvene this evening so that you can meet the new tenor.'

Jonathan looked round the group to gauge reactions to the suggestion and encouraged by the low murmurings of assent, he said: 'We'll obviously want to integrate him as quickly as possible into the company and the production—and Paul and I will work with him a couple of evenings to cover what we did last week—but tonight I suggest we do something completely different.'

He paused a moment for effect.

'Daniel has kindly said we can use one of his sitting rooms upstairs and I'd like us to read aloud the Henry James novel.'

Anna saw Louise raise an eyebrow and smile as if she thought the idea audacious, but amusing.

'As it happens, I'd wanted to do that at the start of rehearsals, but thought we didn't have time, so in a way I'm making a virtue of Harri's misadventure to do something I think could be very helpful for the process—and fun as well.'

'What a super idea,' Elspeth said and encouraged by her lead, everyone else said they were up for it.

'Good. Thank you,' Jonathan said. 'We may skip some sections here and there just to make sure we can get through it.' He turned to Michael and Charlotte: 'Grace will speak to your families to make travel arrangements and so on and before we start rehearsing now, I need you all to tell Emma whether or not you have a copy of the book so that we know how many we have to get hold of by tonight.'

They had made reasonable progress since then, even though the enervating humidity produced conditions that were far from ideal for rehearsals. A motley array of fans had been deployed in an effort to displace and cool the heavy air, but had forced them to stop while the position of the piano was adjusted to move it out of the draught of a fan which was catching the pages of Toby's score.

Anna dabbed at her moist chin with a paper handkerchief and looked round at her visibly wilting colleagues, all of whom, apart from Louise, were involved in the blocking of the scene in the churchyard.

With Jonathan deep in conversation with Elspeth, Anna closed her eyes and breathed deeply, glad of the momentary respite. With her profound fear of thunder and lightning, she dreaded the prospect of being caught in a ferocious storm in a structure which consisted of substantial amounts of glass. When Toby indicated he was happy with his new position, they prepared to run the scene once more from the beginning, and Anna resolved to use her unease at the disharmony of the elements to help her suggest the very real doubts about Miles which are beginning to assail the Governess as she and the boy talk together on the way to Sunday service.

As she moved back into position, she noticed a stranger standing at the far end of the room, watching them, his sudden appearance making her think of the ghosts which haunted Bly. When she looked at him more carefully, she realised with surprise that he was the man she had seen at the end of the concert with Nicholas Kirkby.

The children started singing and processing as if about to go into church and she and Elspeth followed behind them. A few moments later, while responding absently to the comments of Mrs Grose, a glance to the back of the room told Anna that the visitor had vanished as discreetly as he'd appeared.

Chapter 19

The grey morning had suited the mood of the company and everyone was glad to have time away in which to adjust to the loss of Harri and prepare for the arrival of a new tenor that evening.

As she followed Michael through the door onto the terrace, Anna spotted a football lying scuffed and abandoned in a corner where Harri had left it on Saturday morning. The boy was disconsolate, heaving his knapsack wearily onto his shoulder and trudging alongside her across the grass. She put her hand lightly on his arm.

'I feel it, too,' she said. 'I'm really going to miss him.'

Michael looked up at her and nodded, but said nothing.

'Harri's such good fun—he could always make me laugh, even when things were going badly.' She paused. 'I guess you enjoyed having a man to mess around with?'

'Yeah, it was cool,' Michael said, feigning an insouciance he was clearly not feeling and kicking a tuft of dried up mown grass ahead of him as he walked. 'And he supported Arsenal as well. All the boys at school hate them.'

Anna nodded her head, hoping to suggest she understood what that meant, but knew her capacity for making foot-balling small-talk was strictly limited.

'Maybe the new tenor will be good fun, too,' she ventured, though was not encouraged by the sceptical glance he threw her.

'What shall we have for lunch, then?' she said, hoping that the subject of food was one about which a young boy might be enthusiastic.

'I really don't mind, Anna,' he said, sounding polite, but uninterested. 'You choose.'

Anna had offered to give Michael lunch and then drive him home because there would be no one there until his Grandmother returned from a hospital appointment.

'What do you think of the idea of reading the book together?' she asked as she put the key into her front door.

Michael brightened. 'It could be really good—especially if the storm's got going by then.' He grinned. 'Just what you need for a ghost story!'

'Yes, that's what I'm afraid of,' Anna moaned, walking through to the back of the cottage to open the double doors, hoping to let in some cooler air.

'Why, what are you afraid of—storms or ghosts—or both?'

And at that he came up behind her making a ghostly whooshing noise which made her jump before she turned round laughing.

'That's more like it,' she said, ruffling his hair. 'I don't like to see you looking so sad.'

She opened the fridge and seeing an unfinished packet of cooked salmon flakes, she said, 'What about some salmon with a salad? Do you fancy that?'

Michael pulled a face. 'Could I just have a salmon sandwich without any salad please?'

Anna laughed.

'I get it. Salad's a bit too healthy for your liking is it?'

Michael blushed and muttered, 'sort of.'

Anna busied herself in the kitchen while he looked along the shelves of books, flicked through the pile of CDs she'd brought with her and then wandered down the garden towards the water's edge.

'What do you talk to a twelve-year-old boy about?' she worried as she buttered slices of brown bread—at the same time wondering whether he would have chosen white if given the choice. All week she'd found herself watching Michael and listening to him with interest and curiosity; she realised that with her almost non-existent experience of young boys, she had no idea what he was thinking or feeling or what he would say next.

She glanced over her shoulder and saw that he was standing by the water's edge with his hands in his pockets, apparently gazing across the lake to the house. He really was small for his age—might he pass for a nine-year-old she wondered, the age her own child would have been.

Childlessness was a state she had come to accept, and she rarely thought of that egg, settled in the wrong place, as a little person, but watching Michael, looking so lonely and out of sorts, old feelings came flooding back.

She had barely had time to rejoice in the much-wanted pregnancy before it was over and the chance of a child seemingly lost forever. The kindly surgeon had not ruled out another attempt, but had warned of possible difficulties and risks. And Edwyn, hearing only predictions of danger not reasons for perseverance, had put an end to their hopes for a family.

Or, she wondered now, was it—in reality—*her* hopes for a family?

She turned back to the half-made sandwich and forced herself to think only of the child standing in her back garden, not the one who might have been. After a few moments, Michael came and stood in the doorway, holding onto the sides of the door frame with both hands and leaning back and forth, and as he so often did, humming *Malo, Malo* quietly to himself.

'Anna, can we sit outside to have lunch, please?'

'Of course,' she said. 'We can sit on the grass by the water and have a picnic if you like.'

'Great stuff!' he said. 'Would you like me to take anything out for you?'

'Why don't you get the rug off the back seat of my car,' she said, fishing out her keys from the bottom of her handbag.

With his help, they had soon gathered together a simple feast on the blue and black checked travel rug. Michael confined himself to the sandwiches, crisps and orange juice, while Anna picked at some salad and cold potatoes. The heat was still oppressive, but for now the distant rumblings of thunder had ceased and the air was still.

'So how were *The Horrible Histories* on Saturday?' Anna asked, remembering that Michael's mother had taken him to the theatre after rehearsals had finished.

Michael grinned.

'Really gruesome and gory.'

'Oh, great!' Anna said in mock horror.

'And,' Michael enthused, 'we were sitting in the stalls and there were cannonballs from Spanish ships whizzing over our heads.'

Anna laughed and shuddered.

'I'm so sorry I missed it.'

She looked round when she heard the shriek of a small child close by. There were new holiday-makers at Bailiff's Cottage, this time with young children—twin boys of about seven years old and another boy of less than three, Anna guessed. As she and Michael ate their lunch, settling into comfortable silence, the father was standing at the bottom of their garden holding the small child in his arms and pointing out the sights to him—ducks, water, trees, grass and so on—and Anna became aware that Michael was studying them closely.

'So what does your mother do?' she asked him at last.

'She works for the Crown Prosecution Service,' he said. 'She's called a Casework Support Officer.' He shrugged and pulled a face as if to suggest he wasn't that interested.

Anna wondered how much she could ask without appearing prying.

'So, have you never met your father, Michael?'

The boy had saved a few of his crusts and was lobbing them towards the ducks which were making their way towards them.

'Well...' he said deliberately. 'I think I may have met him once, but I'm not sure.'

Anna raised her eyebrows to indicate she was interested.

'It's one of the very first things I can remember,' he said, 'from when I was three years old. My mum and I were walking in a park near where we lived then. It was freezing and everyone was wrapped up against the cold.'

He pursed his lips and frowned.

'I didn't really like the park,' he explained. 'It was very overgrown—I remember there were lots of rhododendrons —and I always thought that someone nasty would come out of the bushes and get me.'

He laughed.

'Course—it wouldn't scare me now.'

The moment of lightness was brief; he was soon serious again.

'A man came up to us. My mother didn't seem pleased to see him and she put me to sit on a roundabout while they talked. I could hear them arguing and then they moved away until I couldn't see them.'

Anna heard the quiver in the boy's voice as he recalled this memory. He was staring out over the lake and shaking his head.

'I was afraid they'd forget about me and not come back for me and that I'd be alone and lost in the park.'

He bit his lip and when he spoke again, his voice made a hoarse, choked sound that she'd never heard before.

'My mother came back, but I never saw the man again and she wouldn't tell me who he was.'

'So what made you think he might be your father, rather than, say, another boyfriend of your mum's?'

He had a ready answer for that.

'I reckon, if he was just another boyfriend she'd have said that.' He paused. 'And anyway, my mum doesn't have boyfriends.'

'What did he look like?'

Michael thought for a moment and frowned.

'I can't remember,' he said sadly.

He stopped to nibble at some crisps, some of which he threw to the ducks.

'I decided that he came to see what I was like, but didn't like me so he went away again and forgot about me.'

Anna was shocked to think that he had lived his young life believing such a bitter and destructive thought.

'I'm sure that's not what it was,' she said and reached over to touch his shoulder. 'I doubt it was anything to do with you—it must have been something between him and your mother.'

'Then why doesn't she just tell me?' he cried, and chucked a handful of crisps at the startled ducks.

Anna laid her hand gently over his and looked into his face which was flushed with anger and unhappiness.

'I don't know, Michael. I don't know.'

She wondered what stopped Lizzie Manning from telling her son the truth and dispelling the fictions with which he tortured himself.

She held his hand lightly in hers, seeing at close quarters the jagged finger nails she'd noticed on the first day of rehearsals. With his other hand he banged at his thin legs which Anna saw bore the bruises caused by the spectacular dives he had made when fielding penalty kicks from Harri.

People say you can't miss what you haven't had, she thought, but as she rubbed the top of his hand with her thumb, she realised that this complete blank about his father had left a hole he wanted to fill. Perhaps it was this that gave him the aura of sadness which had struck her so forcibly when they had first met—for all his grownup observations on Miles and *his* lost loved ones.

Anna felt herself holding onto his hand more firmly.

He had not grieved as a child might grieve for a parent who had died, because he still held onto the hope of one day finding his absent father.

Chapter 20

He stared out of the car window as they made their way from Myddleton to Abingdon, some of his normal equanimity restored, but looking strangely peaky as if he might be going down with something.

Anna cleared her throat.

'I'm sorry if my questions upset you, Michael. Really I am.'

'It's OK,' he said, smiling and nodding his head to reassure her. 'It's nice to have someone to talk to about it who'll listen to me.'

He turned away to look out of the window again, occasionally humming the *Malo* tune under his breath.

'You know,' he said all of a sudden. 'I loved Harri. I can't believe I'm not going to see him again.'

Though momentarily taken aback, Anna was not surprised that Harri could provoke such a fervent declaration from a boy so badly in want of a father. She thought back to the last scene the two had rehearsed together on Saturday morning, when Quint has lured the boy out into the garden in his night clothes and is intent on seducing him with his dizzying word play. Though Jonathan was keen to suggest something homo-erotic in the exchanges between them, as if the valet was encouraging the boy's sexual awakening, the relationship between Harri and Michael remained resolutely straightforward, despite the demands their roles had made on them.

'I'm sure you will see him again,' she said. 'I'm sure he'd love to hear from you. Why don't you ask Grace for his phone number and give him a ring to see how he's doing?' She glanced over at him. 'He'll be fed up about not being able to play golf for a while—you could try and cheer him up!'

Michael nodded and smiled and for a while they drove on in silence.

'You're always thinking, thinking,' Anna sang at last, when the boy appeared lost in thought again.

'Hey,' he cried. 'That's my line.'

And he repeated it, his rendering more plaintive than hers had been.

'What are you thinking about?' she asked.

'Sometimes,' he said, 'I dream that my father's a musician and that one day he might come and hear me sing or play the clarinet.' He brightened. 'That would be brill.'

Anna could tell that he was struggling to find a more complete identity and that knowledge of his mother's family was not enough to explain his place in the world.

She thought of the parents she knew best—hers and Edwyn's—and realised she'd never spent much time analysing her own enlightened, hardworking mum and dad, whereas the distant, emotionally inexpressive Maxwell family had given her hours of thankless speculation. How, she had asked herself after every visit, did Brenda turn into that demanding, frustrated woman? How did Jim become the submissive, unhappy man who tried to please by keeping quiet?

Was this, she wondered, the real reason for Edwyn's readiness to abandon their plans for a family and not a mangled fallopian tube? Did he lack the courage to take on the challenges and pitfalls of parenthood and fear he was condemned to repeat other people's mistakes?

They had reached the outskirts of Abingdon and Michael guided her expertly round the town's one-way system until they turned off the Oxford Road and he told her to stop at a 1930s semi with a small front garden. She thought he might invite her in to meet his grandmother, who she could see standing in the window waiting for them, but he said nothing.

'So how are you getting back to the house tonight?' she asked, as he opened the passenger door.

'Oh, Sarah's coming for me—or maybe Emma, I'm not sure, and then one of them's bringing me back as well.'

'OK then—see you later.'

'Thanks for lunch, Anna. It was really nice.'

She waited while he let himself into the house before she drove away.

She thought how frustrating it must be for Michael to know that someone else held the key to the information he wanted so badly, yet refused to give it up.

What power this gave Lizzie Manning.

Did she not realise that when such a crucial relationship is shrouded in secrecy, that so much else must also be cast into doubt?

Chapter 21

Hugging her light raincoat around her shoulders, she hesitated on her front door step, debating about playing safe and taking the car, but looking at the sky she judged that she could make the short walk through the park while it was still dry, and if it was raining at the end of the evening, she knew that one of the others would drive her home. She would be early, but by leaving now she hoped to reach the house ahead of the storm that was almost upon them.

The air felt ominously still, and the birds—who normally twittered away until well past this time—were silent, the ducks on the lake tucked up in their hideaways.

'They know it's coming,' she muttered to herself and, beginning to regret her decision to walk, she picked up her speed and fell into a sort of stop-start run. Her breath came in rasping bursts and she could feel her heart pounding. Through the trees she could see that the sky had gone black and in the distance heard the first crash of thunder followed by a flash of white light which momentarily lit up the horizon. From the trees to her right she heard the sound of undergrowth being disturbed.

'A fox?' she thought—'or something else?'

She could feel the panic rising and though her instincts told her to run as hard as she could, she was forced to slow down to allow her breathing to steady.

'Fat lot of good you'd be if there were ghosts about,' she chided herself.

The branches of the trees above her began to rustle and she held out a bare arm from under her coat to check whether it was rain or just a gathering wind that was making them move.

Even through the heavy foliage, she knew it was definitely rain—large cold droplets that landed with force on her warm skin.

'Damn!'

She was half way there now, and just about to move from out of the clump of trees into an open stretch of parkland that led over to the house. She stopped at the edge of the copse deliberating what to do: go on and almost certainly get drenched despite her coat; or stay where she was and risk being struck by lightning.

'Great choice,' she muttered.

The rain was falling in torrents, but her fear of lightning far outstripped her dislike of getting soaked and she decided to run. She pulled her raincoat up so that it covered her hair and prepared to launch herself into the open space that lay between her and safety.

'Wait! Stop!'

She froze, not sure from where the call came and knowing it was not a voice she recognised.

She waited for someone to appear and to her right she saw a man wearing only jeans and a short-sleeved shirt making his way towards her. She could see that he was smiling and something about him was reassuring. She felt herself relax a little.

'Hi,' he called. 'Sorry if I alarmed you, but I thought if I warned you then, I could save you from getting a soaking.'

As he held out his hand to shake hers, she recognised him as the man at last night's concert and the visitor from this morning.

'It's Anna, isn't it? Hello, I'm Daniel,' he said. 'Daniel Ennis.'

'Oh,' she said with relief. 'How do you do?'

'Like you,' he laughed, 'I misjudged how soon the storm would get here. I'd been down to leave some light bulbs in Bailiff's Cottage—they rang to say three had blown in the

139

same fitting—and I got caught here. I saw you from the Folly, where I'd gone to take shelter.

'Ah,' she said. 'I thought I heard something—but then I am playing the Governess, so I'm prone to hearing things.'

He laughed, and his face was so open and kind that she laughed too.

'I can take you there, if you like, and we can wait for it to pass.'

Anna hesitated.

'But I have to be up at the house in fifteen minutes—do you really think it will have passed by then?'

'No, not passed completely,' he agreed, 'but I think this really heavy spell will ease up in about five or ten minutes.'

'OK then—let's go.'

By now the rain was clattering against the trees and even under the cover of the branches Anna's coat was soon streaked with wet marks. She followed him back in the direction from which he'd come until they emerged into a clearing, in the centre of which was a small, round single-storey building that was something between a gazebo and a bandstand. There was an inner 'room' and outside it a covered veranda on which there was a bench which ran all the way round.

They ran the last short distance until they reached shelter and then leaned back with relief on the bench.

'Not exactly salubrious,' he apologised, looking round at the debris of dirt and leaves that littered the floor and the interior, 'but it will keep us dry.'

Anna looked at her watch—it was still only twenty to seven, so with luck she would make it in time.

Daniel sensed her anxiety.

'Don't worry—I won't let you be late.'

She smiled.

'Thanks.'

She was quiet for a moment, wondering if he knew that she was Edwyn's wife, and that they were now separated.

He was looking at her closely and, as if he had read her mind, said: 'I was sorry to hear about you and Edwyn—I know you were together a long time. It must be very hard for you.'

She nodded

'Yes,' she sighed. 'It's a big readjustment. All my adult life has been spent with Edwyn.'

She rubbed the finger on her left hand on which she had for so long worn her wedding and engagement rings and thought how naked that hand now looked.

She shivered as from beyond the house she heard more thunder and saw the sky illuminated by the dreaded white streaks of lightning.

She shut her eyes and tried to sound calm. The rain was pounding in what she hoped would be one great deluge before it stopped.

'Just the night to be reading a ghost story.'

Daniel said nothing, perhaps sensing her embarrassment at him seeing her fear of the storm and her awkwardness because of his acquaintance with Edwyn.

She looked up at him.

He was tall and slim, in his late forties she guessed, and with his intelligent, but somewhat bland face he was attractive in a sexless, unthreatening sort of way.

'Have you heard from Edwyn since he moved to Wales?' she asked.

He was unperturbed by the question, as if it was natural she would ask him such a thing, and when he answered his voice was low and gentle.

'Yes, we've spoken a couple of times.'

Anna looked at him with surprise and added interest, but when Daniel didn't volunteer anything more, a shocking possibility struck her for the first time.

'Has he met someone else?' she gasped. 'Is he with someone in north Wales?'

'No, I'm sure not,' Daniel said with emphasis.

Mollified, Anna asked: 'How is he, do you think?'

Daniel paused.

'I think he's a lot of things all at the same time.'

'Go on,' she urged.

'I think he's very sad about how things turned out, but relieved to be away from here. And I think he's wracked with guilt and regret—but feels he did the right thing in going.'

How did that make any sense, she wondered.

'I fear he'll never forgive them—Jim and Brenda, I mean.'

She turned to him surprised, but he was looking at the ground, kicking at a jumble of twigs and moss, and shaking his head with concern.

'When the truth came out—well, I mean—what a shock —everything he assumed to be true about himself turned out not to be true.'

She caught her breath as the impact of his words hit her full force.

He was quick to see her confusion.

'I'm so sorry, I felt sure you must have known all about it.'

The words stung her as hard as if he had wielded his hand against her face: this man barely knew her husband, yet was aware of secrets that Edwyn had chosen not to share with her, his wife and life's companion for over sixteen years.

Daniel realised his mistake and clasped his right hand to his forehead and shook his head.

'I'm sorry, that was so crass. Please forgive me.'

She was staring at him, wondering what would come next and he took a breath to compose himself.

'What I should have said is, that I felt sure you would have known that the couple who brought Edwyn up were not his parents.'

She let her head drop and felt the tears build.

'No,' she said. 'I didn't know that.'

Nearby, she heard the chattering of some blackbirds, and looked up to see that the rain was easing.

'I don't know the details,' Daniel said, 'but it seems to me that for years Edwyn has devoted huge parts of his life to pursuit of the past.'

He was looking through the trees to peer up at the sky.

'I mean his personal past,' he added. 'I'm afraid his life has become consumed by the search for who he might have been.'

Anna guessed what he meant: that her historian husband had not only gone in search of the stories of long-dead rulers and rebels, of revolutions and the clash of empires, but of the life he might have lived with different parents.

She looked up at him aghast.

'I had no idea about this,' she cried.

It didn't make sense, though she could imagine Louise saying: "Just because you love someone doesn't mean you know them."

Anna reached into her coat pocket for a handkerchief, but the thought of Louise made her look at her watch.

'We should go,' she said, dragging herself to her feet.

Daniel took her lightly by the arm and led her back through the trees and across the grass towards the house.

She knew that this patently decent man felt bad about the shock he had unwittingly inflicted and as they made their way round to the front entrance, she wanted to say something to show she had recovered herself a little.

'Do you know whether we have a new Quint tonight?'

'Ah yes,' he said, with some of the brightness back in his voice. 'There he is. Come and meet him.'

At that moment, the man he pointed to on the gravel outside the front door, turned round to stub out a cigarette in the sand-filled urn next to the bench.

When he looked up, Anna saw that it was Nicholas Kirkby.

Chapter 22

The setting they had created was ingeniously theatrical.

The stage management team had been tasked to transform Daniel's upstairs drawing room into one where ghost stories might credibly be exchanged amongst friends on a winter's evening before Christmas at the end of the nineteenth century.

The room lent itself to such treatment: it was at a corner of the house and on two sides it had tall windows covered by dramatic black and red drapes to match the burgundy embossed wallpaper, while one of the windows which overlooked the lake had been left bare, the curtains tied back to make the rain and the lightning visible to them as they read.

Eight high-backed red chairs were arranged in a semi-circle around an ornate fire place, in which, despite the warmth of the evening, a fire had been lit. In front of the fire, on a large, low square table a tray had been set containing tumblers of mulled wine and cranberry juice and plates of savoury canapés. In the hearth and on every available flat surface, flickered candles of all shapes and sizes.

Anna had heard a clock striking seven as Daniel led her and Nicholas up the stairs and down a long corridor to the red drawing room. He had introduced her quickly to Nicholas and she noticed the evident warmth between the two men. She was struck, too, by how tense and pale Nicholas looked and guessed that the hurried cigarette and his last-minute arrival to join the others were a sign of nerves and insecurity, as was the slightly agitated way in which he clasped her hand when she was introduced and said he was pleased to meet her.

Daniel stood aside to let Anna enter the room ahead of them and she saw that Louise, Elspeth, Charlotte and

Michael were already seated, while Jonathan and Paul stood with their backs to the fire, enjoying a drink and apparently celebrating the fact they had come by a replacement Quint with such ease and relatively little disruption to their well-laid rehearsal plans.

Though—or perhaps because—he looked decidedly ashen-faced, Anna could see that as he made his entry, Nicholas would cut a striking figure in his black jeans, grey top and Slavic appearance. His large, pale, slightly bulging eyes scanned the group quickly and while he took them all in, Anna could see that Michael was appraising him keenly, though she was gratified, too, when the boy smiled at her and indicated he wanted her to come and sit next to him, leaving Nicholas to join Louise, and allowing the director and conductor to take the chairs in the centre of the semi-circle.

Grace, Emma and Sarah made sure that everyone had drinks and then withdrew to chairs at the side, from where they could observe the reading. Jonathan stayed standing and waited until everyone was seated and had a glass in their hand.

'Welcome everyone,' he said. 'Thank you all for coming and giving up an evening at such short notice. Can I start by raising a glass to our wounded warrior? To Harri: get well soon!'

'To Harri,' they all concurred, with Anna and Michael turning to face each other and chink glasses as they made the toast to their absent friend.

'And now a warm welcome to Nicholas Kirkby, who we're delighted is joining us to play Quint. To Nicholas!'

'To Nicholas! Welcome,' they chorused.

Though her head was still reeling with thoughts of Edwyn and the secrets at which Daniel had only been able to hint, Anna forced herself to concentrate. The company were opening their copies of the Henry James novella, and while Elspeth was typically taking the arrival of the newcomer in her stride, Anna could see that he strangely excited the rest of the group.

Despite her lascivious bravado of the previous evening, Louise was eyeing him discreetly. Charlotte had blushed and hung her head when he'd acknowledged her, but quickly assumed the quiet and studious air she displayed in rehearsals. Michael was visibly intrigued, his wide-eyed curiosity undisguised.

Though the rain had been easing as Anna and Daniel made their way across the park, it was once more torrential, lashing at the windows with vicious force, the skies dark and unfriendly. Anna was relieved that despite the glowing fire, the room was not over-warm, as in another cunning act of stage setting the girls had opened the windows behind the closed drapes, meaning that what little air there was occasionally moved the curtains, suggesting the presence of invisible guests.

They agreed to take it in turns to read, starting with Nicholas, and with people stopping when they wanted their neighbour to continue the story or when Jonathan indicated they should make a cut.

Nicholas's speaking voice was mellow and cultured and though at first he was a little hesitant, he soon grew in confidence and proved an accomplished storyteller, using colour and inflexion to capture the suspenseful atmosphere of the book's compelling opening.

As they read on together, deeper and deeper into the story, with its dense and florid language, its tantalising refusal to be clearly explicit, Anna was struck by the terrible sense of not knowing that stood at the heart of both the novella and the opera.

Why has Miles been expelled from school? Why did Miss Jessel have to go away and how did she die? In what way, precisely, was Peter Quint "much too free" with the household?

As the evening passed, for the most part her attention was held by the mounting tension, by the great struggle taking place between the forces of good and evil and the Governess's increasing awareness of her inability to oppose the supernatural and save the children, but all the while she was tormented by her own not knowing, by new questions about Edwyn which assailed her.

The candles gave barely enough light to read by and when it was her turn, she at first stumbled over the wordy, convoluted sentences and realised that in her own recent reading of the book she had skimmed the more obtuse passages, whereas in reading it aloud she had to focus hard so that she could master and give meaning to the archaic language and the long-breathed rhythms of the ambiguous prose. When others were reading, she studied their faces, listening closely to what they were saying, just as those house guests in the story would have strained to follow every fearful twist in the tale as they heard it unfold for the first time.

Everyone had their turn to read once, the children both contributing surprisingly dramatic renditions, with Michael's boyish voice and his precise enunciation seeming ill-matched to the novel's sexually suggestive style and the troubling allusions with which the text was peppered.

They had started at the beginning of the half circle again and Nicholas had once more taken up the story, reaching the end of chapter 10—about half way through the book—at the point when the Governess looks out of her bedroom window at night to see Miles standing on the lawn, motionless and fascinated, looking up at a person on the tower.

In the opera, this incident took place in the last scene they'd rehearsed with Harri on Saturday morning. She had watched as Quint lured Miles away from his bed and out of doors, his dazzling command of language bewildering the child, so that as if sleepwalking, Miles latches on to key words in Quint's rhymes and intones them back to him.

'Secrets, O secrets!' Michael had cried with almost religious fervour.

Anna let the book drop momentarily onto her lap and gazed out of the window, through which she could see clouds scudding across the leaden sky as if to escape the relentless onslaught of the storm. They had been reading without a break for over an hour and a half and she guessed it was not yet nine o'clock, but it seemed much later, not just because it was dark so unseasonably early, but because she felt depleted in so many ways, a sign that she was exhausted and overwrought, that her senses, like those of the beleaguered Governess, were overloaded.

Secrets, forbidden subjects, the loss of innocence, the realisation that all is not what it seemed.

She closed her eyes and sighed.

'Secrets, O secrets,' she inwardly intoned, wondering whether her husband's secrets would ever give up their answers.

Chapter 23

Cypress trees surrounded the perimeter of the cemetery and though it was only mid-morning, it was already hot, and here and there, Edwyn could see people seeking shade under the trees or resting on some of the white concrete benches.

Though the grave looked bedraggled and the headstone was dusty, the black marble had weathered well and the inscription was clear:

The LORD gave, and the LORD hath taken away.

He laid his flowers carefully across the grave.

'She's been here a good while then. Nice to see someone taking an interest after this long.'

It was meant as a friendly pleasantry, but Edwyn felt the remark as a criticism.

'We'll soon have this tidy, don't you worry. We'll keep it nice for her.'

The Head Gardener was a local man, but like many people in that part of Shropshire, he spoke with a Welsh accent.

Edwyn nodded and murmured his thanks.

'I'll set up a standing order as soon as I get home,' he said, folding up the sheet of paper he'd been given in the cemetery office.

The man pulled a cloth out of his jacket pocket and gave the headstone a quick, but efficient wipe.

'Next time you come, you'll see a difference, I tell you.'

Next time.

Yes, he would come again.

The man held out his hand to say goodbye and Edwyn watched him shuffle off down the path, humming quietly to himself, and feeling in his pocket for his peaked cap.

Edwyn was glad to be alone, to have a few moments of private contemplation before he set off for north Wales.

He gazed at the inscription, remembering his other visits here—once with Jim and twice alone.

He recalled that first time, bemused that Jim had decided to come here on the day they were moving house and heading south. He'd been uninterested and viewed it as yet another example of the perverse behaviour of which grown-ups were capable.

On his second visit, in the autumn of 1990, he'd had to concentrate hard to find his way through the expanse of gravestones. He had a plan of the cemetery to guide him, but it was not easy to follow and in the end he came on the black marble headstone almost by chance, his eye caught by a lavish grave nearby, with an ornate statue of a weeping woman with a baby in her arms adorning the top of a stone whose inscription entreated: *Rest in peace beloved husband.*

This corner of the cemetery was quiet and on that chilly grey day sixteen years earlier it had been almost deserted. He remembered the desolation that hung in the air, made worse by the ragtag of weeds intent on attacking the grave and half concealing the black marble headstone, as if they knew that no one cared enough to rid this resting place of their encroachment.

His thoughts skipped back to that first visit with Jim, his small hand in his father's larger one and Jack Rabbit swinging carelessly in his other hand. He was carefree then. He and Jack Rabbit were off to a new home and he longed to get going: he was impatient to *get* there.

Jack Rabbit—his constant companion—had been made for him with such care and skill, such attention to the detail of Jack's ears and paws and whiskers, but as far as he could recall, no one had ever been credited with that craftsmanship.

Now he guessed why.

He looked again at the sculpture depicting the grieving widow and her fatherless child and wondered if she had knitted woolly toys for her son.

It was the third visit, two years ago, that was the most strangely memorable.

It was Easter Sunday and the graveyard was busy, with groups of mourners moving among the graves, some kneeling in quiet communion with their dead. This time he'd found the grave with the black marble headstone without difficulty, but he'd been taken aback to see that though it was still overgrown and neglected, someone had laid fresh flowers there. In his surprise, he at first registered regret for the thoughtlessness that meant that he had come empty-handed. But then he reached down and touched the white tissue wrapped round the bottom of the stems, to discover it was still damp, as if the blooms had only recently been taken out of water.

A dozen Easter lilies with showy white trumpet-shaped flowers.

He stood up quickly and looked round to see if he could identify the person who had left them, and for a moment all the brightly coloured figures amongst the graves seemed to freeze like statues. Then the air shifted and they once more breathed and moved and murmured. A child ran along a path to his left, calling to his mother. A baby cried in the distance. Two men got up from a bench and made their slow way up the path towards the entrance gates.

When he'd first arrived, Edwyn had noticed a young woman sitting on a bench nearby and he looked round for her. She was no longer there, but he spotted her sitting by a plot marked only by a wooden cross.

He spun round, but apart from the girl there had been no one else anywhere near the grave when he'd first approached. He glanced down at the flowers and looked up again as he heard the sound of shoes disturbing gravel. The girl was scurrying away up the path, as if in a hurry, and he saw the two men stand aside to let her pass, giving him the chance to study them. They were walking arm-in-arm, the younger of them a man in his early sixties, the older—the father Edwyn presumed—sporting an eye-catching multi-coloured scarf against the chill spring air, a man of still upright bearing despite his advanced age and frailty.

A screech of blackbirds squabbling in a nearby tree brought him back to the present. He knelt and passed his hand over the inscription on the headstone: the name, the dates marking the beginning and end of life, the biblical quotation. He tried to push aside his resentment at the inadequacy of the description: this woman had been more than *daughter and sister*.

He adjusted the position of the flowers and stood back to take a last look at them before he, too, walked away up the path towards the entrance.

Easter lilies for Lily.

Chapter 24

His calls to Miles were at once inviting and bloodcurdling.

"In me secrets, and half-formed desires meet."

Anna watched from the side, enthralled as Nicholas strode restlessly about the stage area, as seemingly haunted as the boy he had come to haunt, the bedazzling text sung with devilish fluency.

"I am the hidden life that stirs when the candle is out," he sang and Michael, his face lit by an unsettling rapture, conveyed the eager expectation of a boy excited by the secrets that Quint's visit promised.

"I'm here... O I'm here!" he cried, feeling the fleeting touch of Quint's hands on his face and spinning round in search of his deathly visitor.

Jonathan had resumed rehearsals with the scene in the garden at the end of Act 1 so that Nicholas could start work at the point when Quint sings for the first time, in a scene that involved all six singers.

The night storms had brought relief, having carried away the oppressive heat that had made working so tiring, but it was not the fact that the air in the Orangery was cooler that created a frisson in the room, but the arrival of a man whose unnerving intensity had transformed the dynamic of the group.

Anna had never seen Michael concentrate so hard or move so convincingly towards the path of corruption. Even Jonathan, whose stamina was seemingly boundless, appeared re-energised and unperturbed at losing a day's rehearsal going over work he had done the previous week.

'These words are really important—they must come through,' he said, shuffling a sheaf of notes until he found the reference he wanted. 'Listen to what Myfanwy Piper said about the words she gives Quint: *"What Quint actually sings is an expression of the kind of mystery that could surround a half-known grown-up in the thoughts of a romantic and isolated boy... What I tried to evoke was the fascination a small boy could have had for a mysterious adult outside his usual experience".'*

Michael frowned as he took in and made sense of this note and then gazed at Nicholas as if already entranced.

Jonathan turned towards Paul and Toby.

'We'll need to be careful about the tempo here—fast enough to capture the vitality of the music, but not so fast that the words sound garbled, especially in the final section where Quint and Miss Jessel sing the same words in unison.'

Paul nodded and sang a few lines to suggest the speed he had in mind, beating time with his right hand, and continuing long enough for Toby to pick up the piano accompaniment and Nicholas to join in and take over.

'How does that feel?' asked Paul.

The two singers looked at each other for agreement and nodded their heads.

This was a big scene for Louise as well and Anna noticed that she, too, was rejuvenated—the jet-lag gone, replaced by alert engagement with the work in hand. She had tied her dark hair back with a green ribbon and, with a fly-away strand escaping and clinging to her neck and with her cheek-bones emphasised, she began to look the part of Quint's partner in sin: beautiful, but undoubtedly fallen.

Anna watched Louise and Nicholas together and sensed an electricity between them that Jonathan would surely capitalise on. He drew them together at one point and beckoned Anna to join them.

'We can't ignore the massive sexual charge that Britten and Piper injected into the story when they made the ghosts not just real, but actively seductive.' He looked from one to the other of them. 'I'll need you all to be open to this.'

The three singers looked at each other, and while Louise indicated her understanding by a raised eyebrow and a flash of her eye, Anna could feel herself flushing, visibly apprehensive about what would be demanded of her—and how she would react.

She moved quickly back to the side to wait for her entrance, wondering what the others had noticed and not for the first time curious to know whether the men— Jonathan, Paul and now Nicholas—knew about the sudden ending of her marriage or sensed from her demeanour and behaviour that she was a woman heavy with heartache, trying to conceal the humiliation she felt so keenly. She knew that Grace would have been discreet, but feared that when this role forced her to relinquish her defences and allow herself to be vulnerable, she might struggle to maintain her self-control.

She was disconcerted to see that Nicholas was still looking at her and she turned away to pick up her score. When she glanced up again, he was back into the action of the scene.

Jonathan was choreographing the early part as if it was a solemn court dance between the two children and the ghosts, the young people moving slowly and uncertainly as if locked in a trance, the adults sweeping and gliding around them, in and out of the shadows in which they would be lit.

'That's fantastic, Nicholas,' said Jonathan, stopping them for a moment to block something differently, while Paul tapped the side of his music stand with a pencil to show his approval. 'The romance and the danger of those words— the hero, highwayman, Midas, Mercury—are really coming through now as I want so that the audience should see that a master charlatan is at work. Well done.'

It was a long scene and Anna's appearance came only in the closing moments, so she had ample time to watch as the interplay between the children and the ghosts became more threatening and disturbing. She sensed what a huge challenge the role of Quint represented for a singer who had been away from the stage for some time, but saw that Nicholas's distinctive, almost tortured appearance and his febrile nervous energy made him perfect for the part, while his expressive voice would make him an utterly credible seducer.

Watching how others in the room reacted to him—the women of cast and crew, the teenage girl, the pre-teen boy and the director, conductor and pianist—she realised that Nicholas was that rare animal, a man whose sexuality was not immediately obvious and yet was attractive and intriguing to both sexes.

For the first time, Anna experienced a tingle of anticipation as she realised that this man would challenge and stretch her as Harri could not have done, that he might help her unlock the key to this fearful young woman and enable her to attempt the descent into hysteria and despair of which she had been so afraid.

Chapter 25

The next day they began to block the beginning of Act 2, when Quint and Miss Jessel lock in a bitter exchange of reproach and remembered desire, of troubled passion and gruesome plans.

Anna spent the morning wrestling with self-consciousness and anxiety, yet striving to achieve the complex amalgam of common sense, hysteria and obsessive protectiveness that Jonathan was trying to coax from her—and all the while struggling to cope with the new and unexpected questions about Edwyn.

She was tired, her sleep disrupted, her appetite lost since Daniel's unwitting revelations. She had not seen him since he left her at the read-through on Monday, and wondered if he'd told Nicholas about their awkward exchange at the Folly, whether this was the reason for his apparent fascination with her, why he looked at her so often and with such unconcealed interest. Or was she imagining it and did that look signify nothing of importance?

She had told Grace about her conversation with Daniel and knew that her friend was concerned for her, but there had been little time to talk properly as Grace was preoccupied with the task of settling a late arrival into the company—getting his measurements to the costume-maker and his biography to the programme editor and revising the rehearsal schedule as Jonathan required.

Though Jonathan had told Michael and Charlotte they would almost certainly not be needed on the Wednesday, they had both opted to come in and watch. Anna was glad to see the boy and appreciated his cheery smile and the shy hug he had taken to giving her at the start and finish of every day, but as the rehearsal developed, she felt increasingly uncomfortable that he was there, because

Jonathan's direction was at times explicitly sexual in ways she had not foreseen.

Jonathan proposed that while the ghosts revealed their intentions for the children, the Governess should be seen lying in a bed at the edge of the stage area, half-asleep, but tossing and turning, as if somewhere in her subconscious she could hear and see the dangerous images the former servants were calling up.

Before they rehearsed that, Jonathan suggested that Anna first of all watch the scene so that later on, with her eyes closed, she would know how to react; not only to what they were saying, but what they were doing.

She sat on the edge of the bed and watched as the dream-bound figure of Miss Jessel was roused and tormented by Quint and ultimately responded to him as he wanted her to.

Jonathan urged Louise to appear edgy and needy, desperately longing for Quint to acknowledge what had once passed between them.

"Why did you call me from my schoolroom dreams?" she cried, trying to engage him in some sort of dance of love.

Anna admired the confidence with which Louise, with minimal coaching from Jonathan, stood behind Nicholas and wrapped her arms round his waist, while nuzzling his neck before pulling him round to face her.

"Ah! Quint, Quint, do you forget?" she gasped, head back, as if with anticipation of ecstasy to come, while Quint ran his hands suggestively across her hips, teasing her before, at Jonathan's prompting on the words *"The ceremony of innocence is drowned,"* he pushed her roughly away.

"I seek a friend—he shall feed my mounting power."

The danger that Quint posed to Miles was unmistakable and it was not long before Miss Jessel revealed similar plans for Flora, to bind her to the chains of the afterlife.

Anna glanced over at Michael and Charlotte to see that both were mesmerised, he wide-eyed, she willing and excited.

With no trace of nostalgia, the ghosts described how innocence and childhood would be brought to an end.

"The ceremony of innocence is drowned."

With the repetition of that one line, sung in unison, the ghosts promised nothing more for the children than joylessness and the "breaking" of love.

When they finished, the whole room was silent for several moments. Even for a first attempt at a difficult scene—Nicholas, with his eerily plangent singing and Louise, with her throbbing, tortured longing—had cast a spell on everyone present.

They broke for coffee, but the mood held. Often at such moments, someone would say something to dispel the tension, but Nicholas and Louise appeared to want to stay with their characters and sat together quietly, talking about ways they could change and improve on what they'd done.

The others took their lead from them and the mood in the room was muted, but expectant, as if a screw had been turned and the tragedy would escalate inexorably.

Having no desire to intrude on Nicholas and Louise, Anna took her coffee and sat on the bed, easing off her shoes and thinking that by staying in situ she, too, would absorb some of the atmosphere that had been established. When Jonathan called her and Nicholas together after the break, she felt the impending crisis for her character—and perhaps for herself.

'So,' Jonathan said, as the rest of the company took their seats at the edge of the acting area, 'when the Governess sings at the end of the scene, what I want us to show is that while she has lain on the bed during what's gone before, she has felt the presence of evil. Now she's feeling suffocated by helplessness against the evil enclosing her.'

He looked at them both and Anna and Nicholas nodded solemnly.

'Right then. When the ghosts have finished singing in unison, the lights will slowly fade out on them and fade in on the Governess, who'll be lying in the bed.' He stood between them with a hand on each of their arms to draw them in closer to him. 'We'll think that Quint has gone, but a little more light coming up will reveal that he's still there, at first standing at the bed head looking down on you Anna as you start singing, but then moving round to sit on the edge of the bed—so you'll need to make sure that at this point you're not lying in the middle of the bed, but to one side. And while you're singing Anna, you need to convey how agitated and disturbed you are. Shall we just try that first without music? And then I'll talk you through what I think might happen next.'

Anna lay on the bed and she and Nicholas mimed what Jonathan had described while he spoke the words Anna would sing.

"Lost in my labyrinth I see no truth, only the foggy walls of evil press upon me."

'Nicholas, don't take your eyes off her as you move round now—I want you to seem transfixed, full of intent.'

"Lost in my labyrinth I see no truth."

Nicholas sat on the bed and Anna adjusted her position so that he was not touching her.

'OK,' Jonathan said. 'Stop there.'

He knelt on the floor on the other side of the bed.

'When Anna sings the next bit: *"O innocence, you have corrupted me, which way shall I turn? I know nothing of evil, yet I feel it, I fear it, worse—imagine it,"* Nicholas, I want you to lean over her and appear to caress her. You don't need to touch her more than a little—just suggest it, so that as she continues to writhe it's not clear whether it's because she's still in her earlier tormented state or whether she's now aroused by something she's not fully aware of.'

Nicholas and Anna smiled awkwardly at each other and once again, they mimed what was asked of them, Anna feeling doubly uncomfortable because of the close proximity of both men as she lay prone between them.

'Good, stop there,' Jonathan said getting to his feet. 'Nicholas, as she sings the words *"imagine it,"* get up and move away, so that by the time she sits up and sings the final words: *"Lost in my labyrinth which way shall I turn?"* you're back in the shadows behind the head of the bed. OK? Do you feel ready to try that with music?'

Anna nodded to signal her agreement, but was worried that the rising lump in her throat would make singing impossible. For reasons she could not explain, she felt her pent-up emotions fighting for release and could only hope that enacting the scene would provide that release while allowing her to remain true to her character.

Paul had been listening and watching intently, staying on the sidelines, saying nothing. Now he walked over to Anna and sat next to her.

'You'll really need to keep breathing for this, otherwise you won't be able to cope with the line.' He patted her hand. 'OK?'

She was horrified to feel her eyes fill up and turned away quickly before he could notice—these men were all being so kind and gentle and yet it felt impossibly intimate and exposed.

But she did as Paul counselled and concentrated on her breathing, experimenting to see which positions worked best to allow her to sustain both the line and the tone, and working with Nicholas so that he knew why she was moving and when.

Even with her eyes closed, she felt him hovering over her body and at one point, when she jerked abruptly away from him, one of his hands brushed her breast, causing her body to shudder and her voice to catch.

161

When at the end of the scene she sat up to sing her final lines, she was flushed and her hair was damp at the back of her neck. Jonathan and Paul both came over at that point to give notes and after a few moments' discussion, they prepared to run the whole scene from the top.

Anna lay back on the bed and Nicholas and Louise once more engaged in their lurid colloquy. Everyone else in the room was perfectly still, the only sounds coming from the whirring of the fans and the distant whine of a grass strimmer. Anna twitched and shook, wincing at their wicked words, but sinking back as if in despair as they finally joined in unison to describe the moment of innocence lost.

"The Ceremony of Innocence is drowned."

She listened to the repetition of that one line, which proclaimed that something wonderful had been replaced by the realisation that, in fact, everything was lost.

Once again, she felt her throat tighten, and as she prepared to sing, it occurred to her that those words could apply not only to the loss of childhood innocence, but to her marriage. The thought threatened to overwhelm her, but somehow she was able to keep singing.

She felt the thin mattress sag as Nicholas took his place beside her.

"Which way shall I turn?" she cried and almost involuntarily half rose to turn over, meaning that she met Nicholas's embrace coming down on her, so that she found herself briefly in his arms. He pulled away and the contact was soon over, but her next words were swallowed and her breathing was short and shallow.

She could sing no more and Toby, realising she was not going to continue, stopped playing, the dying chords echoing in the silent room.

Nicholas looked at her in confusion, but she turned away from him onto her other side and with no warning to him or even herself, began to weep uncontrollably.

Chapter 26

The fans droned on and somewhere in the large room a bluebottle buzzed intermittently, settling quietly now and then before zooming off again in noisy agitation. Even within the sound of her sobs, Anna could tell that the people around her had frozen and were silent.

'I'm so sorry,' Nicholas whispered, shying away before jumping to his feet. 'So sorry.'

Anna's voice was muffled.

'It's not your fault, really. I'm sorry.'

The next thing she knew was that Grace and Jonathan had come to sit by her on the bed, Grace at her left hand side by her shoulder and Jonathan at her feet.

'Do you want to take some time out?' he asked. 'Or would you like to talk about it? Might that help?'

Grace leant over her to pass her a paper tissue and she pulled herself up onto her elbow so that she could blow her nose properly. She looked over to where Elspeth and Louise were sitting with two empty chairs beside them and was grateful that someone had had the presence of mind to usher the children out. She saw Nicholas hovering close by, his face creased with anxiety and she waved her hanky at him and then the others.

'Sorry everyone.'

She took a deep juddering breath and felt calmer, Grace's warm arm round her shoulder serving to relax and quieten her. She looked up at her friend and managed a watery smile.

'I'm OK, really.'

Then to Jonathan she said, 'I'd like to continue, but I'd like to try and explain—understand—what just happened.'

Nicholas looked at her with real concern in his face, as if fearing that she would lay the blame for her distress at his door.

She shook her head.

'Really, Nicholas, it's not your fault. Please don't think that.'

He nodded and took that as his cue to go and sit next to Louise.

Anna blew her nose again and sat fully upright, bringing her knees up to her chin and covering her bare feet with her long cotton skirt. Grace squeezed her shoulder before getting up to go and sit with Sarah who had put down her score and was gazing over towards her with a mixture of concern and incomprehension.

'Shall I sit here?' Jonathan asked quietly. 'Is that alright?'

Anna nodded her head, now feeling she wanted him close as she tried to understand what had caused her to break down, finding his presence reassuring rather than embarrassing.

'Are you happy for everyone else to stay? Michael and Charlotte have gone off with Emma, so you don't need to worry about them.'

She nodded, glad Michael was not there to see what must have looked like unaccountable anguish, but feeling that one of his hugs would have been welcome.

'What was so hard for you about that?' Jonathan asked at last.

She looked into his face and thought how young he looked, and yet how wise, as if there was nothing she could say that would surprise or shock him.

She sniffed and shook her head as if it was too difficult to find the words, but he waited patiently until she could.

'It's all mixed up—it's not just one thing,' she said at last. 'I just feel I'm dealing with so many conflicting emotions— which is good for the Governess, I know,' she laughed, 'and I'm trying to use all that for the part, I really am, but it's not easy for me.'

'I'm sure,' he said, and when after a long pause he spoke again, his voice sounded unusually tentative. 'Your husband?'

'You knew?' she asked, almost with relief.

He nodded.

'Harri—not gossiping: just saying how well you were doing considering what you were going through.'

'Dear Harri,' she thought.

'And he's right,' Jonathan was saying. 'Just the fact that you're prepared to be open about what happened in front of us all takes real courage. Real courage.'

The unexpected compliment bolstered her, but she was unprepared for what he said next.

'You seem so resilient, enjoying your work and your colleagues, being creative and committed—surviving.'

She looked at him in astonishment.

'Is that how he—they—saw her?' she wondered and looked across to where everyone else was sitting and saw them nodding and murmuring support.

'Thanks,' she said with surprise. 'Thanks.'

'I guess that today, though, the painful feelings were taking centre stage for a while?' Jonathan said.

'Yes.'

She paused.

'That line—*"The ceremony of innocence is drowned"*—it struck me differently when I heard it just now. Like it was me facing up to the loss of my innocence, the loss of my marriage.'

The words were hard to say out loud and her voice wavered. In her mind's eye she saw Edwyn's handsome face smiling at her, heard him telling her how much he loved her, how proud he was of her.

'And I thought I was immune,' she hurried on, while she could, 'immune to any prospects of loving again—of even feeling again, let alone loving.'

She looked around and saw that Toby had got up from the piano and gone to lean against the wall, as if to see and hear her better.

'And today, I felt surrounded by all you men and you were all being so gentle and kind,' the words were coming out in a rush now, 'and I felt overwhelmed by this terrible loss, this fear of never ever being able to be close to anyone ever again.'

She let her chin drop onto her knees and stared down at the bed.

Jonathan was sitting close to her, but being careful not to touch her, guessing that it might not be what she wanted.

She looked up.

'And I'm scared—scared of all this pent-up emotion that the Governess is carrying round inside her that in the end will come out as full-blown hysteria and I know that I've got to go with all that, but it's scary because in other ways, I'm trying to keep myself, my life together.'

She was crying again, but this time quietly and with a welcome release, having faced and admitted her challenges, both personally and professionally.

She looked at the soggy, screwed up ball of tissue in her hand and laughed—her tears had defeated it.

Jonathan reached into his pocket and brought out a crumpled, but clean-looking cotton handkerchief.

She took it and smiled.

'I think I'm OK now, thanks.'

'Sure?' he said.

'Sure.'

'OK.'

He was about to stand up, but then stopped and turned back to her.

'Anna,' he said, 'take support and comfort from wherever you can find it, whenever you need it—from us, from companionship, from poetry—and of course from music. Never underestimate the healing power of words and music.'

And at that moment, she realised that all her years on the stage and on the road had lent her a resilience she had underestimated.

Maybe, she thought, it's time to take some of my power back.

Chapter 27

'Wrong address, no post code—been round the houses it has! When they showed it me and I saw your name, I knew Lilac Cottage was wrong and it was meant for you here at Lavender. The Morgans live at Lilac.'

Huw had knocked at the door to hand him the envelope, and having said his thank yous, Edwyn took the letter through to his study, smiling at the thought that Huw was like Willy Nilly, the postman in Under Milk Wood who knows everyone's news.

He looked down at the expensive cream envelope: the address was incomplete and muddled, but the handwriting was familiar.

Anna, writing to him from Myddleton.

He'd been expecting her to get in touch, guessing his text would have provided excuse or provocation, but the unexpected formality of a letter surprised him. He laid the sheets of paper in front of him on the desk and began to read.

The first paragraph suggested she was hoping that some cathartic release would be achieved by an outpouring of emotion, but as he read on, he was stung by the hint of defiance, the implicit rebukes, until towards the end, the tone softened and he saw care and compassion in her words of concern.

He could tell, though, that she resented him for throwing away their love, that she hovered between tenderness and frustration, and that coping with work while still in a state of emotional meltdown must be costing her dear.

He pushed the letter away and rubbed his eyes, knowing he was to blame for the distress and confusion she was feeling. It touched him to think that in spite of this, she could still find it in her heart to worry about what he might be going through.

He knew she was right to press for a decision on the house in Richmond and knew he must reply.

He looked out of the window and gazed at the unusually becalmed waters. A seagull sat on the window ledge, unblinking eyes fixed on him, as if questioning his right to be there. He shooed it away with his hands, but it was back within moments.

He looked down at the letter, skimming its contents once more. They would need to meet; there were decisions to make and he could delay it no longer.

He stood up, feeling the need to get out of the cottage. He opened the front door and stepped onto the small paved area that served as front garden, where the seagull was now tottering around the circular rockery that provided the only greenery. He sat on the seat outside his study window, looking across the bay to where wet-skin-clad surfers floated listlessly on their boards, waiting for a wave and looking like shiny black sharks ready to pounce.

The seagull at last flew off to find new pickings, leaving him alone with his unquiet thoughts. He could tell that Anna was trapped in a bewildering limbo-land in which she still harboured hopes of a way back to the life they'd once shared, but at the same time, was mourning their marriage like a death.

But she was not a widow; she was a wife forsaken by a husband who could barely explain to himself the crisis that had waylaid him.

He had learnt with dismay how profound and unpredictable grief could be; how in the end it will out, however hard you try to lock it away.

Why could he not move on, get on with his life as Wendy had urged? Even she, with all her compassion and understanding, expected him to disregard and discard his past as if it was a skin and not a pervasion of his entire being.

He remembered her parting words, just before Christmas:

'Please don't let this search take over any more of your life. It's one thing to want to achieve some sort of closure, but not if it becomes a destructive obsession. Why pursue it further? To what end? To blame and shame?' She'd squeezed his hand at this point and said more gently: 'They're dead—you can hardly confront them now.'

Dear kind, loyal Wendy.

He knew she feared he would risk his happiness in a fruitless quest for the truth. But the discoveries had changed his entire narrative about himself. His sense of self, his place in the world had been swept away and unless he could uncover the full story, drawing a line seemed impossible.

Chapter 28

She could hardly have refused him, but now that they were there in the garden at the Vine, Anna was glad she'd come. The evening was warm and the garden busy, but the tables were well spaced and they'd found one away from the corner where locals were throwing batons at a wooden skittle which looked like a doll.

'Have you ever seen that before?' Nicholas asked.

Anna looked on in amusement and shook her head.

'What is it?'

'Aunt Sally,' he replied. 'It's an Oxfordshire game—they say it may have been introduced by Royalist soldiers during the English Civil war when Charles I set up court in Oxford.'

'I'm glad we're not any closer!'

'I know—it looks a bit vicious the way they go at it, doesn't it?'

He was a gentle, thoughtful companion, self-effacing and intense, undoubtedly marked by life, but not at all the man she had so recently dismissed as aloof and stand-offish.

'So what made you come back to England?' she asked. 'I'd have thought a house in the Dordogne was far too nice to leave, even for one in as lovely a place as Oxford.'

Nicholas reflected. 'I suppose I thought it was time to draw a line, try to move on.' As he drew his index finger through the condensation on the side of his glass he looked tired and his voice sounded hoarse. 'I think I'd been heading for some kind of breakdown for ages. The travelling got to me so much.' He closed his eyes and groaned. 'You go from Paris to Munich to Rome and you spend your life talking in school French and school German and holiday Italian and a sort of pidgin English, and your personality shrinks to a size commensurate with your ability to communicate.' Anna recognised the truth of his words. 'You know what I mean?'

She nodded and grimaced. Her command of languages was limited and working in Europe was taxing.

'And the stage fright had become crippling, almost pathological—but when my brother died, that was the tipping point.'

'Oh, I'm so sorry,' Anna said. 'I didn't know.'

She had no idea that a question designed to be purely conversational would elicit such a raw and candid response and she hesitated to ask more for fear of stirring up feelings he was holding back.

'What happened?' she said after a while.

Nicholas's eyes were pale and blue and a little watery-looking, but he showed no danger of losing control.

'I'd been in trouble for a while, really—probably doing too much, and becoming paranoid about the top of my voice.'

Anna nodded in sympathy.

'Composers have no pity for sopranos and tenors—that's a fact.'

'I was singing parts I should never have been singing in houses that were too big and struggling with roles I should have taken in my stride.'

He tugged open the bags of crisps and nuts he'd bought, laying them out flat so that they could both help themselves.

'It was early in 2004. I'd been singing Tamino and finding it difficult—not helped by some sort of virus I couldn't shake off—and got into the habit of asking for announcements—which the management got pretty fed up with—and then I cancelled a few—which is never good.' He was studying a handful of nuts. 'And then they sacked me from the *Traviata* I was booked to do—which was ridiculous casting anyway and I should never have agreed to it—and a few days later Charlie died in the Madrid train bombings.' He took a large gulp of lager. 'We were twins—but I didn't even know he was in Spain.'

Anna gasped, appalled at the savage sequence of events.

'We never found out why he was there or what he was doing. My dad and I went to Madrid to see what we could find out—we thought that if we could discover the truth it would help us, but...'

He stopped and shrugged.

'There were no answers, so I took myself off to Charlie's house in the Dordogne, thinking that the answer might lie there.' He bit his lip. 'Of course it didn't, but then I found I couldn't leave the place, I lacked the courage to face the world again.'

He looked at her hard, and Anna felt he was checking to see whether she understood—which of course, she did, all too well.

'Unfinished business,' she said. 'It's natural to want to find out the truth.'

'Yes, but why do we assume the truth will set us free?' he asked.

'I guess we want to achieve some sort of closure and we associate that with knowing the truth.'

'That's right.'

'And have you?' she asked. 'Achieved closure?'

'I'm getting there. It was Daniel who helped me to see that as long as we believe there's unfinished business, we can postpone the day when we finally have to accept that someone has left us for good.'

'Daniel?'

'Yes, he came to see me. He and Charlie were friends—worked together for a while—and he was grieving for him, too, but he could see that I was becoming obsessed and that it had become an excuse for me to say I couldn't move on, when in truth, I wasn't really trying to.'

He had a habit of looking away as if overcome by shyness or self-consciousness and then shifting his focus back onto whoever he was speaking to with the searching quality Anna had previously found so disconcerting.

'And,' he went on, 'of course I felt I had nothing to come back to—that my career was dead in the water because I'd got a name for being flaky and unreliable.'

'It takes real courage to start again, I think, particularly when stress and nerves have been such an issue for you.' She was thinking that if she had stopped working in those awful first days and weeks after Edwyn left, she might never have sung in public again.

Nicholas nodded to acknowledge what she'd said.

'It was Daniel who encouraged me to give it another go. The plan was to start with a gentle programme of concerts and recitals and build things up gradually'—he grinned unexpectedly—'I hadn't expected to be thrown into *The Turn of the Screw*, but that was down to Daniel. He put my name forward to Paul and Jonathan as soon as he heard about Harri.'

He smiled and blushed and then looked away again as if in sudden embarrassment.

'Was Charlie married or with someone when he died?' she asked, wondering what exactly was the nature of the relationships between these men.

'He'd been married briefly in his twenties to an Argentinean woman he met on holiday, but as far as we know he wasn't involved with anyone when he died.' He bit his lip. 'I did wonder whether it was a woman that had taken him to Madrid, but no one ever came forward to claim him, so to speak.'

The lowering sun was dipping behind some trees in the corner of the garden and the dappled sunlight on her face made Anna shift her position on the long bench seat to move into shade.

She thought about what he'd said and wondered whether she was in danger of allowing obsession to get in the way of facing the reality of Edwyn's permanent separation.

She shifted her position again and leant across to take a handful of nuts.

He was scrutinising her closely, and she wondered if he could read her thoughts.

'Grieving's a complex process isn't it?' he said. 'It simply defies rational explanation—as you must have felt this morning.'

Anna realised he no longer thought himself to blame for her outburst and was offering her the opportunity to talk about her loss as he had spoken about his.

'Being left by someone I loved very much....' Her voice trailed away. 'Since he went away the way he did...' She paused. 'I've asked myself how much of my life have I wasted in delusion?'

'But surely,' he said, 'you can't discredit all the years you had together.'

'No,' she said. 'I don't want to do that—that would be just too painful to bear.'

He was looking at her in that way of his she found so unsettling, but he was also ill-at-ease himself, and when she forced herself to hold his gaze, she saw he had something to admit.

She raised her eyebrows in expectation.

'Daniel told me about the conversation you and he had in the Folly.'

'Ah...'

'But what he didn't tell you is that I knew Edwyn well when I was a student, that he was my tutor at New College.'

Her eyes widened with surprise.

'Yes, 1987-90. He never actually taught me, but he was my moral tutor, and was incredibly supportive when I had a crisis at the end of my first term.'

He downed the remains of his drink.

'My parents separated a few weeks after Charlie and I came up, but I had History Prelims at the end of the Michaelmas term and I completely flunked them and had to retake them the following term.' He paused, as if looking back at that unhappy time. 'Edwyn was brilliant—he really seemed to understand what I was going through—not at all the dry, dusty Oxford academic.'

Anna did a quick mental calculation: in 1987, Edwyn would have been 41.

Nicholas drew a packet of cigarettes out of his pocket.

'Just one a day, before you ask.' he quipped.

'But how can you?' she asked aghast. 'You and Louise!'

'I justify it now by saying it stops me getting too precious about my voice. But actually I quite enjoy it as well.'

He lit up quickly and expertly, but as he screwed up his eyes to take his first hungry puff, Anna saw once again the weary, ravaged look she had noticed at the concert a few nights earlier.

'Let's have another drink,' he said, taking a few more puffs before propping the cigarette on the ashtray and heading to the bar.

Chapter 29

The Aunt Sally players had packed and gone and the garden was emptying, some people retreating inside to the warmth of the bar, others scooping up their small children and taking them home. The sun had disappeared and the air was cooler, and though Anna shivered and pulled on her cardigan, she had no desire to move as there was still more she hoped to learn. She felt her forehead tighten, and as she waited for Nicholas to come back, she prepared herself for the truth that Edwyn had denied her.

'Will you tell me what you know please?' she asked as he sat down.

He continued to puff away at his cigarette in deep, greedy breaths and when he spoke, it was to ask a question. 'When did you and Edwyn meet?'

'February 1991,' she replied. 'I was in my final year.'

Nicholas hesitated for a moment.

'It was August 1990,' he said. 'I'd graduated in the summer and had got a place at Cambridge to do a PhD. I remember that Edwyn wasn't around at the end of term—after exams—because his mother had died and he'd gone home to be with his father. I was about to leave Oxford for the last time and wanted to say goodbye to Edwyn and thank him for all his support.'

He squashed the stub of his cigarette hard against the ashtray and took a sip of lager. Anna waited, holding her breath, resolved to let him tell the story in his own time.

'I hadn't told him I was coming, I just knocked on his door in the hope that he was there. He didn't answer, so I knocked again and tried the handle and popped my head round the door. He was sitting at his desk, wading through paperwork, I thought at first, but he was in a state of some agitation, and even when he saw me, he didn't really cover it up. I assumed he was still upset about his mother and I made to leave, but he beckoned me to come in.'

Anna pictured the scene in her mind's eye, the handsome room with its generous bay window and deep window seat covered in cushions, the comfy sofas, the book-lined shelves and the orderly desk.

'We sat on one of the sofas, but I couldn't help noticing the disarray on his desk.'

Anna raised an eyebrow in surprise.

'It was covered with what looked like letters, diaries, newspaper cuttings, photographs, sketches and other stuff I couldn't make out. It was as if he was trying to put it in some sort of order. He offered me a sherry and I noticed he'd already got a glass on the go. I started to say something about his mother, how sorry I was, to ask about his father. I could see he was subdued, though he made an attempt to talk about my degree, my place at Cambridge, but I could see his heart wasn't in it, so I asked him straight out, was he alright. I remember his answer because it was such a bizarre *non sequitur*. "I always wondered about the spelling of my name. Apparently my mother wanted to call me Dafydd, but Brenda worried it would be too difficult for them to explain away such a Welsh name when they weren't Welsh, so they compromised on the Welsh spelling of Edwin".'

Anna shook her head in puzzlement.

'I know,' Nicholas said, 'it didn't make sense to me either and I'm sure I must have looked taken aback, but before I could say anything, Edwyn said: "You see Brenda wasn't my mother after all. She was my aunt. Lily—her sister—was my mother."'

Anna frowned. 'But Brenda didn't have a sister.'

'It seems she did,' Nicholas said, 'a younger sister, but she'd been written out of Brenda's story.' He paused. 'It was a strange position to be in, a tutor using you as a confidant for something so profound, but I guess I just happened to turn up at the right moment.'

'So did he tell you anything else?' Anna asked.

'Oh yes,' Nicholas replied. 'After that it all came pouring out. It was like a reversal of the time when I'd told him about the bitter breakup of my parents.'

Anna shivered and put her jacket round her shoulders.

'Are you warm enough to stay out here?' she asked him.

He nodded, but put on the jumper that he'd had draped round his shoulders.

'It seems that with Brenda's death, Jim felt released from the promise he'd made to never talk about Lily. He'd always felt uneasy about keeping the truth from Edwyn, but didn't want to go against his wife. She sounds quite formidable, I must say.'

'She was,' Anna agreed. 'She always seemed so resentful and discontented and I could never understand why. Jim was so kind and decent.'

'Was he rather submissive?' Nicholas asked.

'Yes, he was. He could appear quite passive, but I suspect he just preferred a quiet life.'

'But without Brenda knowing, Jim had kept a memory box for Edwyn—quite an act of defiance you could say. And having broken the news to Edwyn, Jim handed it over to him.'

'So, can you remember what Edwyn told you?'

''I think so, but forgive me if there are gaps or if I mis-remember anything.'

Anna nodded reassuringly.

'Lily was Brenda's younger sister—ten years younger and an unexpected—and for Brenda, unwanted—arrival in the family. It sounds as if Brenda was jealous of her—even resented her prettier name. And to make it worse, Lily was popular and talented—wanted to be a costume designer. That's how she met Edwyn's father.'

Anna's eyes widened. As she'd listened to the story unfolding, she'd begun to speculate that Jim was Lily's lover, but no, clearly not.

179

'He was an actor called David Demery—I remember the name because there was a French master at school with that surname. He was part of a touring company, performing *Yeoman of the Guard* at the theatre where Lily was learning her trade as a dresser. David was the understudy for Jack Point the jester and had to take over the role. Lily had to alter the costume to fit him.'

'Ah!' said Anna.

'Lily told Jim that David had a lovely light baritone voice, ideal for operetta and musicals. He sounds like quite a character and not surprisingly Lily was charmed by him—said he was really funny in the role, but very touching too, hiding his love for Elsie behind this extrovert comic persona.'

'I love that role,' Anna said. 'He has that wonderful aria, *"I have a song to sing, Oh!"*'

"Sing me a song, Oh!" crooned Nicholas. 'Yes, it's a lovely number.'

So caught up was he in recalling what he knew that he'd forgotten his lager, but now he paused to take a few sips.

Anna waited, not wanting to break the spell of his storytelling.

'So, Lily and David fell in love and the inevitable happened. She fell pregnant, told no one apart from David and took herself off to North Wales to have the baby in secret. David was meant to collect her from a boarding house where she and Brenda had been taken for family holidays.'

'Don't tell me he didn't turn up?'

'Fraid so. Lily had written to David—who was on tour somewhere—to tell him that the baby had come slightly early, but he didn't show up. In desperation, she turned to her sister and brother-in-law for help and they agreed to take in the baby and register him as their own.'

'But what happened to Lily?' Anna cried.

'She had been unwell on and off for a while and put it down to her pregnancy, but she died in an isolation hospital of TB during the bad winter of 1947 when Edwyn was just a few months old. I suppose Brenda and Jim hid her shame —and their deception—by denying her existence.'

'Oh God, how sad,' Anna said.

'I know, it's awful. It sounds as if Jim tried to describe the story with real care and sensitivity, but Edwyn was shattered.'

'Poor Edwyn!'

They were silent for a moment. A young couple who'd been sitting in the opposite corner of the garden, walked past them on their way out to the car park and called a cheery goodnight. The woman was heavily pregnant and walked with an uneven waddle, her partner's hand gently steering her from behind. Anna watched them go and then remembered something Nicholas had said at the start.

'What was in the memory box?' she asked. 'Do you know?'

'Well, I suspect much of the contents were on Edwyn's desk. On the floor by the side of the desk, I noticed a carved wooden box with flowers painted all over it—lilies I think they were. I assumed that was the memory box.'

Anna nodded. 'It would have been. Jim loved making those boxes.'

'Edwyn said Lily had kept David's letters and memorabilia from his life in the theatre. So he had something of both his parents.'

He paused. 'I'm not sure how much consolation it was at the time. He was very angry with Jim and Brenda for keeping the truth from him, for denying him his true identity.'

Anna winced.

'I knew nothing about any of this,' she said, 'and from what Daniel said, it sounds as if Edwyn spent years delving into the past. I assume he was looking for his father. Why would he keep that from me?'

The question upset and angered her and she leant her elbows on the table and clasped her hand to her head.

'I've thought about that, too,' Nicholas replied, 'ever since Daniel told me that you were in the dark.'

He looked grave and concerned and she could tell he understood how let down she felt by Edwyn's failure to include her in something so fundamental.

'Sharing most of my life with an identical twin who I lost in a way I still can't make sense of, I've thought a lot about identity.'

She nodded.

'I think Edwyn's anger and hurt stemmed not only from the information that had been kept from him, but also the lies that surrounded it. After 40 years, he may have felt he was OK with who he was, where he'd come from, but then all that was pulled away from him, and he felt powerless and vulnerable.' He paused. 'And I suspect he wouldn't have wanted you to see that in him. So he hid it from you.'

'Someone with a hidden side, a side that remained in shadow,' she murmured, 'that's what Grace said,' remembering their conversation over dinner, and closing her eyes to try and recall what she had said next: 'only to appear when a problem emerged that he saw as personal only to him and couldn't share with you.'

She looked at him quizzically.

'Do you think that something else recently came to light that triggered another crisis for him?'

Nicholas shook his head.

'I don't know,' he said. 'I guess only Edwyn can answer that.'

'If only he would,' she said. 'If only he would.'

'I'm sorry, Anna, I feel I've told you only the most garbled précis of what must have happened—but it's all I know, or all I can remember.' He frowned. 'It must be tantalising—I mean to know so much, and yet so little.'

He looked so genuinely regretful that she felt sorry for him. They were both silent for a moment, before a thought occurred to her.

'When you met him again at reunions after you'd left Oxford, did you get the impression that he'd got anywhere with his search for his father?'

Nicholas thought for a moment.

'Yes, a little. We only spoke about it once, several years later, and he was nothing like as forthcoming as he had been, but I remember him telling me that he'd been helped by a former colleague—she used to be the College Librarian. She had an interest in genealogy apparently and knew how to go about these things.'

'Wendy Wainwright. Yes, I remember her. I think she had a soft spot for Edwyn, actually.'

'Yes, I gathered that, too. What happened to her, do you know? I know she's not at College anymore, or you could perhaps have gone and talked to her.'

'She got married, out of the blue, to Francis Tyler, Fellow in English at Trinity College—a specialist in Thomas Hardy—just before he took up a post at Cambridge. I sang a duet with Wendy's nephew at the wedding.'

'So, she'll remember you then,' he said.

'Oh, yes,' Anna said. 'She'll remember me.'

Wendy Wainwright, well-organised and warm-hearted, ran the College Library with as much interest in the students' emotional welfare as in their academic achievements and her unexpected marriage provoked a mixture of delight for her and dismay for the academic community she left behind. To mark her marriage and her departure, the Organist at New College had written a setting of *Love Divine all love's excelling* for soprano and tenor.

It was the last time Anna had ever sung with Mark.

Chapter 30

He emptied the contents of the folder onto his desk and began to sort through the materials he'd picked up from Richmond. Fragile originals—not transcripts or photocopies—their unearthing had marked a turning point in his research; the moment when his subject became more than prime minister and reformer and emerged three-dimensional, a man of flesh and blood, a side of his life revealed that he had successfully kept hidden.

The documents were an unexpected gift from William Loudon, a distant relative of Lord John Russell, and an obsessional family historian. Edwyn recalled the thrilling moment in Loudon's cluttered, overheated sitting room when he had held this momentous hoard for the first time. Loudon had amassed not only old photos and press cuttings, but a stash of yellowing letters between Russell and Charles Dickens; a candid correspondence that threw light on the premier's unknown personal distractions and helped explain his failure of leadership at times of duress. Loudon was prepared to lend this archive to Edwyn, realising that a professional historian could put it to meaningful use and allow a more complete story of his illustrious ancestor to be told at last.

Edwyn was looking for a particular letter he needed to check and in sifting gently through the piles, his elbow caught the framed wedding photograph of Jim and Brenda and knocked it over. As he righted it and moved it to safety at the back of the desk, he was reminded that history could sometimes give up its secrets more readily than the recent past.

The photograph was in black and white and he wondered if it was only in his imagination that the smiling bridesmaid looked unnaturally flushed, her heightened colour a sign of future illness. He gazed at her, struck as always by the simple power of a still image of someone long dead, staring out at you, holding your gaze.

He sighed.

It stung him to acknowledge that though remarkable discoveries could be made about someone born before the French Revolution, a man who had vanished scarcely sixty years earlier remained veiled in mystery.

How do you begin to fathom parents you have never known? All he had of them, he realised, were fragments of imagined lives; fantasies which with time became dangerously entrenched as facts. He had explored every strand of available evidence, but had to accept that sometimes no amount of detective work will demystify the past.

He had never before attempted biography, but what had begun as a study of the transition of the Whigs into the Liberals had turned into a life of the last Whig Prime Minister. The research was done, but he was finding the writing slow and arduous.

Needing a break and a change of scene, he walked his usual route into Criccieth, leaving the car at the Feathers. As he headed towards the ruined castle that had once intimidated prospective attackers, he remembered why he had been drawn to the study of history. He'd always been fascinated by the link between past and present; it suited his analytic mindset. In another life he might have been a detective, so much did he enjoy unravelling the complex web of causes that help explain why particular events and phenomena occurred. But more than that, he loved the challenge of communicating those findings in narratives that make the past come alive, that reveal who we are and explain where we came from.

He walked along Marine Parade until he was standing under the shadow of the castle. Some disgruntled visitors passed him, complaining how little there was to see.

'It's not exactly Edinburgh is it?' a woman said peevishly.

Edwyn smiled. It was true that little remained, but the views from the top of the mound were spectacular and the castle's history—deeply entwined in the age-old conflict between Wales and England—was a fascinating testament to the fluctuating fortunes of war.

From behind him he heard a shout, a child calling his father to come look at the sea. Edwyn walked away from the castle and drew close to where the man and the boy were pointing. He could feel his breathing quickening as he guessed what they had seen. He moved a little distance away from them and peered into the sunshine. As the child and his father cheered in unison, Edwyn caught sight of two sleek grey dolphins at play. There was an unmistakable flash of light as they leapt above the waves as if in unison before briefly disappearing under the surface, then diving high again, away from the shoreline.

Edwyn turned and saw that he was standing just a few doors away from number 9. This was the sign he had waited for, the bargain he had made with himself. With only a momentary hesitation, he walked up to the royal blue door and rapped hard on the cast iron door-knob.

Chapter 31

She had slept fitfully, her rest disrupted by anxious hours of wakefulness followed by uneasy dreams in which Edwyn and Brenda and a man she couldn't make out lured her into bizarre situations and taunted her with fragments of surreal and unsettling conversations.

As she tried to revive herself with mugs of tea and buttery toast, she studied the call-sheet for the day, relieved to have a later start that morning. She had her first costume fitting at 12.30 after which she'd return to the cottage for lunch before going back to the House for the afternoon rehearsal.

Her eyes ached and her skin felt tight and dry. She went upstairs to finish dressing and, catching sight of herself in the dressing table mirror, she groaned to see how wan she looked. She started to apply some makeup, hoping to disguise the ravages of a sleepless night, but all the while, mulling over what Nicholas had told her, trying to piece the story together.

She was particularly troubled to learn that Edwyn had known the truth about his parentage throughout the time they had been together, had lived with those secrets for as long as he had lived with her. Without success, she trawled her memory for some clue that would help her recognise what crisis had precipitated his abrupt departure.

She studied her efforts in cosmetic concealment and sighed. Even with the help of blusher and lipstick, she still looked tired and drawn. Thinking some colour at her neck might help to lift her jaded appearance, she opened her jewellery box in search of her emerald green beads. As she secured the clasp at the nape of her neck, she glanced down at the swarms of tiny white butterflies with which Jim had covered the small casket and thought of the chest he'd made for Lily. She ran her fingers across the smooth wooden surface of the box and wondered for the first time about the girl in the wedding photograph. Until now, she'd speculated that grief and guilt had led Edwyn to give the photograph of his parents such prominence, but she guessed the smiling girl hanging on to Brenda's arm, was Lily, the younger sister.

Edwyn's mother.

How cheerful and childlike she had looked, yet she was only a few short years away from so much pain and sorrow. Anna's heart ached for this long dead girl, with her faithless lover and broken health. How Edwyn must grieve for her; and how bitter, by contrast, his feelings for his father might be.

With Wendy's help, did he now know more than he had told Nicholas all those years before? Anna couldn't remember to which college Francis had gone, but guessed he would have since retired and wondered where he and Wendy lived now. There seemed no easy way of finding out.

She made her way round the Orangery, where Jonathan and Paul were working with Nicholas alone, and headed towards the front entrance and into a set of interconnecting rooms just off the hall that were occupied by the staff and volunteers who ran the Festival and which, during the event, doubled as sewing and fitting rooms.

The outer office was empty, but through an open door at the back Anna could see Jane the costume maker on her knees at Louise's feet, pinning up the hem of a striking black dress. The skirt and closely fitting bodice were shot through with narrow panels of silvery coloured silk, some of which Patrick had explained would be pulled through raggedly as Miss Jessel becomes more agitated and dishevelled.

Jane looked up and smiled. She was small and sporty-looking with an eye-catching pair of red ankle boots making a striking match with her black leggings and black bolero jacket.

'I'll be with you in two minutes Anna—I just need to get this hem sorted.'

'That's fine,' Anna said. 'I'm early.'

Louise looked over her shoulder.

'You OK?' she asked, scrutinising Anna closely. 'You look a bit more like Miss Jessel than's good for you—a bit too much haggard beauty if you don't mind me saying. You should leave that to me!'

Anna laughed and pulled a face and Jane looked up again, her expression showing she was bemused by the exchange.

'I'm fine—and you look fabulous: that dress is stunning. What a fantastic cut. Well done Jane.'

'Thanks. Let's hope Patrick thinks so…'

Anna found herself excited at the prospect of seeing her own costumes.

A voice behind her calling her name made her jump and she turned round to see Emma, the Assistant Stage Manager.

'I saw you heading this way,' the girl said, 'and thought I'd bring you this—it came this morning.'

Anna's heart fluttered as Emma handed her a small package. Surely, she thought, it was too soon for Edwyn to have replied?

'Thanks,' she called distractedly as the girl headed back towards the Orangery, leaving her alone in the office holding the small white jiffy bag.

She sat on one of the comfy chairs arranged around a low coffee table and turned the package over, her curiosity aroused. The label was addressed to her, care of Myddleton, but it was not Edwyn's writing and the postmark was local.

The flourish of the capital letters was unmistakable.

She took an intake of breath and eased open the flap. She could tell that Jane and Louise had finished and that Louise was getting dressed and was almost ready to leave. She had time to do no more than peer inside the envelope and half remove the contents for a quick glance before Louise came out.

Though she feared her tired mind might be playing tricks on her, she could see that the package held her missing address book nestled within a sheet of writing paper bearing a short letter in Mark's distinctive handwriting.

Chapter 32

Somewhere from within the house he heard a woman's voice and the sound of footsteps hurrying towards the door. Though many times in his head he'd rehearsed this moment, he felt tongue-tied, and realised he had no idea how he would explain his visit. He could feel his colour rising and his heart thudding, but there was no time to retreat because the door swung open to reveal a woman in an oversized man's shirt and faded jeans with flecks of blue paint in her dark brown hair.

She looked at him quizzically, but her manner was friendly and she was quick to spot his uncertainty.

'Hello,' she said. 'Do you need directions?'

'No, no,' he replied quickly.

She waited, with no trace of impatience or irritation, and he felt his resolve return. Something about her good-humoured expression gave him the confidence to be direct.

'I'm tracing my family tree,' he said, 'and I know that my mother stayed here with me for a few days when I was first born.'

'Oh really?' the woman said. 'Fancy!'

'Yes,' Edwyn went on, 'I never knew her—my mother—she died when I was a baby—and I wondered if I could prevail on you to show me the room she rented please.'

The woman smiled and without hesitation invited him in.

'I'm sorry to bother you—I can see you're in the thick of things.'

'Don't worry,' she said. 'I'm glad of an excuse to stop for a minute. I'm Jenny, by the way, and my husband on the ladder up there is Steffan. I won't shake your hand because I seem to have got blue paint in places where I shouldn't have blue paint!'

She laughed and from the landing at the top of the first flight of stairs, her husband laughed too and signalled a friendly welcome with a wave of his paintbrush.

'Come through to the kitchen,' she said. 'We're not too bad in there.'

He followed her across a square-shaped hall that had large rooms off it on both sides, down a short corridor that led to the back of the house. At a glance he could see that the interior was an empty shell—no carpets or furniture—but its renovation and decoration were well-advanced, giving a sense of light and spaciousness. The kitchen was large and newly fitted with stainless steel appliances and black marbled work tops. A large farmhouse style table was a jumble of brochures and colour charts, in the midst of which were a couple of mugs and plates bearing traces of a recent snack.

'Cup of tea?' she asked. 'There's still some in the pot.'

'No, no. I really don't want to disturb you for long. It's very kind of you to let me come in.'

'Not at all,' she said, moving some fabric samples off a chair and inviting him to sit down. 'I'm interested, and to be honest, Steffan prefers it if I leave the practicalities to him and stick to the designing side of things.' She pointed at her hair. 'I know I should wear a scarf or a hair net or something equally unflattering, but I'm vain.' She laughed again and Edwyn relaxed and laughed with her.

She sat on the other side of the table and pushed the crockery to one side. He guessed she was in her mid-thirties and, from her accent, Welsh, but not local. She was studying him closely.

'So when would this have been then?' she asked. 'I only ask because I've been clearing out a cupboard under the stairs and I've come across a whole load of visitor books going back years.'

Edwyn heard his breathing quicken.

'Well, my mother first came here as a girl, with her parents and her older sister. Hannigan was the name and they'd have come as a family in the late 1920s, early 30s. My mother would have come here with me in late June 1946.'

'There's nothing before the 1940s, but you could be in luck for the later visit. Wait here and I'll go and fetch them.'

She went through to the front of the house and returned carrying a pile of hard-backed ledgers.

'Right old state they were in, thick with dust. I've cleaned them off as best I can, but look here, the dust is ingrained in this raised stubbly effect on the covers.'

She put them down on the table and picked up the one on the top.

'How long have you been here?' Edwyn asked, hoping to disguise his excitement and apprehension.

'We bought the house about a year ago, but we had to finish our jobs down south before we could move up here full-time. Steffan's from Criccieth, I'm from Cardiff, and we were both teaching down there when the house came on the market and we decided to make a complete change. We were both fed up with teaching and Steffan's always wanted to run a bed and breakfast on Marine Terrace, so here we are.'

She was flicking through the book in her hand before putting it to one side and picking up the next in the pile.

'It was in a very sorry mess when we bought it so we got it cheap. It had been empty for a few years and before that it had been a bed and breakfast under a string of different owners. None of them seemed to be able to keep going at it.'

The pile of rejected books was building as she talked and Edwyn felt his hopes fading.

'I understand the woman who owned the house in 1946 had been here for decades and had got to know the Hannigan family well because they came so regularly.' He paused. 'I think that's why my mother came back here—it was familiar and the landlady was kind-hearted.'

Jenny looked up and nodded, but said nothing as she resumed her search.

'Here we are. These are older. Those others were all from the 60s and 70s.'

The next book in the pile had the year 1945 inlaid at the bottom of the right hand corner in gilt that was scratched with age. As she moved it to the other pile, Edwyn held his breath, fearing the next one might be 1944, and the one under that 1943, but with a flourish Jenny declared, '1946—you're in luck!'

She handed it to him.

'Have a look. I'll just clear up some of this mess—give you some space.'

She gathered the mugs and plates together and moved them over to the draining board and busied herself at the sink.

He opened the book, handling it carefully as if it was a priceless exhibit. The book was as old as he was—older even—as the first visitors had stayed in the middle of January 1946. Who were they, he wondered, this Frank and Peggy Ewbank, saying they'd enjoyed their long weekend, but the weather could have been better? Were they newly reunited after the end of the war or newly married? Or not married at all and just having some fun?

He turned the pages and scanned the names and dates. Business was slow in those months after the end of the war: there were a few more visitors in January, none in February, a handful in March, several in April—Easter he guessed—more in May. He saw Jenny glance over her shoulder as he turned the next page.

June.

He ran his index finger down the date column on the left hand side of the page. The guest house had been busy in fits and starts that month—a cluster in one week, then a

194

gap, then another cluster, with just one entry for the last week of June. There it was: the graceful handwriting that had become so familiar: 24th June 1946, Mrs Lily Demery and child.

He had been here. With her. His mother.

He ran his finger over the name that was never to be hers—or his—and sighed.

Jenny looked over at him.

'Any joy?' she asked kindly.

'Yes,' he said. 'It's here.'

She came to stand behind him to see.

'Ah, Room 2,' she said. 'The best room in the house—it even had a bit of a lounge area. I'll show you—the numbers were still on the doors when we first came here so I know which one it was—sea view on the first floor'

Edwyn started to stand up when Steffan's voice called from upstairs.

'Jen—can you help me a minute, love?'

'Hang on,' she said, touching his arm gently. 'I'll be right back.'

He nodded and sat down to wait.

"The best room in the house." A reassuring description, but Edwyn couldn't help wondering what this large room with a good view might have been like in 1946: dingy, threadbare, uncomfortable?

He turned the next few pages of the visitors' book and saw the entries dwindle away until the rest of the pages in the book were empty. No doubt the privations of war had taken their toll on business so that by the time peace arrived, the elderly owner became one of those landladies unable to keep going, unable to prevent the large house slipping into shabbiness and disrepair.

He flipped idly through the blank pages, watching them whir past in a blur, when his eye was caught by a piece of paper slipped in a page towards the back of the book. He turned the pages more slowly until he found it again.

It was a small piece of lined paper that looked as if it had been torn from an exercise book. He turned it over, and to his surprise recognised the handwriting, though this time the script was large and bold:

"As from 10th July 1946, Mrs Lily Demery can be contacted c/o Jim and Brenda Maxwell, 6 Hastings Close, Affcot, near Ludlow."

So Jim had been telling the truth: Lily had left a forwarding address.

Was it never passed on, he wondered, because no one ever came to ask for it, or worse—a bitter thought—because it had been mislaid, stuffed into the back of a redundant visitor book and forgotten?

There was no sign of the dolphins as he made his way along Marine Terrace towards the coastal path. The sun was dipping behind a bank of clouds, but only a few minutes earlier it had illuminated room 2 with a burst of golden light. Spacious and airy—even though some of the room had been lost to incorporate an en-suite bathroom—the view of sea and mountains from the two large bay windows was glorious and he had thrilled to think of his mother—perhaps cradling him in her arms—sitting there watching the sun rise and set, letting the ceaseless turns of the tide soothe her as she waited.

Waited for David; waited for the man who never came to collect his putative wife and their child. The thought chilled him, as it had always done whenever he pictured his mother there alone, her hopes diminishing as every day passed with no news.

There was a straggle of walkers ahead of him on the path and he stepped onto the sand and walked down to the water's edge to avoid them. He wanted to be alone with his thoughts of his mother, to savour having been with her at last in that long-imagined room at 9 Marine Terrace.

He stood for a moment watching the waves break gently in the shallows and peered out at the same horizon his mother would have seen every day from her bedroom window as she kept wait for David Demery.

Demery—where did that name come from that had sent him down so many blind alleys in his search for the truth about his father? Demery, Demory, de Mery, Demere—all had led nowhere in the hunt for someone who had simply disappeared as if he had never existed.

And in a way, he never had.

As Edwyn had discovered on that gloomy day in late January, there was now no one left who could explain the mystery of David Demery's true identity.

Chapter 34

Her costume fitting went well, but took longer than expected as she and Jane experimented with suitable footwear to accompany the two different dresses Anna would wear. Nicholas was not needed for the afternoon, but on his way home, called into the fitting room as Anna was leaving.

He hugged her awkwardly and stood back to look at her.

'Mm,' he said dubiously. 'I don't need to ask how you are.'

'Do I look that bad?' she laughed and hugged him again.

'Well, I don't suppose you slept that well,' he replied.

'Very diplomatic,' she teased. 'Another way of saying, I'd frighten any passing horses.'

He was about to protest when she stopped him.

No, really,' she insisted. 'I'll be fine once I get going this afternoon. Don't worry. Enjoy your afternoon off and I'll see you tomorrow.'

'OK.' He smiled. 'Have a good session—and get an early night!'

She looked at her watch and realised she had little time left for lunch, so she decided to stay at the House and pick at some sandwiches that she ate alone on the bench near the bothy. Only she and Louise were called for the afternoon session and the place felt deserted, with no sign of Grace, whose company she would have welcomed.

The letter from Mark was tucked away in her handbag and would remain unread, she'd decided, until she was back at the cottage at the end of the day. She could face no more distractions while she had work to do and was already fighting with tiredness and a mind clogged with secrets and untruths.

She opened her score and flicked through it till she came to the scene in Act 2 in which the Governess confronts her ghostly predecessor in the schoolroom and finds the courage to challenge her and drive her from the room.

She knew she would need to summon similar strength and determination to get through the afternoon. She gathered her things together musing that it was at times like this she almost regretted choosing a profession in which so much self-disclosure was expected and where there was little opportunity to hide raw emotions behind a seemingly unruffled façade.

'So how was it then?' a voice called to her left.

Louise had been lying on the grass in the sunshine, but joined her as she made her way to the Orangery.

'Tell me about your costumes,' she said, linking arms and singing one of Mrs Grose's lines:

"A good young lady, I'll be bound, and a pretty one too."

Anna laughed, feeling instantly more cheerful.

'I really like them,' she enthused. 'And I simply love my little ankle boots—soft black leather and a solid heel I can walk on.'

Louise pulled a face.

'They sound terribly sensible. But tell me about your dresses.'

'Well, they're nothing like as glamorous as yours, but they feel just right. There's a pale dove-grey outfit, trimmed with cream, for her arrival at Bly and the opening few scenes; and the other's more severe in a darker grey, trimmed with mauve. Beautifully cut—Jane's a star.'

'I know—and what style. I've told her I want those funky red boots off her.'

They walked into the Orangery in companionable good humour, still arm-in-arm, and Anna sensed that Jonathan and Paul and the rest of the team were relieved to see she'd recovered the composure she'd lost the day before. Grace was there to make sure everyone was okay and to get the rehearsal started, but soon disappeared, leaving the rehearsal in Sarah's charge.

Anna and Louise set to work on the powerful encounter between the two governesses, the living one seeing the other as competition and resenting her for it.

'This is an important moment,' Jonathan said to Anna at one point. 'You sense the presence of Miss Jessel and the growing danger she poses convinces you that you must not abandon the children. You need to show us that the Governess's resolve to oppose the evil intentions of the ghosts is now equally strong and that you're determined to save the children.'

Louise proved an exciting sparring partner and even in her everyday clothes was magnetic as a tormented sexy Miss Jessel, producing a haunting velvety tone in her fearsome lament of tragedy and revenge and an anguished cry of *"alas"* when she disappeared in despair.

The afternoon sped by in a blur and Anna noticed this was one of those times a strange blend of energy and exhaustion prevailed, when she felt almost Amazonian, willing to challenge herself in her work at the same time as riding a personal emotional roller-coaster.

When Miss Jessel had made her exit and Louise had gone, they worked on the scene where the Governess breaks the promise she made to her employer and writes a letter to him, beseeching him to see her at once.

Anna was seated at the small table preparing to write, when Jonathan leapt over to move the table further away from the bed so that the focus would be on the Governess as she wrote. While Emma made a mark on the floor to denote the table's new position, Anna found her thoughts wandering to other letters, other letter-writing scenes, and thought she could draw on the agitated, conflicted state in which she had composed her letter to Edwyn a few days earlier.

'OK, that's better,' said Jonathan, as Anna sat again. 'So Anna, after that encounter, you're in quite a state, driven increasingly mad by the isolation of the house and the strange happenings. Show us that, but at the same time, we still need to sense the ambiguity of her character—determined saviour of the children in her care, or a fantasist steadily falling apart?'

Anna nodded and tightened the ribbon with which she'd loosely tied her hair into a ponytail.

'The ensemble music can help you there,' Paul said. 'It's increasingly agitated before you start singing, but relaxes when you start to explain you've not forgotten his charge of silence, but there are things which he must know.'

Jonathan nodded.

'That's good. You should start writing with the orchestral passage—that will help you to convey her fervour with the right level of intensity.'

Anna looked down at her score to find the passage he meant, trying to focus on notes that swam in front of her eyes.

'Ready Anna?' Paul asked, with baton raised, as if sensing her distraction.

She nodded again, but as Toby began to play her mind drifted back to the other letter lying unread in her bag.

Chapter 34

It was starting to rain as she arrived back at Forester's cottage. She stood at the double doors watching the raindrops dance off the waters of the lake, the sky darkening, the earlier brightness vanquished by black clouds. She felt weary, lack of sleep and a demanding afternoon catching up with her. She lit the lamps, intending to slump on the sofa, but decided to go upstairs to lie on the bed and rest.

The light in the bedroom was dim and the curtains fluttered as the wind got up outside the open window. She took off her shoes, plumped up the pillows and lay back, listening to the rain pattering against the glass, glad she was inside, the rigours of the day safely negotiated.

She closed her eyes and sighed deeply.

'Let's hope we don't have this sort of downpour during performances,' she thought, smiling at the memory of Harri's warning about soggy ghosts.

She propped herself on one elbow and leant over to grab her bag, which she'd dropped on the bed beside her. She reached inside for the small padded envelope and took out the red-covered address book, wondering where she'd lost it and how Mark could have found it.

She usually kept it with her when she was away from home and had not realised it was missing until she came to write Edwyn's new address and had to recall it as best she could from memory. That was on the first day of rehearsals, so either she'd lost it in London before she left for Myddleton or...

Then she guessed: it must have fallen out of her bag as she made her flurried escape from New College, perhaps displaced by the umbrella she'd shoved inside when she ran from her car to the chapel.

She switched on the bedside lamp and opened the single folded sheet of paper, scanning the stylish, flowing writing she remembered so well. He gave a postal address near Hinksey Park, an email address and a phone number.

Dear Anna,

You'll be surprised to hear from me after all this time, just as I was surprised to see you in the audience at New College last week. I often go to the choir's concerts and think of us, all those years ago in that other lifetime. I saw you leave during The Turtle Dove and wondered if you were unwell—though perhaps you were simply unsettled by too many memories?

I saw this little red notebook on the floor where you'd been sitting, but though it had your name on the front page, it didn't have your address, so I took it to the lodge at New College, intending to leave it for Edwyn to collect for you, but a new young porter told me that Edwyn retired in January. (He's old Fred's grandson, by the way, keeping it in the family he said, three generations now of New College porters).

I held on to it for a few days, not sure what to do, when I saw a poster advertising the Myddleton Festival with you listed as one of the artists appearing.

So I hope it reaches you safely and that if it does, you might have time to meet for a drink while you're here.

I'd like that.

Mark

So there had been ghosts at New College after all and one of them had watched her hasty exit.

She shivered, disconcerted that their paths had crossed again at a time when she was feeling so vulnerable.

She imagined him living in one of the streets that surrounded the lake and the park off the Abingdon road, and wondered what or who had brought him back to Oxford.

She thought, too, of Wendy and Francis. Might Oxford have lured them back, also? Mark would know and that, she thought, was reason enough to meet him, but part of her thrilled at the chance to see him again, to learn about his life and his work, to reconnect with her student friend and discover the man he'd become.

And she owed him an apology for the churlish way in which she'd rejected his gift of the book all those years earlier and she welcomed the chance to make amends. But the timing felt uncomfortable: how could she disguise her humiliation that the man Mark had envied and resented had in the end abandoned her?

Chapter 35

Daniel's call had taken him by surprise and left him ruing the years of silence and dissemblance.

Sitting at the kitchen table, a cup of tea pushed to one side, cold and forgotten, Edwyn felt his forehead tighten. He felt wretched; embarrassed and ashamed that his weakness had exposed Anna to such a humiliating shock.

Though Daniel had told her only the stark fact of Jim and Brenda's deception, he felt he should tell Edwyn what he had said and warn him that an accident of fate meant that Nicholas Kirkby and Anna were unexpectedly working together.

And that Anna now knew much more.

How small the world was, Edwyn thought, and how naive he had been to think his secret could be kept from her indefinitely.

He knew he could put off replying to her letter no longer, that a meeting must be arranged as soon as she had finished at Myddleton. He got up and walked through to his desk in the study where Anna's letter lay in its envelope propped against the box covered with lilies.

He re-read the torrent of emotion her letter contained, sensed the compulsion to pour out her feelings that had propelled her to write, and in his mind's eye he saw her as Tatyana, so young and vulnerable, heard her voice so fresh and touching, and felt a lump rise in his throat. He had seen her sing the role a number of times in her career, and as the years passed, he found it more profoundly upsetting each time, as if he realised that like Onegin, he too might have made wrong choices and lost the *"happiness that was once so near"*.

He reached into a drawer; he had no writing paper so a sheet of A4 printer paper would have to suffice. He started to write, searching for words that were just out of reach.

Chapter 36

As she walked to the Orangery on Friday morning, Anna felt surprisingly expectant, as if something had shifted inside her; that her distress of a few days earlier had been a cathartic turning point leaving her more resilient.

She knew there was hard work ahead, but hoped she might now enjoy it rather than viewing it as a necessary and welcome distraction. Jonathan still wanted to complete Act 2 by the time they finished at Saturday lunchtime, and since a vital session had been lost while he and Paul worked with Nicholas alone, it would be a busy day and a half, working from scene 4 through to the end.

'Let's see how we get on,' he said to Anna, Nicholas and Michael at the start of the morning. 'We may not be able to stop and start as much as before—but let's see if we can at least block everything before we break for the weekend.'

Emma and Sarah were setting the props while Toby moved the piano into position. When they were ready, Jonathan introduced the scene.

'So this is where we are,' he said. 'Scene 4: Miles is in his bedroom before undressing for bed. The Governess warns the boy of her letter to his guardian in an attempt to force him to confess his relationship to the ghosts. Quint's voice orders the boy to stay silent. A candle in the room is blown out.'

'Jonathan, will I really have to undress?' asked Michael, frowning anxiously.

Anna put her hand on his shoulder, sensing his unease, and was relieved to see that Jonathan, too, recognised the self-consciousness of a pubescent boy.

'No, I think we can do it without you needing to undress,' Jonathan reassured him. 'The Governess sings *"Why Miles, not yet in bed? Not even undressed."* We'll have you without your jacket and your shoes on, as if you started to get ready for bed. Is that OK?'

Michael nodded and Anna squeezed the top of his arm before moving aside to get into position.

The scene was a conversation between governess and boy and went well, Michael note and word perfect and suitably agitated and distracted when he heard Quint's disembodied voice. After a few notes from Paul about tempo, they ran without a break into scene 5 when Quint coaxes Miles to steal the Governess's letter.

Quint was to be shown in silhouette throughout the two scenes and Nicholas, standing a short distance away from the bed, sounded both sinister and irresistible in his urgent, plaintive calls to the boy. Jonathan showed Michael how to convey the confusion and hesitation of the boy before he creeps across to the desk to seize the letter and take it back to the bed. Michael had to time his run across the 'room' so that it worked with the music and he needed a couple of attempts before he got it to Jonathan's satisfaction. Anna sitting at the side, watching the business with the letter, was struck that letters were a feature of both her life and the art they were creating.

They broke for lunch at the end of the scene and while Michael and Nicholas went off with Jane to try on shoes, and the others gathered round one of the tables on the terrace for a production meeting, Anna helped herself to some sandwiches and went outside on her own.

She wandered down to the slope of grass where she had met Michael reading his detective story the previous week. There was no sign of the rain that had been relentless throughout the night and the lawns looked lush and green after their generous watering and had dried enough in the sunshine for her to sit down. She breathed in the sweet smell of cut grass wafting from further down the slope and hoped the weather would hold, knowing her plans for the next afternoon depended on it.

From behind her in the Orangery she heard Louise practising a passage from scene 7, picking out the occasional note on the piano, warming up her voice for the rehearsal ahead.

She was lost in thought when Michael slithered down next to her, holding out a mug of coffee and a parcel of greaseproof paper.

'My grandmother made it,' he said, smiling up at her. 'She makes fantastic cakes, but this is my favourite, so I brought some for you.'

She took the mug from him and put her other arm around his shoulder as he settled himself next to her.

'Well done in there,' she said. 'You were brilliant. It's good to have you back—I missed you yesterday.'

He looked at her intently as if checking for any tell-tale signs of lurking distress and then handed her the neat package.

'Grace thought you might like some coffee,' he explained.

'How thoughtful of you both,' she said, thinking the thick slice of lemon drizzle cake and the sweet strong coffee would provide a sugar-burst of energy for the afternoon session.

'Mmm—lovely,' she said, opening the greaseproof paper and breaking off a corner. 'This looks really good—just perfect to go with the coffee.'

'Are you OK now?' he asked, his dark eyes like saucers in his small face.

'I was a bit wobbly yesterday,' she conceded, 'but I'm much better today.'

He nodded and continued to study her.

'Aren't you having any ?' she asked.

'I ate when I was waiting for Jane to finish with Nicholas. She's had to get me some bigger shoes—my feet must have grown since mum sent in my measurements.'

Mention of his mother made Anna ask: 'How's your book coming on?'

'Finished it yesterday,' he said, looking perplexed. 'I didn't learn much—it was too confusing.'

Anna laughed in agreement. 'Those sorts of book often are. Perhaps you'd get on better with Sherlock Holmes? I like those stories.'

There was a companionable silence between them before Michael said something that had obviously been weighing on his mind.

'What happened?' he asked. 'Did Nicholas do something to upset you?'

'No!' she said with emphasis. 'It really wasn't his fault— poor chap just happened to be in the wrong place at the wrong time.'

She looked at the boy and sensed he was old enough to be told at least some of her story.

'No, I was feeling a bit sad and it all felt too much for me to cope with—the music's so hard and so high and the story's so intense, so claustrophobic.' She perched the cake on her lap and ran her hand through her hair. 'It all just came out without me being able to stop it.'

He nodded his understanding, but was still curious.

'Why are you sad?'

'My husband and I have split up.' She paused. 'I miss him.'

'So you're all on your own?'

The straightforward question and his visible concern brought a lump to her throat.

'Yes, I suppose I am,' she said at last. 'But I'm not lonely,' she assured him. 'Well, not lonely in the way most people use the word—after all, I have friends here like Grace and you, and everyone else is very nice and very kind.'

He smiled and looked pleased and she felt him edge a little closer beside her.

'And tomorrow,' she continued, 'I'm meeting up with an old friend I haven't seen for fifteen years and that will be lovely.'

As she heard herself say those last words out loud, she felt again that quiet sense of shift.

Chapter 37

The Friday afternoon session had been gruelling, with all six singers involved in two of the most demanding scenes of the opera and by the end everyone was exhausted and most of the company decided to forgo the planned meal in the pub. Louise, the most enthusiastic socialiser, was not called on Saturday morning; so was heading straight back to her flat in London for the weekend. The others decided to conserve their energies for the powerful final scene they would tackle for the first time the next day.

Michael and Charlotte looked dull-eyed and weary as they sat waiting for the last rehearsal of the week to start. The day before, they had only had time to discuss and then block Miles's virtuoso piano recital and the vicious tussle between Flora and the Governess, but both children had been tested to their limits by the demands of the music and the drama. Charlotte had little to do in the final scene, but the confrontation between Miles, Quint and the Governess was a major challenge for a young, inexperienced performer and Anna, watching him as he unpacked his score and a carton of Ribena, felt a rush of concern for him.

'So,' Jonathan said. 'One last push this morning and then a deserved break for everyone. Let's see how we go, but if we can we'll finish before 1.30pm. It's been a hell of a week, one way or another!'

Even he, thought Anna, looked drained and she realised that the equanimity with which he had navigated the company through the change of Quint had no doubt concealed a fair amount of inner anxiety.

'We're at the end of the opera now and the final Variation starts with a terrific clash of sounds from the orchestra, setting a mood of building doom. Flora's angry outburst the day before means she can no longer stay at Bly so Mrs Grose will deliver her back to her uncle, but before leaving, the housekeeper warns the Governess that her letter was never delivered. The Governess steels herself for a confrontation with Miles while Quint warns Miles to beware of her. She tries to ask Miles about the letter and it soon becomes obvious that Miles is torn between making a confession and his allegiance to Quint. The Governess and Quint appear to play out a dangerous tug of war, with Miles caught in the middle with disastrous results.'

As he set the scene in his typically clear and vivid way, Anna saw his usual animation return and invigorate the company and when they all moved into position to start, she sensed a more positive energy pervade the room.

'So, Mrs Grose and Flora have left and you three are alone together,' Jonathan said to Anna, Michael and Nicholas after they'd gone through the opening of the scene. 'The state of Miles's soul is the underlying, unanswered question. We've seen this boy veering between angel and demon, but as Quint and the Governess assert their possession of him, we need to feel the final struggle for Miles's soul as a painful, almost visceral experience.'

The physical tug of war between Miles and the Governess was hard to rehearse, with Anna concerned not to be too rough with Michael, but knowing that it had to look like a realistic struggle between them. They were both flushed and breathing hard when they got to the point when Quint attempts to lure Miles away and the boy shrieks and collapses. As Toby on the piano imitated the plangent sounds of the cor anglais, the moment arrived when the Governess realises that she is holding Miles's lifeless body in her arms.

Anna cradled Michael gently, rocking back and forth and began a sorrowful repeat of a strain from his 'Malo' song:

"What have we done between us? Malo Malo Malo Malo."

She looked down at Michael's crumpled figure, lying still in her arms as she stroked his hair and hugged him to her. As she had foreseen, he was the perfect heart-tugging Miles

—confused and complex, stranded between innocence and corruption, a disquieting blend of vulnerability and wisdom beyond his years.

They finished a little before 1.30 and Paul and Grace left promptly to get the train to London for a first rehearsal with the orchestra. Emma and Sarah tidied up the room as the rest went their separate ways until Monday.

'No climbing ladders Mr Kirkby!' Anna called after Nicholas, who feigned a dramatic limp as he waved goodbye.

Michael was waiting for his mother to come and collect him and Anna agreed to wait with him.

'I'm in no hurry to get away,' she smiled, glad to have some normal time with him after the disturbing scene they'd just rehearsed.

She gathered her things together and Michael wandered round the now empty room singing quietly to himself. She saw him pick something off the piano.

'What's this?' he asked.

She went over to look and saw that it was a book that Toby had been reading, a biography of Benjamin Britten, which focused on the composer's relationships with the various boys in his life.

'*Britten's Children,*' Michael said as he fingered the spine and turned to the back cover.

Anna caught her breath, feeling awkward about the subject matter.

'Shall we wander round to the front?' she suggested.

Michael nodded and put the book back on the piano. The sun was high and hot and Anna reached into her bag for her sunglasses. At the front door they sat together on the bench, from where they would see Lizzie Manning's car arrive.

'Have you read that book?' he asked at last.

'Only in parts,' she said. 'I dipped into it when Toby brought it in last week.'

'What's it about?'

She hesitated.

'Well,' she said, not meeting his eye, 'the book says that Britten had very clear ideas about good parenting and he regretted that because... because he never married, he couldn't be a parent. But when he worked with children on his music, he could be *in loco parentis* and could offer the boys care and encouragement.'

She hesitated again.

'The book says that many of these boys had absent fathers.'

She looked away as she heard the sound of a car making its way up the drive. A battered white Fiat pulled up on the gravel and Michael picked up his score and stood up to go.

'Will you come and say hello?' he asked.

Lizzie Manning was leaning over the passenger seat to clear away a pile of papers. When she sat up and Anna saw her face in profile for the first time, she knew that her mind's eye image was mistaken.

This woman was certainly not young and did not appear to be either flighty or bohemian. Anna estimated that Lizzie was at least fifty years old and though she might once have been pretty, she made few concessions to either fashion or vanity. Her brown hair was scraped back from her forehead with a black Alice band and her dun-coloured clothes were ill-fitting and unseasonal. The woman acknowledged her and smiled, but what struck Anna most forcibly was the contrast between the determined set of her mouth and the wary, almost guarded look in her eyes.

'Have a good weekend,' she said to Michael, unsure whether to give him a quick hug, but while she was deliberating he leant up and gave her a peck on the cheek.

'Malo!' he called cheerily as he clambered into the passenger seat.

As she walked back to the cottage, she wondered what his home life was like, would he have friends nearby to play with, or was he a solitary child who preferred the company of adults? He was a resourceful boy, but she hoped he wasn't lonely.

Alone at last, she began to think about Mark. She was meeting him at four o'clock at Port Meadow for a picnic tea so she had plenty of time to relax and change. The cottage felt airless and she left the front door ajar as she went to open the double-doors. A gentle draft cooled the air and the stuffiness lifted as she looked down the garden to the shimmering lake. She turned to close the front door and saw a slim white envelope hanging from the inside of the letterbox.

Chapter 38

Dear Anna,

I owe you apologies on so many fronts it's hard to know where to begin. I'm truly sorry that I've caused you not only grief and bewilderment, but anxiety too. I don't deserve your concern, but I can at least reassure you that I'm not ill.

First, I must apologise for exposing you to the shock and embarrassment of hearing so much of my story from others when I realise you should have heard it from me. Daniel is a good, decent man and he felt bound to let me know about the conversation you and he had and I'm sorry you are now grappling with these revelations during a challenging rehearsal period. (He also told me about the change of Quint and Nicholas's unwitting part in all this).

When Jim told me that he and Brenda were not my real parents, that Brenda had had a sister I had never known about who was my birth mother, it was devastating. I felt as if the scaffolding of my life had collapsed and everything that rested on my relationship with Jim and Brenda was cast into doubt. There's so much talk about similarities in looks, mannerisms and behaviours between parents and their offspring, and no wonder, because these similarities confirm a child's place within their family and in the world. Having that place swept away was very confusing and I felt very vulnerable. All of a sudden there was no firm ground anywhere in my life and I came to fear that if this most elemental thing that I believed about myself was a lie, then why should I believe in anything?

I tried to protect myself—prop myself up—by switching my mind away from examining my feelings too closely. I know you worried that I worked too hard—even on holidays —but work was more than just my passion. It was a safety valve; I was doing something satisfying, taking myself out of myself, involving myself in other people's stories and struggles.

Meanwhile, as you now know, I've been trying to find all the missing bits of the jigsaw and put them together, to make sense of who I am. I've learnt a certain amount, especially about my mother, but I've had to accept that I now have no hope of finding out who my father really was and what happened to him.

I'm sorry I kept all this from you. Please don't doubt that I loved you and was happy with you, but the more I delved into the past the more fragile I became and I found it hard to live with the intensity of your love when I felt so hollow. You may have idealised me and I felt pressurised by that and feared I couldn't live up to your perceptions of me. That's why I so often sought space whereas you made huge efforts for us to be together, despite all your travelling.

Towards the end, not even work helped me as much as it once did. I'm enjoying my research into Lord Russell, but I've come to realise that what's important in most people's lives is not governments or politics, but a longing for nothing more than health and a loving family; and to deal with all the joys and disappointments—the marriages that work or fail, the jobs that flourish or founder, the children who are born or lost—and still lead happy, productive lives.

It was hard to pull away from you, but everything had got too much for me and I simply needed to deal with this in my own way. I know it's been wretched for you and I won't offer you platitudes about things getting easier for you as time passes. But please promise me that you won't blame yourself for any of this or discredit the years we had together.

I know we have big decisions to make and we need to meet, but you have enough to deal with right now, so I suggest we wait until you've finished at Myddleton and are back in London. I can come down at any time that suits you in the week after you get back—just let me know when and I'll be there.

Until then, take care of yourself. I wish for nothing more than for you to be happy.

Love, Edwyn

Anna read the letter twice; she was relieved Edwyn knew that his secret was out as she suspected he had written more openly than he might otherwise have done. His despair grieved her and she wondered if all those emotions he couldn't express had caused him to suffer from depression—well-disguised—through which he'd functioned professionally, but which had cost him dearly. It was as if the pain of the search had tainted his enjoyment of life; his personality defined by this hunt for the past.

She sat at the patio table gazing over the lake towards the Orangery and tried to visualise Edwyn far away in his water-side cottage, his existence now so separate from hers. She had a saddening picture of him disconnected from the life he had once appeared to embrace, frustrated by a past now based on fracture when once it had appeared whole.

From somewhere outside she heard the gravelly voice of one of the gardeners, calling gruffly to his barking dog, urging him to come to heel and be quiet. The dog whimpered and fell silent and the disembodied voice became instantly affectionate, murmuring words of approval. Unable to see them, Anna marvelled at the suggestiveness of the human voice, its ability to galvanise, to terrify, to console, to beguile. Edwyn's voice, with its low register and cultured intonation, was often in her ears and she knew that they had both—no less than any lawyer, preacher, or politician—cultivated the possibilities of the voice. While she had captivated him with her silvery soprano, it was with honeyed, confiding cadences that he had wooed and charmed her.

The memory served to reinforce her sense that something special had been wasted, that a future together might yet have been possible if only he had shared his predicament with her. But his letter wished her future happiness in a way that suggested he would play no part in it, and that probability felt more than she could bear. She squeezed her eyes tight shut to force away the tears and when that failed, tilted her head as if to tip the brimming tears back into her eyes.

She'd heard the theory that if you have loved well and have thrived as part of a couple, you are likely to love again.

It made sense, but she doubted she could ever be so lucky twice and anyway, it smacked of an inconstancy she found hard to contemplate.

She wiped her wrist across her nose and sniffed. Outside the gardener was once more calling to his dog: 'Come on my lovely, in you get. In you get.'

She heard the sound of a car door slamming and an engine starting up, the gardener pulling slowly away towards the main drive.

In the silence that followed, her thoughts turned to Michael and his cheerful cry of 'Malo' as they parted. And at that moment she feared for him just as the Governess feared for Miles.

'Malo, a naughty boy in adversity.'

Time and again, whenever it recurred, his spine-tingling piping of the haunting refrain unnervingly suggested the sadness of a boy badly in need of a father figure. Might his life—like Edwyn's—be blighted by an unfulfilled sense of identity and a longing for something he might never find?

Chapter 39

Anna drove round the green and continued to the far end of Wolvercote village. Recalling that the car park in Godstow was frequently requisitioned by travellers, she had set off early, wanting to allow enough time to find somewhere else to park if need be. She was relieved to see that the entrance was unblocked, though the parking area still bore the marks of a recent sojourn and a hasty, careless departure. Stepping past the detritus of used nappies, soggy chips in crushed polystyrene cartons, and flimsy carrier bags fluttering in corners, she walked onto the long stretch of common land and prepared to wait for Mark to arrive.

Edwyn's letter had saddened her, but she felt calmer than she'd expected, as if his candour had helped banish some of the uncertainty. She stood enjoying the beauty of the landscape, hoping to absorb some of its serenity, and resolved not to spoil the reunion with Mark. In the hazy afternoon sun, the colours over Port Meadow were a pastel blur of pale yellows and greens and bluey-greys. The ancient flood plain had the River Thames stretching down it on one side and a stream along another, while at the north end, to the right of where she had entered, stood the ruins of Godstow Abbey.

To the left, her eye was caught by two small children running ahead of a man and a woman, walking and laughing together as they strode off in the direction of Jericho. Even from a distance their closeness was visible.

She turned to face the other way and saw a man talking into a mobile phone, a rucksack on his back and something rolled up under his free arm. She put on her sunglasses and narrowed her eyes to make him out more clearly.

It was Mark.

She took off her glasses and started to walk towards him just as he put his phone away and looked up. She quickened her step and as she got closer he came more clearly into focus. His face was tanned, as were his legs beneath his long linen shorts, and his once floppy fair hair was cropped short and was now a surprising platinum grey.

'Anna,' he called, his voice unmistakably the same as she remembered.

'Hello!'

They embraced clumsily, his one free arm pulling her towards him before he took a step back to look at her.

'It's so good to see you,' he cried. 'You look wonderful!'

She laughed, hardly able to believe him, but enjoying the compliment. She thought how well he looked; as if he had grown into himself.

'You too,' she said, nodding at his hair. 'Very distinguished.'

He rolled his eyes. 'Mmm. I think you mean old, but I'll take distinguished.'

She laughed again and blushed under his scrutiny.

'Shall we walk?' he asked. 'We could go left and do a circular walk and end up near the remains of the Nunnery for our picnic.'

'Sounds good to me,' Anna said as they set off.

'There are usually a hundred or so horses and cows grazing here,' he said, 'and if we're lucky, we'll see some new foals.'

'I'd forgotten how beautiful it is' Anna murmured, letting her head drop back so that she could feel the warm sun on her face.

They walked on with the river on their right, and the spires of Oxford on the far horizon, making easy conversation, the years of silence slipping away, and for the most part Anna felt any moments of reserve between them were companionable rather than uncomfortable.

They stopped to watch a family of ducks paddling lazily downstream.

'They look like a set of bath-time toys, don't they?' Mark said, reaching into the pocket of his shorts for a handful of breadcrumbs which he scattered into the water, the mother duck scuttling round her chicks as they fed eagerly on the wilting crusts.

'And not a word of thanks,' Anna said as the ducks disappeared downstream, followed in stately fashion by a couple of snooty looking swans who eyed them with what looked like disdain. Mark mimicked their haughty expressions and called after them:

'La-di-da!'

They turned away from Oxford and headed back towards the ruins of the Abbey. Godstow Lock was busy, with boats in both directions waiting to pass through, and people waiting patiently on the tow path for their turn.

'We can cross at Godstow Bridge, just beyond the Lock,' Mark said, 'to get to the Abbey.'

Half way across the bridge, they stood for a moment looking down across the meadow.

'Look' said Anna, 'some foals. I wondered where they all were.'

The mares and their young had gathered in groups in the vicinity of the ruins, which, as they crossed the river, now lay ahead of them. They walked on towards the abandoned Nunnery and Anna noticed an elderly woman sitting with her back against one of the walls, her eyes closed and her face tense with either pain or grief. Anna felt a pang of sympathy for her as she realised how much her own mood had lifted.

Mark put his arm out to indicate they should keep still and they watched as a young foal with brown eyes too big for its tiny head wandered over to the woman and whinnied at her. The woman opened her eyes and jolted forward with a start, before relaxing back against the wall. The foal gazed at her and Anna saw the woman smile back and enjoy a moment of quiet connection with the gawky, Bambi-like creature. The spell was broken when the foal looked up to see her mother trotting towards her. In a flash, the foal had gambolled away and the woman was once more alone with her thoughts.

Anna and Mark walked past her unnoticed before laying the rug on a patch of soft grass, just beyond the Abbey. Anna settled herself on one edge of the rug and watched as Mark unpacked the contents of the rucksack.

'So, in memory of picnics long past,' he said, with a flourish, 'we have cheese and cucumber sandwiches, some wedges of lardy cake and a flask of tea.'

'Lardy cake,' Anna cried. 'I haven't had that since I last ate it at one of our picnics.'

'An Oxfordshire speciality, madam!'

'Wonderful. Thank you.'

She was amused and touched that he had thought to replicate their student picnics, but for a moment felt dejected by the memory.

It was such a long time ago.

She gazed around at the lovely flowery meadows, their rug surrounded by splashes of buttercups and daisies and yellow rattle.

'Tuck in,' he said, pouring tea into a couple of china mugs.

She helped herself to a sandwich and took the mug of tea he handed her.

'Cheers!' he said. 'Did I say how good it is to see you?'

She laughed. 'I think you might have mentioned it.'

'I love it here,' he said. 'So much history, such a strong sense of place.' He munched at a sandwich. 'It's pre-historic, you know. Bronze Age people buried their dead here.'

Anna nodded and shivered. Edwyn had once told her that this was Oxford's oldest monument and contained well-preserved burial places, some of which were visible on the ground as shallow circular ditches and banks.

'Lewis Carroll used to row Alice Liddell out here for picnics and read her extracts from *Alice in Wonderland.*'

'I didn't know that,' Anna replied with interest, relieved he had not yet broached the subject of Edwyn. 'Do you still read as much?'

'Avidly,' he said. 'Whenever time allows. What about you?'

'I do now, though for a long time after I left Oxford I thought doing an English degree had killed off my love of reading. I was worn out with having to read so many books on such a pressurised timetable, but now that I travel so much and am away from home for stretches of time, I find books a real comfort.'

He nodded in understanding and poured them some more tea. They'd finished the sandwiches and he had started to tackle a large chunk of lardy cake.

Still wanting to deflect the conversation away from herself she said, 'So, tell me about your work and what brought you back to Oxford.'

He swallowed a piece of cake and plucked at the grass, like he used to do wherever they picnicked.

'Well, after I'd done my VSO in India,' he said, 'I came back to the UK and did teacher training for a year before going back to India to work in a school on the outskirts of Calcutta.'

'I'd heard that,' Anna said. 'How long were you there?'

'Ten years altogether,' he replied. 'Then my father fell ill and though he was really quite poorly a lot of the time, he was determined to keep his independence so I came back to be near him and help him out.'

'So you moved back to Birkenhead?' Anna asked with surprise.

'I did,' he replied. 'I taught at first, but I got involved with a homeless charity in Liverpool and after a couple of years, I gave up teaching and worked for them full-time.'

He poured out the dregs of the tea and took a sip.

'Dad died a few years later and by then I was ready for a change. There was nothing to keep me in Liverpool after he'd gone, so about two years ago, I took up a similar job in Oxford: we run a hostel, but we also provide medical services to people living rough.'

Anna listened with growing admiration. 'That's fantastic,' she said. 'Very tough, I'm sure, but so worthwhile. I don't think many people realise there's another side of Oxford—they think it's all high table and dreaming spires.'

'That's right,' Mark agreed, 'but Oxford's always had an above average quota of eccentrics and vagrants who take up residence on the streets for a few weeks and then disappear, but we see people who've been homeless for ages and some of them have serious health issues.'

'It must be very demanding work,' Anna said. 'Do you find time to sing?'

'Oh yes,' he said. 'Choir's an absolute lifeline—I never miss it unless there's a real emergency. And I play a bit of cricket, too. I used to play with the kids at school in India and discovered I was quite good.'

Anna thought what different paths he and she had taken and yet here they were, those paths having unexpectedly crossed by dint of her dropping her address book. It was as if she had left a trail for him.

He was tearing off another piece of cake, and she studied him closely for the first time. There were lines around his eyes, but he looked fit and lean, and his honest face still shone with the good nature she had recalled in the gloaming of New College chapel.

He glanced up and saw her looking at him.

'And how are you?' he asked at last. 'I was surprised to hear that Edwyn had retired…'

His voice trailed away and she wondered what else the friendly new porter might have told him. She avoided his gaze and adjusted her position, feeling the beginnings of pins and needles in her left leg.

She turned to face him at last, knowing she could avoid the subject no longer, and tentatively at first she began to tell him her story.

'What a wretched time for both of you,' Mark said when Anna at last stopped. 'You know, you look around here, surrounded by the graves of people who were buried here by people who loved them and mourned them and you realise that in so many ways they were just like us and we are like them. And in thousands of years' time, nothing will really have changed. People will still love and yearn and hurt.' He paused. 'And I think you should try and hold on to the belief that for you this pain will eventually pass.'

Anna looked at him with surprise.

'You sound as if you're speaking from experience?'

'I think it's one of the most important lessons life has taught me.'

Anna was still nibbling on the rich, fruity lardy cake and for a while they were both silent, before she asked: 'When did you learn that?'

He looked uncomfortable, but at last replied: 'Let's just say, I've had to learn it more than once.'

Anna reached over and touched the back of his hand lightly.

'Thank you for being such a sympathetic listener. I feel self-centred going on about myself like this.'

He smiled. 'That's fine. Your hurt is more current than mine.'

There was another silence, during which they watched a couple of cows idle past them.

'How did you feel about leaving India?' she asked at last.

He flushed momentarily.

'Very mixed feelings. I wanted to be with my dad, wanted to help him out—he sacrificed so much to help me

226

get to Oxford—but I had a life in India, too, and I felt I was doing important work. So it was a wrench to leave.'

'And was there someone to keep you there, perhaps?' Anna suggested.

'I thought so,' he said quietly. 'She was a doctor in the same suburb my school was in so our work coincided—that's how we met.'

'Where is she now?' Anna asked.

'Still there, I assume. She was committed to her medical practice and to her community—she'd grown up there—and our obligations took us in different directions.'

'That's sad,' Anna said, feeling sorry that Mark's loyalty to his father had involved such personal sacrifice.

He said nothing and she realised she might have been the cause of earlier hurt.

'You know,' she said, 'I owe you an apology for my churlishness when I sent you back your gift of *Far from the Madding Crowd.*'

He looked surprised and flushed again.

'I felt bad about our last meeting; felt I'd behaved badly. I'd always been quite touched and flattered that you could consider me as enticing as Bathsheba, but afterwards, when I looked at the book and saw what you'd underlined, it somehow seemed disloyal to Edwyn.'

He nodded his head and said, 'I guessed that, but really I never felt you were churlish about it. I just thought I'd gone too far and had irritated you.'

She was surprised by the rush of relief she felt and realised she had always feared that the encounter at St Hugh's had cost her his friendship.

'There's a battered old copy of the book at the cottage I'm renting,' she said. 'It made me think of you.'

'Now it's my turn to be flattered!'

She laughed, but didn't volunteer anything about the feelings the book had aroused or admit that it remained unread on the shelf above her bed, its themes too painful to confront.

As if he had read her mind, he said: 'Some of the book's themes—coincidence, catastrophe, fate—make me think of Fanny Robin and I wonder if something similar went wrong for Edwyn's father.'

Anna looked puzzled.

'You remember Fanny went to the wrong church for her marriage to Troy? She went to All Souls instead of All Saints,' he explained. 'Perhaps some calamity prevented David getting to Criccieth in time to collect Lily and the baby?'

Anna considered the possibility and sighed.

'Will we ever find out?'

'It's getting chilly,' he said. 'Let's pack up before you get cold.'

She helped him tidy away the remains of their picnic and waited as he repacked his rucksack.

'What are you going to do next?' he asked.

She brightened and said, 'I wondered about asking Wendy if she or Edwyn had been able to find out anything more.'

'Well you're in luck,' he said. 'She's happily ensconced just down the road from you in Abingdon.'

Anna gasped.

'That's wonderful news.'

In the distance, she heard the screech of peacocks on the riverside terrace of *The Trout*.

'How about a drink before we go home?' he said, taking her arm and wheeling her away across the meadow. 'We can call Wendy from the pub.'

Chapter 40

Though the house was not far from the centre of town, Wendy's garden had the old-fashioned charm Anna remembered of her grandparents' picture book country cottage in Suffolk. It was a riotous mix of wild flowers, sweet-scented roses, climbing shrubs and herbaceous borders, and on the large paved patio Wendy had placed a cluster of terracotta pots overflowing with scarlet geraniums and orange busy-lizzies.

Anna was sitting in a corner under the shade of a silver birch tree, the sunlight playing through the branches and leaving splashes of white on her bare arms. Wendy had moved a black wrought iron table from the patio and placed it between two wicker-backed chairs and was now heading towards her with a tray of coffee.

'It's so kind of you to see me,' Anna said, leaning forward to take the mug Wendy offered her and spooning in some sugar.

'Not at all, Anna. It's a pleasure to see you again after all these years.'

Wendy eased herself into her seat, adjusting the cushion so that it supported her back.

'You haven't changed, Wendy. You look so well.'

'I try and keep reasonably fit. I love this time of year when there's so much to enjoy in the garden. I'm up most mornings at six o'clock doing something or other out here —hence the stiff back today.'

'Are you still working?' Anna asked.

'Oh yes,' Wendy replied. 'We both are. Frank's retired from teaching, but he's working on some new editions of Hardy's less well-known novels and I'm working part-time for the Oxford Dictionary of National Biography as an associate editor. There's a team of us, working on updates, new entries, corrections and so on. I love it.'

Wendy still had the cheery, round face Anna remembered and it shone with enthusiasm as she talked about her work. She was in her early sixties and Anna noticed that her pale blue eyes were as bright as ever, with the canny yet caring look of old. Her skin was smooth and unlined, though her fine brown hair was now streaked with white and grey, creating an eccentric speckled effect.

'I've heard news of you from Edwyn over the years,' Wendy said. 'You've done extremely well—I gather you sing all over the world?'

'I certainly seem to get around' Anna laughed. 'I've been lucky—sung the right roles at the right time in the right places.'

Wendy scrutinised her closely.

'But I'm guessing things haven't been easy these last few months. It must be hard coming back to work in Oxford so soon, with Edwyn not here anymore.'

Anna nodded.

'He'd been my friend as well as my husband.'

Wendy shook her head in sympathy.

'It's horrible for you. You said on the phone that you're working with Nick Kirkby and that he was able to tell you some of the story?'

'That's right. He's been very kind. Do you remember him?'

'Oh yes, I do. He seemed a rather sad young man when he was an undergraduate—I'm glad to hear he's found his way.'

'He's going to be brilliant as Quint.'

Wendy sipped her coffee and smiled.

'You said you wondered if there's more to know.'

'That's right,' Anna said. 'I've wondered why Edwyn left when he did, having lived with his secret and its impact for so long. Did something happen to tip him over the edge— perhaps some new revelation around the time of Jim's death?'

'Yes, I think that's what did happen, though it wasn't linked to Jim's death.'

The answer intrigued her and Anna raised her eyebrows in expectation, waiting for Wendy to begin.

'After Brenda died, Jim gave Edwyn quite a lot of material,' Wendy explained. 'He used a box that had been Lily's to create a memory box. First of all, like the seasoned historian he is, Edwyn tried to organise this "evidence" (as he saw it) into a coherent and chronological order. He read the letters that David wrote to Lily and some of his preconceptions of David were seriously challenged when he realised they were not the work of a feckless waster: they were well-written, humorous and vividly described David's life on the road as a touring player.'

'Have you read them?' Anna asked with surprise.

'I have,' Wendy replied. 'They're very affectionate and there's no sign that he shied away from the prospect of the baby. But he wanted to train professionally as a singer and he did seem to realise that this would be a challenge with a wife and child to support. Edwyn wondered if, in the end, ambition and selfishness got the better of him.'

'When did he come to you for help?' Anna asked.

'It was about seven years after Jim told him the truth—around the time of your ectopic pregnancy, when Edwyn was particularly troubled and confused. I think the thought of a child of his own had thrown up a lot of conflicting feelings which seemed to make him even more inquisitive about his father and determined to try and find out what happened to him.'

Anna thought back to that difficult time nine years ago. It had been painful for both of them—and she had taken months to recover physically and emotionally—but now she realised that throughout that period, Edwyn was dealing with other losses about which she had no inkling.

She bit her lip.

'Did he show you the memory box?' she asked.

'He did. It was beautiful, full of mementoes that helped to give an insight into the people Lily and David were. There was a lock of Lily's hair intertwined with Edwyn's baby hair; a pale blue matinee jacket, which Lily had knitted for him; a silver necklace which Jim and Brenda gave her on their wedding day when she was their bridesmaid; letters she wrote to Jim and Brenda, and of course the letters from David to Lily. There were even some of Lily's costume designs plus a sketch she did of David in his costume as Jack Point. I must say, her drawings showed real skill.'

Anna pondered this.

'Edwyn's idea of where he came from must have been completely overturned.'

Wendy nodded as Anna went on.

'So, he wasn't the high-achieving son of a bank clerk and a water board engineer after all, but the product of an aspiring costume designer and an actor. I wonder how he felt about that.'

Wendy nodded again.

'Of course the paradox about Jim's revelation,' she said, 'is that everything changed and yet nothing changed. Edwyn had known no other parents than Jim and Brenda, had loved no others, and yet he decided to pursue the parents that might have been his.'

'And he hoped you could help?'

'That's right,' said Wendy. 'He knew I had an interest in genealogy and that I knew how to set about this sort of research. It's a national pastime now, you know. We're all at it: tracing our family trees, delving into history, finding out what we can about who we are. When I first dabbled with my own family tree it was a matter of hard slog, long drives to distant parishes, yellowing certificates in faded ink and barely legible censuses—and there's still quite a lot of that —but of course now we've got online search engines it's become much easier and more efficient. Though I confess for a long time we kept hitting brick walls and Edwyn frequently wanted to give up.'

She paused and smiled.

'We've got a visitor. I wondered where she'd got to.'

Anna looked up to see a marmalade-coloured cat perched on the wall behind them, eyeing her closely through half-closed slits.

'The frustrating thing is,' Wendy continued, 'we found no record of a birth, marriage or death for anyone called David Demery who could have been Edwyn's father. We think his last engagement was with the Harold Ingram Players, whose summer tour in 1946 was due to end in Swansea at the beginning of July. After that I could find no mention of David in their playbills—or anywhere else for that matter. He simply seemed to have vanished.'

'How strange—and how frustrating,' Anna said, watching the cat slither down the other side of the wall and disappear.

'Then, about a year ago,' Wendy continued, 'I found press cuttings reporting the week in Swansea, which said that an understudy had played David's role, so I thought maybe he was ill or been sacked, but it seemed possible that he never made it to Swansea.'

Anna listened intently while Wendy topped up their mugs from the cafetière and continued the story.

'I decided to try and track down anyone from that final cast who might know what happened to him. That was difficult—many of them were dead—but just before Christmas I found one of the actresses. She was living with a niece not far from Winchester and Edwyn went to see her in January.'

'Was she able to remember anything about David?' Anna asked.

'She told Edwyn that David left the company abruptly at the end of the previous week when they were in Cardiff. The day before they finished the run there he received a letter that had been mis-addressed and sent to the wrong theatre in Cardiff. Apparently, he left immediately after the show on the Saturday night saying he had urgent family business to attend to. From the dates of these performances, Edwyn worked out that he had been born just before the company got to Cardiff, so the sudden departure might suggest David was rushing away to be with Lily—though the non-appearance in Criccieth might suggest he couldn't after all face up to the responsibility…'

'How awful for Lily,' Anna said, 'never knowing what happened to him.'

'Indeed,' said Wendy, 'and for Edwyn, too.'

The marmalade cat had returned to her perch and this time, Wendy reached up and lifted her down onto her lap. The cat curled up, tail and ears twitching rhythmically, until eventually she fell asleep.

'Many people,' she said, stroking the cat's neck, 'who have no knowledge about their fathers feel unsettled and ill at ease with themselves. It comes down to a confused sense of identity.'

'It certainly seems to have had a devastating effect on Edwyn,' said Anna. She hesitated, recalling Edwyn's letter. 'What I hadn't expected was how much our separation would challenge my view of the past. I can't stop the doubts, the questions. I've been driving myself mad trying to identify the turning point.'

'My dear, you've also suffered in the fallout from this,' Wendy said, reaching forward to touch Anna's hand. 'You can't blame yourself. I think Edwyn is one of those people who pull into themselves just when they need their loved ones most.'

She swatted away a wasp, which was heading towards the sleeping cat.

'Most of us need to know where we've come from,' she went on at last, 'and I think any unresolved issues from the past can have a big impact on our present and our future lives. When the facts about our identity are denied us—as Edwyn's were—it's bound to have repercussions not only on our own lives, but on the lives of those we love…'

Anna swallowed hard, for the moment unable to speak.

'Do you know why he didn't share any of this with me?' she asked at last.

Wendy shook her head.

'I did ask him that,' she said, 'because I felt uncomfortable being taken into his confidence when I knew you were completely in the dark. I'm sure you feel hurt at that and I'm sorry.'

Anna coloured, but smiled, grateful for the acknowledgement.

'When you and he first met,' Wendy said, 'he was bowled over, said he couldn't believe someone as lovely as you could fall for someone like him, so the last thing he wanted to do was to give you the impression he was damaged goods. He kept quiet, and the longer he said nothing the more impossible it became to broach it.'

Anna frowned, her thoughts racing back to January and the sequence of events leading up to Edwyn's departure.

'Do you know,' she asked, 'when exactly Edwyn went to visit the actress?'

Wendy thought for a moment before replying.

'It was towards the end of the month. I can't tell you the exact date, but I remember him telling me afterwards that it was the day a whale swam up the Thames.'

Anna gasped.

'The whale! We went to watch the attempts to save it and as the day went on, I sensed this inexplicable detachment from me, as if he was drifting away.'

Wendy grimaced in sympathy.

'The separation shocked everyone we knew,' said Anna, 'but the fact has to be faced that he was desperately unhappy and none of us realised. I do feel bad about that.'

The cat awoke with a series of yawns and jerks and Anna watched her slide to the ground and retreat to the shade in another corner of the garden to begin the long process of washing and grooming herself.

Wendy leaned forward to put her mug on the tray.

'Men and women handle emotional crises differently,' she said. 'Women can fall apart totally, let all the feelings out, then just get on with things. Most men aren't used to handling intense emotions so a grieving man can lose his way, behave irrationally.'

Along the road, the church bells of St Michael's chimed twelve times, slightly ahead of those at All Saints, which were a few moments behind.

'We just can't find the missing piece of the jigsaw,' Wendy said with a shake of her head. 'I've sometimes wondered if something happened to David on his journey to Criccieth.'

'I can see it could be tricky to find that out,' Anna agreed, 'but why would Edwyn write so categorically: *"I've had to accept that I now have no hope of finding out who my father really was and what happened to him."* '

Chapter 41

"I expect this will make bitter-sweet reading for you. I'm sorry if it leaves you with a sense of unfinished business. Perhaps now is the time to move on and accept that there are bits of this jigsaw that are lost, perhaps forever."

Edwyn frowned. So long as there was unfinished business, he would find it hard to move on. He had become convinced that only the truth would enable him to get on with his life and achieve the connectedness he longed for.

He put Wendy's note back into the envelope and opened the newspaper cuttings, smoothing away the creases where they'd been folded. The news of Ursula's unexpected death was a blow, coming so soon after she'd summoned him to return.

'She has something for you,' her niece had said on the phone. 'Something she says you must come for in person.'

A date was agreed for the following week, but before he could make the journey down to Winchester, Ursula Saunders died in her sleep, the remembered detail—if that's what it was—lost forever.

It was, he feared, a final setback.

Without knowing what he hoped to find, he had scoured the broadsheets for obituaries, but they appeared to ignore the long-retired starlet of the 1940s. Wendy kept looking, her search at last rewarded by tributes in *The Stage* and *The Hampshire Chronicle*.

He read the local paper first, the writer remarking on Ursula's debut performance at Winchester Theatre Royal:

"In the role that established her as the leading soubrette of the day, Ursula Saunders was delightfully goofy and wonderfully bawdy as the hysterical flapper girl niece."

He smiled. Even in her late seventies, there remained traces of the coquettish personality she displayed on stage.

He folded the cutting carefully and put it to one side, reaching for the other larger piece that carried a black and white production photograph of Ursula wearing an expression of doltish bemusement as Audrey in *As You Like It.*

He glanced through the article, looking for more about the show that launched her career, when a name caught his eye: a surprise reference to his father and the role that linked him with Ursula:

"Ursula Saunders made a memorable stage debut in Agatha Christie's Black Coffee when she was terrific as Sir Claude's niece Barbara, the dishy, fizzy ingénue with a taste for sensation. Her scenes with the innocent, but beguiling David Demery as Hastings—to whom she takes a shine—were a hoot."

'He was marvellous in that role,' she'd told him. 'Too young for it really, but he seemed to *become* Hastings as soon as he stepped on stage. He imbued him with this wonderful mix of embarrassment, awkwardness and Tigger-like enthusiasm—he made it easy for me to play off him and look good.'

She'd sighed then.

'I did so miss him. It wasn't anything like as much fun after he'd gone.'

Edwyn had visited her in the house she'd been brought up in and to which she returned when she became too ill to work. Her parents were still alive then, but after their deaths she lived alone for many years, until her widowed niece Doreen moved in to keep an eye on her.

She sat in a high-backed chair, holding court in her little sitting room, one wall given over to portrait shots and production photographs mounted in identical brass frames. She had talked without affectation and with great humour about her brief time in the theatre, her career cut short by the onset of rheumatoid arthritis when she was still in her thirties.

'Do you know what happened to David?' he'd asked, when she paused for breath after one of her rambling stories.

She shook her head sadly: 'No one knew what happened to him, dearie. He just disappeared, said he had a family matter to deal with.'

She took a cotton handkerchief from the sleeve of her cardigan and dabbed the corner of her mouth.

'In the twelve years I spent in the theatre, I never heard of him again. He just seemed to vanish.'

Her arthritic hands were cruelly misshapen, but she was elegantly dressed and carefully made up, as if preparing for a performance.

'He was sweet and funny and very handsome,' she said, with a faraway look of fondness. 'Something about him reminded me of a boy I was in love with when I was seven years old and needed a best friend in my new school. Philip Markham.' She shook her head sadly. 'Philip and his family emigrated to Australia when he was twelve years old, but I've never forgotten his bright little face and cheeky grin.' She paused and, for a moment, her eyes clouded as if peering into a distant past. 'I could chat away to David like I used to talk to Philip and sometimes I imagined that the face that looked back at me was Philip's.'

Edwyn guessed she'd been a little in love with David, too, and as if she'd read his mind she said: 'Of course, he never gave me a second thought, dear. I knew he had a sweetheart; he was always on the lookout for the post, waiting for the next letter from her.' She laughed. 'He used to keep them together tied up in a brown rubber band so I gave him one of my satin hair ribbons to use instead. Far more romantic.'

Edwyn was struck that this elderly woman remembered his father so vividly, and found himself blushing at the thought of such innocent intimacy between them.

She was studying him closely.

'You have his nose,' she said. 'But your eyes and mouth are quite different.'

He nodded, calling up in his mind's eye his pictures of Lily, with her even features and wide smile.

'So you can't find him, dearie?' she said after a long silence.

'No,' he replied. 'I can't find a record of a birth, marriage or death for anyone called David Demery who could have been my father.'

'But dearie, you wouldn't,' she cried in surprise.

He looked at her in confusion.

'What do you mean?' he asked.

'Well, Demery wasn't his real name.' she said, as if he must have known that. 'Oh no, dearie, he had to change his name when he went on the stage.' She laughed. 'He used to joke that his *alter ego* was some Hollywood big shot.'

'Do you remember who that was?' Edwyn asked, hardly daring to breathe as he waited for her to answer.

She pulled a face as if struggling to recall the once known name, then shook her head.

'I don't, I'm afraid,' she said at last, tapping the side of her head. 'My memory's not what it was and I was never very good at names.'

Edwyn covered his face with his hands as he remembered his disappointment at hearing those words, the sinking feeling as he took his leave of her and headed home to London.

He lifted his head and looked down at the news cuttings. They had told him no more than he already knew, but he placed them carefully in a folder, which he stored away in the top drawer of a shiny black filing cabinet.

'No Name,' he thought.

Like Wilkie Collins's illegitimate sisters, he too remained nameless.

Chapter 42

As she approached the main entrance to Myddleton, restless and unready to return to the cottage, she decided to leave the car outside the gates and walk up to the house. She turned into the long tree-lined avenue, recalling Henry James's description of the summer sweetness that offered a friendly welcome for his heroine arriving with trepidation at Bly.

She made her way towards the house and studied the façade, soon to represent the grand mansion at Bly, removed from the world in a rural idyll of apparent purity. She was struck by the silence, the place seemingly deserted. She turned onto the terrace, empty now, but in a week's time she knew it would be a hive of activity as banks of audience seating were erected and cables, lighting rig and other paraphernalia installed.

She sat at one of the tables that looked across the park to the lake and breathed in the sweet warm air and reflected on how much had happened in the last two weeks; how she, like the Governess, had experienced *"the whole beginning as a series of flights and drops, a little seesaw of the right throbs and the wrong."*

Looking over to the woods from which the ghosts of Quint and Miss Jessel would sometimes emerge Anna thought about Edwyn and his ghosts, the restless dead he had allowed to haunt him for so long. She sighed and looked away, aware of her solitude, the only sounds to break the silence the trill of contented birdsong and the occasional roar of a motorbike going past on the road at the bottom of the drive.

She remembered what Mark had said about the role of fate in *Far from the Madding Crowd* and wondered if each twist and turn in the sad story of David and Lily was more luck—or bad luck—than choice; if misfortune, not inconstancy, had cast them apart.

Inevitably, Edwyn had looked at his reconfigured family tree and seen illegitimacy, a concealed adoption, false names and betrayal, but what if there were other surprises to come? Though she sympathised with his frustration at drawing a blank about his biological father, she couldn't help thinking that he could have made a different choice: to find contentment in the present rather than to forage ever further into the unhappy past.

She thought back to that January day on the banks of the Thames that was more than ever a milestone for what happened next. She flinched as she recalled Edwyn's displeasure at her display of Jim's boxes; imagined Jim, full of guilt and regret, trying to make amends to his son in a gesture of love and contrition. Jim, setting aside a collection of mementoes for the son he had brought up, offering him glimpses of the people who had given him life.

In her mind's eye, she conjured the array of pretty boxes, remembered the task of gathering them together from all over Jim's house and arranging them on the narrow alcove shelves and wondered if they might yet have more secrets to surrender.

Chapter 43

"I thought you were miles away or dead! Why didn't you write to me?"

The book had slipped to the floor; Troy's *"strangely gentle"* words to Fanny as she trudged to her death in the workhouse were the last Anna could remember reading before sleep overtook her. She woke early, and with the messiness of their thwarted love affair still turning in her mind, she could not stop wondering if David had loved Lily and been separated from her by cruel fate or if she was the victim of his falsity.

The sky was overcast, but the air warm as she walked through the park towards the Orangery. She'd arrived early, keen to warm up her voice before the others appeared and planning to use the time alone to clear her mind of personal distractions and centre herself in the character of the Governess. The external doors to the Orangery were still locked so she went round to the front door. The Festival staff was busy at computers, but stopped to greet her and exchange friendly chitchat.

The Orangery was still and echoey as she made her way to the piano. Reaching into her bag for her vocal score, she dislodged her copy of the Henry James novel, which splayed open as it fell to the floor. She leant to retrieve it and her eye was caught by a passage in the preface, which she'd underlined in green pen:

" *'A trap for the unwary' is how Henry James once dubbed his tale, preparing the audience for their steady, but ineluctable journey into a territory where they can never quite discover the truth they seek. Within that terrifying chasm between what they know and what they cannot be sure of lies the troubling power of the piece.* "

"A trap for the unwary", indeed, she sighed, as she thought how Edwyn's dogged attempts to unearth the truth about

his roots was to have brought him only emotional anguish, not the understanding he craved.

'You're in bright and early,' a voice called and Anna swung round to see Grace walking across the room, keys in hand. 'How are you? I hoped I might have got back early enough yesterday to check in on you and ask how Saturday went, but events overtook me. Did you have a decent weekend?'

Anna stepped away from the piano and waited for her friend to unlock the doors and turn round.

'I'm fine,' she said, as Grace came towards her, 'but by last night, my head felt fit to burst, and now here I am trying to focus on my overwrought alter-ego. It's enough to drive a girl mad.'

'It is,' agreed Grace studying her closely, 'but if I may say so, you're looking surprisingly well on it.' She raised an eyebrow in expectation.

'I need to warm up,' Anna laughed, taking Grace's arm, 'but could we do something tonight and catch up? A drink perhaps?'

'Good idea,' Grace said. 'Let's fix something later.'

There was a different rhythm about rehearsals now. They had reached the halfway mark and this was their last week indoors before they moved outside for the final week of technical rehearsals, when they'd be working at night as well. Jonathan planned to work through both acts in the first four days of the week, with a floor run in costume planned for Friday afternoon.

Nicholas had spent the weekend fully memorising his part and everyone was now able to work without their scores so there was greater attention to the drama and to the detail and nuances that Jonathan demanded.

Anna could see the strong individual performances of the cast beginning to mesh to form a single claustrophobic community. Michael and Charlotte conveyed a wonderful sense of children growing up too fast, with Charlotte proving an excellent Flora, plausibly pubescent and with a nasty temper, her blossoming but youthful voice suiting the role perfectly; Michael an ostensibly angelic Miles, but hinting at shocking depths of experience; Elspeth as Mrs Grose was utterly real as a sensible woman increasingly out of her depth; Louise a tormented and sexy Miss Jessel and Nicholas's Quint—a magnetically attractive man adept at control and manipulation. He had a way, she noticed, of gathering all his resources for one big, brave outburst and she realised what mettle it took to make this comeback after such a severe breakdown.

In a way, his courage inspired her, and Anna felt herself more confident and at ease, as if she had learnt how to characterise the Governess as a woman with more going on in her troubled hinterland than watchers could possibly guess at and at the same time, to assimilate her own fluctuating emotions with the demands of the role.

After supper at home on her own, Anna was enjoying a drink with Grace at a pub to which she could walk from the cottage. Grace had been working late and was grateful for the hummus and salad the pub had rustled up for her, even though the kitchen was closed. She ate and listened as Anna recounted the events of the last few days: the letters, the meetings, the revelations, the nagging guilt, the new confusion. It all came pouring out and, as ever, Grace was a patient listener and astute commentator.

'I still beat myself up about Edwyn leaving, because at times it seems obvious that it must have been my fault,' Anna said as the barman took away Grace's empty plate. 'We were happy, but perhaps only superficially.' She hesitated and shrugged. 'It wasn't a quarrelling, obviously bad sort of marriage, but the fact has to be faced that he was so miserable that he turned his life—and mine—upside down in his desperation to be free.' She paused and took a sip of lager. 'That's the shadow that's difficult to shift.'

'Oh Anna, that's too harsh,' Grace said, seizing Anna's hand and squeezing it hard. 'I think he must bear the brunt of the responsibility for the mess he's made of your love.' She squeezed Anna's hand again, as if for emphasis. 'And I don't think you should give him the chance to make a mess of you. You're too good for that. You deserve better.' She held Anna's startled gaze. 'And you will find it,' she said. 'And whatever you do, don't think of yourself as unlovable.'

The barman came back with more drinks and Anna blushed, fearing he had heard Grace's last words.

'And will you see Mark again?' Grace asked. 'I must say he sounds like a good thing right now.'

Anna paused.

'It was lovely seeing him on Saturday. I wasn't sure what it would be like—what *he'd* be like—but he seemed more *solid* than when we were students—not in a bad or boring way—less of a boy, but still with a lovely sense of humour. He made me *laugh*,' she said with a flourish.

Grace laughed.

'Well, that is a good thing,' Grace said with feeling. 'And I ask again: will you see him again?'

Anna ran her finger through the condensation on the side of her glass and looked up shyly.

'We're going out for a meal tomorrow night, as a matter of fact.'

'Excellent.' Grace said and helped herself to one of Anna's crisps.

For a moment neither spoke, until Grace asked: 'Is there a problem?'

Anna hesitated, fearing she would sound conceited.

'I just don't want to lead him on, give him cause to hope when I'm still in such a muddle.'

'I take it he cared for you once before and you suspect he still does?' Grace ventured.

Anna nodded.

Grace thought for a moment before speaking: 'I think it's good to have a period of being alone after a breakup—it allows you to find out the truth about yourself, acquire new insights—as long as you don't close down or build Fort Knox around yourself to keep out all-comers.'

Anna laughed.

'Well, there's hardly a queue.'

'No,' Grace said, 'maybe not yet, but there are no hard and fast rules as to when it's time to move on, so just stay open to possibilities. Listen to your feelings.'

'Oh I don't know if that's such a good idea—they're all over the place at the moment.'

She took a gulp of lager and wiped her mouth on the back of her hand.

'Mark used to say that *Far from the Madding Crowd* was his favourite novel because Gabriel Oak got his Bathsheba in the end—after she'd worked her way through two unsuitable suitors.' She grimaced. 'He took to calling me Bathsheba, which I found awkward, because I never thought of him in a romantic way—and then of course I met Edwyn, and that was that.'

Grace nodded and took another crisp.

'I've been re-reading the book,' Anna said at last. 'I haven't read it since I studied it for my degree, but there's a copy at the cottage, and somehow I found myself drawn to it, almost against my will.' She laughed. 'I even fell asleep reading it last night—woke up with the light on and the book on the floor.'

She took a handful of crisps, and nibbled at the corner of one.

'Coming to it again all these years later, and meeting Mark again with Edwyn no longer in my life feels disquieting somehow.'

Grace raised an eyebrow.

'How do you mean?'

'Well, I think in the end, Bathsheba believes that Troy and Boldwood deflected her life from its intended course, from the decent man who truly loves her and won't let her down.'

Grace nodded in understanding.

'Well, who knows what may happen?' she said at last, finishing the last of the crisps. 'Isn't there a saying: "The wrong train may bring you to the right station"...'

Chapter 44

They had agreed on Brown's for old time's sake; as students it was their venue of choice because it was efficient and convenient, and in those days, still thought to be slightly trendy. Mark could walk or cycle there from Trinity and Anna always arrived early so she could browse the shops along Little Clarendon Street beforehand.

With its unchanging décor of cream walls, copious greenery, oversized mirrors and dark wood tables and chairs, Brown's was still something of an Oxford institution, despite long ago being overtaken in the culinary league.

Anna was late and Mark was sitting at a table in the window with a glass of red wine and *The Guardian* folded over so that he could do the crossword. She hurried inside and slipped into the chair next to him before he'd even realised she was there.

'Hello!' he said, pleased to see her.

'So sorry I'm late. The ring road was almost at a standstill.'

'No problem. I've enjoyed a few minutes of unwinding with a glass of wine and today's uber-cryptic crossword.'

He opened the paper out in full and then folded it neatly back together. After taking an order to the table next to them, a waitress stopped by to see if Anna wanted a drink.

'Sparkling water, please. A large bottle.'

She relaxed and sat back in her chair.

'It's good to see you again,' she said smiling as she smoothed away some stray strands of hair and retied her pony-tail. 'It's good to get away from Myddleton, too. It's exhausting—so intense. I need some light relief from the haunted house.'

'Then light relief you shall have,' he said, raising his glass to her.

The waitress arrived with a large bottle of water and two glasses stacked with crushed ice.

'Are you ready to order?' she asked.

'I'm going to have my usual,' Anna said. 'Bacon and avocado salad please.'

'Mushroom risotto for me, please, and a green salad.'

Anna poured some water and drank greedily.

'That's better. I needed that. Cheers.'

'So how are rehearsals going?' Mark asked, chinking his glass with hers.

'Good,' Anna replied. 'It'll be full-on this week as we try to pull it all together before the distractions of being outside, dealing with the dark and the elements, get in the way.' She took another drink of water. 'There are always bumps in the rehearsal process at some point, but we seem to have navigated our way through a couple of those— losing our Quint, me having the screaming hab-dabs, that sort of thing—so hopefully we're on track now.'

Mark's cheerful expression was momentarily clouded by a look of concern and she was aware that he was studying her closely.

'And how did it go with Wendy?' he asked. 'Was she able to help at all?'

Anna paused as the waitress came back to lay the table, her manner slick and professional, not personal. She fiddled with her cutlery for a moment before telling Mark what she'd learnt from his aunt.

Mark listened carefully and swirled his wine round in the glass before taking a sip.

'It's natural to want to find out the truth, achieve closure,' he said at last, 'but after all this time, I guess the full facts can never be established with any certainty.' He stared into his glass. 'And people find uncertainty hard to accept.'

Anna nodded, but frowned.

'I know,' she said sadly 'but what starts out as a healthy desire can easily turn into an unhealthy obsession.' She sighed. 'He could have stopped at any point and taken the decision to delve no further and accept the life he had.'

She poured herself another glass of water, looking up as the waitress appeared with their meals.

Mark speared a couple of mushrooms and looked thoughtful as he steered them into his mouth.

'That's the theory of *amor fati* then,' he said after chewing for a while.

Anna was stirring up her salad so that the dressing was more evenly distributed and she could get at the chopped bacon, which was buried at the bottom.

'What's that?' she asked, looking up with interest.

'It's the acceptance, or even embrace, of one's fate, and the rejection of the idea that anything could, or should, have unfolded differently.'

To her surprise, Anna found herself thinking about Gabriel Oak and the vicissitudes he endured so stoically before Bathsheba became his wife. She felt herself colouring and to add to her disquiet, Mark started quoting from a poem by Hardy.

'Do you remember *Night in the Old Home*?' he asked. 'I can't recall the exact words, but it went something like: *"Take of life what it grants, without question…"* He paused, struggling to remember the words. *"Enjoy, suffer, wait."* Or something similar.'

'Do you go along with that?' Anna asked. '*Amor fati?*'

Before he could answer, their waitress stopped to check if they had everything they needed. Mark ordered another glass of wine and persuaded Anna to join him.

He finished his almost empty glass and said: 'Yes, I think I do. After all, even if we wanted to, it's not as if we can venture down the paths not taken or double back and do things differently the next time round.'

The waitress delivered their wine and Anna was glad she'd weakened and agreed to have a small glass. She took a sip and looked at Mark thoughtfully.

'It seems Edwyn couldn't accept that,' she said at last, and wondering if Mark viewed the course his own life had taken with such equanimity.

'But *amor fati* is tough to take,' Mark went on, 'if you feel as Edwyn may have done that if he'd been told the truth sooner, things might have been different.'

Anna munched cautiously on an over-crisp crouton and took a sip of wine. The restaurant was busier now, with many of the customers obviously tourists. At the table next to them, a party of Americans was poring over a street map and arguing noisily over where to go the next day.

'In what way?' she asked, trying to shut out their squabbling.

'Oh I don't know,' Mark said, shaking his head. 'He may have thought that if they'd talked about it sooner, Brenda or Jim might have remembered something that could have led him to his father.' He paused. 'I guess the man may be dead by now, so there's no chance for Edwyn to meet him and get to know him, ask him if he ever thought of the son he walked away from.'

They were both quiet at that; Anna struck by the sad finality of such an ending.

The party at the next table, laden with carrier bags and travel guides, was making heavy weather of leaving and Anna had to move her chair so they could get past her. A small child of about six, the youngest in the group, turned back in alarm, having realised he'd left something behind. Anna followed his gaze and saw a Paddington Bear toppled over on the floor beyond her chair. She reached down to pick it up and smiled as she handed it to the relieved little boy, his grateful father mouthing his thanks.

With several tables around them now empty, the restaurant felt quieter and calmer, and she relaxed back in her chair. She watched through the window as the boy and his family passed along the street.

'Penny for them?' Mark said after a while.

'Michael—Miles,' she said by way of explanation. 'I was thinking about him and his strange family background.'

She took a sip of wine and described him to Mark.

'Poor kid,' Mark said with feeling when she'd finished. 'Perhaps one day, when he's older, his mother will feel able to tell him the truth—or his father will come looking for him…'

'Maybe,' Anna replied. 'I just wonder why his mother can't see the harm she's doing him now by denying him this information. Doesn't she see how hard he's struggling to make sense of his identity?'

Mark pulled a face and shook his head, just as the waitress arrived to take away their plates.

'Coffee?' he asked Anna.

'Cappuccino, please.'

'And an espresso,' he said to the girl, waiting until she'd gone before he went on. 'She must have her reasons, but I agree she could be storing up problems for the future—for them both. He's bound to feel angry at her for keeping this information sealed up, turning it into this big mysterious secret.'

The waitress reappeared with their coffees and Anna nibbled at the almond biscuit that had come with hers, nodding her head in agreement.

'It's interesting to watch him and Nicholas building a relationship,' she said. 'It's quieter, less rumbustious than the one he had with Harri, but the other day I heard them talking about playing the clarinet.'

'Did we know Nicholas at Oxford?' Mark asked. 'Did he sing back then? I don't remember him.'

He had downed his coffee already.

'Do you fancy another coffee? I always forget how small these are.'

Anna shook her head, as he called over to the waitress.

'He did sing,' Anna replied, 'but only in the New College choir. He told me he was much keener then on playing the clarinet and it was when he went to do his PhD at Cambridge that he decided to pursue singing seriously.'

A second coffee was put before Mark and his empty cup removed.

'Ah, that explains it,' he said, leaning back in his chair.

They chatted on for another half an hour and Anna realised how easy he was to talk to, and how much about her he had remembered and was still interested in. He asked after her parents and her brother, quizzed her on her travels, her career, for news of friends from student days. He shared more about India, about his father's death, about how it felt to be an adult 'orphan' and as she listened she knew he, too, had dealt with grief and disappointment.

'You've had a tough few years, haven't you?' she said after a while, resisting a sudden urge to lean over and put her arm round his shoulder.

He didn't contradict her, just shrugged, and when he spoke again, though his voice caught, there was no trace of embarrassment or levity.

'I guess we lumber through life as best we can with our scars and secrets, and they help form who we are.'

She looked at him wide-eyed with surprise at his candour and he held her gaze until she flushed and reached for her bag to hide her confusion.

'I should be going,' she said, opening her purse. 'It's getting late.'

Outside on the pavement, they prepared to go their separate ways, he to his bike tied to some railings further up St Giles, she to her car in Wellington Square. She hesitated and wondered if he would suggest meeting again. As they hugged their farewells, she noticed the distinctive sweet-spicy scent of Pears soap she'd always associated with him and allowed herself to linger in his embrace before pulling gently away.

'Can we do this again?' he asked.

'I'd like that,' she said. 'I'll ring you.'

She turned to go, but he called after her.

'I forgot to ask,' he said. 'What are you reading? How can we have got through an entire evening without discussing our reading matter!'

It was true; they had always spent hours talking about books and writers.

'I fully intended to tell you all about my newly discovered taste for Joanna Trollope and expected to hear you wax lyrical about Proust and Kafka or the like.'

She laughed and walked on, but he called after her again.

'So which is it?'

She laughed again before turning back to call over her shoulder:

'*Far from the Madding Crowd.*'

She heard the wings of a moth fluttering against the inside of the bedroom curtains and wondered where it would settle once she put the bedside lamp off. The book lay face down on the duvet in front of her; she had finished it and was reflecting on the ending. It seemed to her that though Bathsheba does at last marry Gabriel, Hardy was careful to show that the love they share is not the passion of first love, but a wiser, perhaps sadder connection; happiness tempered by all that has gone before.

She picked the book up again and, as she had done on her first night at Forester's Cottage, flicked through it until she found the last pages of Chapter 4 and Gabriel's words to Bathsheba that Mark had once underlined in red ink:

"*I shall do one thing in this life—one thing certain—that is, love you, and long for you, and keep wanting you till I die.*"

Chapter 45

'I loved the scene where Nicole Kidman discovers a photograph album depicting earlier occupants of the house laid out ready for burial.' Louise spread out her hands and made a ghoulish face. 'And then the creepy house-keeper Mrs Mills says: *"The living and dead are part of the same world."*

Anna shivered as she contemplated the scene being described, while Elspeth nodded in agreement.

'We're doing that aren't we? Dealing with the struggle between the world of the living and the world of the dead,' she said.

Louise grinned and laughed.

'The house-keeper in *The Others* isn't at all like the poor kind-hearted soul in *The Turn of the Screw*,' she said. 'Think Judith Danvers in *Rebecca* rather than Megs Jenkins in *The Innocents.*'

The three women were sitting round a table on the terrace sharing sandwiches and ghost stories. They chatted and munched, glad to have a break from the intensity of rehearsals, and diverted by the activity a short distance away from them, as banks of seating were erected and apparently miles of cable were unwound.

Michael and Charlotte were standing further away, examining the contents of a table that was a jumble of clamps and gaffer tape, safety pins and superglue, lanterns and torches that would be used to keep set and singers secure against the challenges of performing outdoors.

Patrick and Graham were now around full-time and had been joined by Ian, the quietly spoken Production Manager, a seeming magician, able to produce anything that was needed, however outlandish the request. He had even sourced and transported an authentic Victorian bandstand, its wooden and wrought iron structure providing surprisingly good acoustics. The three men had been sitting in on rehearsals, talking with Jonathan in the breaks, meeting regularly with Grace and the stage management team at the start and end of each day.

Everyone agreed that Jonathan's ideas were taking shape. At the start of the week they'd gone back to the beginning —always an interesting moment in rehearsals, when the singers ask themselves 'will we remember what we did in the first two weeks, does it work in light of subsequent developments and discoveries, and does it all hang together?'

Anna was feeling more positive than she'd expected, believing they were already conjuring an eerily mysterious atmosphere, to which the stage setting would make as much of a contribution as the music. Going through the blocking a second time enabled them to dig deeper and develop what they'd done earlier with greater insights and subtlety.

Louise and Elspeth talked on about their favourite ghost stories and Anna, absorbed in thoughts of a different struggle, was relieved when her colleagues were called away for further costume fittings and she was left alone, thinking not of the Governess's inner turmoil, but her own.

To her consternation, she was forced to admit that she was confused by her growing affection for Mark and her shifting feelings about her lost marriage. She had met Mark again the previous night, this time for a walk around Hinksey Lake, followed by a simple supper at his little house overlooking the Park. In his own habitat he had looked touchingly self-reliant, a man alone but not solitary, the life he talked about bursting with stories of work and choir and cricket. His bijou terraced house was neat yet stylish, the walls and floors covered with an eclectic range of hangings and rugs, many brought from India, others more typically contemporary western in origin. Inevitably, there were walls lined with books, arranged methodically in alphabetical order of the writers' surnames, a whole row of

Hardy in view between Hammett and Hartley on shelves above a sofa in the cosy front sitting room.

They had talked effortlessly—about the past and the present, but not of the future. She guessed he still cared for her, though any feelings he might have had remained unspoken.

She looked at her watch and, feeling chilly without her cardigan, got up to go inside. Nicholas and Michael were already there, sitting behind the production desk, heads together as Michael turned the pages of what looked like a large battered stamp or photograph album. As she got closer, and heard Michael's excited cries of recognition, Anna guessed it was a scrapbook.

'Oh, this is amazing,' he gasped. 'Pat Jennings, Lee Dixon, Viv Anderson—they're all here.'

Anna stood alongside them, curious to see what they were looking at with such absorption. Michael spotted her and grabbed her arm excitedly.

'Look Anna. It's an Arsenal scrapbook from 1978-1987 and all the greats are here—photos, biographies, autographs.'

Anna looked quizzically at Nicholas. 'I didn't know you were a signed up member of the Arsenal fan club, too. Is it a tenor thing?' she laughed. 'Or—now this would be spooky—a *Quint* thing!'

Nicholas laughed with her as Michael pulled the book towards him and continued turning the pages and letting out occasional squeals of delight.

'No, not exactly,' he said. 'It was Charlie's—he was a fanatic. He had a season ticket from the age of 16—did all sorts of jobs in his spare time to raise the cash.'

Michael looked up and was listening with interest.

'Does he still watch them?' he asked.

'No,' Nicholas said sadly. 'Not anymore.' And as Michael frowned with surprise, added quietly: 'He died a few years ago and I've looked after some of his stuff ever since.'

'Oh,' Michael said quietly. 'You won't want to lose this, then.'

'No,' Nicholas said slowly. 'But why don't you borrow it for a while? In fact,' he went on, seeing Michael's flushed face light up at his words, 'why don't you look after it? I'm sure you'd give it a safe home and Charlie would be glad to know it had gone to a fellow worshipper.'

'Wicked, wicked! Thank you.'

He continued turning the pages when Jane's voice calling him from the inner door of the Orangery made him look up.

'Michael, I've got some different shirts for you to try. Can you come and put them on now please so that Jonathan and Patrick can see you in them?'

He closed the book carefully and scampered away with it tucked under his left arm.

'That's kind of you,' Anna said, looking up at Nicholas as he got to his feet. 'You've made his day—he'll treasure that scrapbook, you can be sure of that.'

Nicholas nodded.

'He reminds me a bit of Charlie at that age,' he said, watching Michael until he disappeared with Jane towards the fitting rooms. 'He and I were so different—me with my clarinet and piano lessons; him with his football and running.' He paused and screwed up his eyes as if struggling to remember. 'Though...' his voice trailed away.

'What?' asked Anna with interest.

'Well, in other ways they're quite different. Charlie was always larger than life, utterly sure of himself. Michael can give the appearance of being unusually grown-up, but in truth, he's none of those things, is he?'

'So, tell me again: what exactly is a Sitzprobe?' Mark asked, struggling over the word and pulling a face to suggest defeat.

Anna laughed.

'It's the first run-through of a show when the singers and the orchestra perform together,' she said patiently.

'Ah-ha! I see... and how did it go?'

Anna was laying the dining table, which they'd moved onto the patio as Mark supervised a barbecue of lamb burgers and sausages.

She handed him a glass of white wine and made him a toast with hers.

'It was good,' she said. 'We did it inside in the theatre, with the Ensemble at the back of the stage and the six singers standing in front.'

Mark looked quizzical.

'So, no costumes or scenery?'

Anna shook her head.

'It's a sort of transition between the rehearsals we've been doing with piano, and staged run-throughs of the entire performance. Everyone was there today: costume, lighting, makeup, technical—all wanting to get an idea of where we are with the piece.'

She walked back to the table, and made space for the dinner plates on which the meat would be served.

'It's an extraordinary score,' she said, gazing across the lake to where the stage crew and the contractors were still hard at work, their activity punctuated by occasional shouts and sounds of clattering and hammering. 'Just thirteen musicians,' she said, 'but the colours and textures Britten achieves are stunning.'

The meat was cooked and Mark brought it over to the table where salad and warm Focaccia were waiting. They ate and talked, and once again the years rolled away, as if there had been no separation, no fracture in their friendship.

Voices in the next door garden made them look up. They saw two women walking arm-in-arm down to the water's edge, laughing and chatting, the sound of a Mozart piano concerto tinkling faintly through the open door.

'Nice neighbours?' Mark whispered.

'They seem so,' Anna replied. 'They were unloading their car when I arrived home. They're twins, having a weekend away from their husbands.'

'I've often wondered what it would be like to be a twin,' Mark said.

'Nicholas had a twin brother who died a couple of years ago.' Anna said. 'It hit him hard.'

'I'm sure it must have,' Mark replied.

'I'm glad I have a brother,' Anna said, 'even though we didn't really grow up together. By the time I was at primary school, he'd left home and was living it up at university. There are limits to the common ground a seven-year-old girl has with a nineteen your old man she doesn't see that often.' She paused. 'I'm sad about that, but I've always loved him and the gap has shrunk as we've got older.'

Mark looked thoughtful. 'It can be lonely being an only child,' he said. He helped himself to another chunk of bread and used it to mop up the juices of the meat. 'I envy the relationships I see my friends having with their siblings, how their shared history forms the narrative of their lives. I see the gentle mocking, the sibling rivalry, and all that, but also the familiarity and the unbreakable bond.'

He looked sad and for once, Anna thought, he did appear lonely.

'Edwyn said that his solitary upbringing made him used to living mainly in his own little world. Much of the time he felt lonely, he said, and passed the time reading or enduring westerns on television with his parents.' She paused again. 'Maybe that solitary childhood has prepared him for a solitary old-age.'

Mark put down his knife and fork and touched her arm gently.

'I can tell you feel concerned for him, sad for him,' he said, 'but remember that choice was his.' He squeezed her hand. 'You have to let him take responsibility for the life he's chosen.'

261

Anna nodded, but for a moment couldn't speak, and stared down at her plate.

'I'm sorry if that sounds harsh—I don't mean to be unkind—to you or to Edwyn. I'm sure he never wanted to hurt you. I bet he feels wretched about it all.'

Anna looked up, surprised by his expression.

How, she asked herself, had she once treated his good, decent kindness—his *love*—as such cheap currency?

She was relieved when Mark turned the subject to his choir and the Mozart *Requiem* they were performing in October. From there on, they returned to the easy, wide-ranging conversation of earlier, but when they said good night and he ambled down the path towards his car, she thought of Daphne du Maurier's analogy with the pack of cards and wondered if it was not mere chance that had brought them together again.

Chapter 46

Anna woke late and after a slow breakfast on the patio, she walked to a nearby garage to buy a Sunday newspaper. The sun was warm, the sky almost cloudless—perfect weather, she thought, for Mark's cricket match in Beaconsfield. She took the picnic rug down to the water's edge and piled it with cushions against which she reclined, surrounded by the multiple supplements.

Ahead of what she knew would be a tiring week, she was glad to have a day alone, indulging herself in indolence. There was no breeze and the water was still and the ducks had temporarily disappeared, her only companion a solitary robin who appeared from time to time to rootle in the grass, as if looking for something there, his tiny breast glowing vermillion in the sunlight.

Across the lake Anna could see that the contractors had finished building the banks of seating and were at work on a green-striped catering marquee. The pagoda-like bandstand stood to one side of the terrace, its ornate structure bringing to mind rented deck chairs and cheerful music, but empty and silent now, awaiting the musicians who would bring to life Britten's pungent, evocative orchestration.

One final concerted effort was required before they would all be ready to face an audience. She felt her stomach flip in apprehension and turned over with her back to the lake to empty her mind of the challenges to come.

'We've had rain once or twice during the festival,' said Daniel the next day, 'but cold weather like this in August is unprecedented.'

Wrapped in blankets and clutching hot-water bottles and mugs of soup, the singers were huddled in the Orangery for warmth, but even there it was draughty. Monday had dawned bright but cold, and though the morning sun had promised warmth, by the time they began their first rehearsal outdoors in the early afternoon, the temperature was dipping steadily, and now, at seven o'clock, it was 10 degrees and falling. The gas heaters placed around the acting area could do little to combat the chill and Jane had produced layers of underclothing and overcoats to supplement what warmth the costumes could provide.

As they drifted outside to start again, Michael and Charlotte looked pinched and wan and Anna put an arm around each of them. They shared a quiet joke about Toby who was huddled over the piano blowing on the tips of his fingers and looking comically sinister in a black and red striped balaclava. Jonathan agreed to let the singers finish work at nine o'clock, an hour earlier than scheduled, but to press on with the overnight lighting session as planned, concerned that if the autumnal chill continued they would lose even more vital rehearsal time.

Anna had wrapped a pashmina shawl around her head and shoulders for added coverage, but was still shivering as they prepared to do a run of Act 2. It wasn't yet dark, but the latish performance start promised a show of gathering shadows and spooky atmospherics. As Patrick had envisaged, the outdoor setting and the nearby thicket allowed the ghosts to materialise with discomfiting suddenness, turning the screw that little bit tighter.

Paul expressed the hope that the temperature would have risen by the time the Ensemble arrived on Thursday afternoon and said he was taking heart from a weather forecast that offered the promise of a return to summer by the weekend.

'Yeah,' said Louise as she headed off towards the trees to wait for her first entry. 'No way you'll get a bunch of musos to play in conditions like this.' She was puffing on a cigarette as she went, assuring the others that it warmed her up and yes, she would make sure she stubbed it out carefully.

'Come on Nicholas,' she called over her shoulder. 'Get your backside off that heater and let's be having you in them there woods pronto.'

Anna had little experience to prepare her for such an unexpected challenge, but took her lead from Elspeth and Nicholas who said little but soldiered on, all three of them glad Louise had assumed the role of comedian, a droll commentator on all their ills, her wry humour cheering everyone and helping to create a bravura *esprit-de-corps*.

They settled into a rhythm of working afternoons and evenings, of hunkering down at home in the chilly mornings and hurrying back to the warmth at the end of the day. Anna found it hard to relax after these strange, wearying days and went to bed later than usual in an attempt to unwind and prepare for sleep. All through the week her dreams were illusory and surreal, snippets of the opera recurring dizzyingly: Michael hiding under a desk, overhearing the letter announcing his expulsion from school, saying over and over *"I am bad, I am bad"*; she and Louise reaching to snatch a doll sitting on the Governess's desk; Nicholas looking particularly crazed, his eye sockets dark and accentuated; Michael's fingers crashing over the piano keys in imitation of a demented virtuoso.

She and Mark exchanged texts and phone calls, which though brief, reinforced their closeness, even while she struggled to understand her own hopes and intentions. Even now, she occasionally fantasised that Edwyn would have a change of heart, but at the same time was not sure how she would react if he did or if they could ever start again. She found Mark attractive in a way she had never noticed as a student, but felt she should not encourage him unless she was certain she would not again disappoint. She sensed, too, he would like children, that he would be a good father, but much as she still hoped for motherhood, she was fearful of another pregnancy. While Mark had so far desisted from calling her Bathsheba, the notion of possible second chances was unspoken between them.

When the Ensemble arrived on Thursday, the weather was still less than clement, but it was warmer than at the start of the week and not so cold that the musicians were unwilling to play. By the time of the first dress rehearsal on Friday night, the weather was balmy again and everyone's anxiety lifted. The team who had worked through the long cold nights designing and plotting the lighting had achieved amazing tricks of light, reflection and shadows. Hearing Britten's orchestrations for the first time in the still, warm air, Anna marvelled at his ability to create images as diverse as the quiet of the Essex countryside, the chiming of church bells and the mystery of Quint's appearance. Earthy bassoons and violas, mournful cello, the chime of harp and chilly glimmer of celeste all haunted the air and laid bare these images with wonderful clarity.

Her body ached with fatigue, her whole being stiff and taut as if the earlier harsh chill had seeped into her bones and lodged there, despite the return of warmer weather. After this last final push, she decided she would leave as soon as the second dress rehearsal on Saturday night was over and go back home to Richmond to rest for a few days; to have a break from Myddleton—and from Mark.

Chapter 47

The slim brown package was propped against the front door, too big to go through the letterbox without being bent, and left there by Huw who had heeded the bold red instruction printed on the front of the reinforced envelope. Edwyn bent to study it, the postmark suggesting it was from Ursula's niece Doreen in Winchester. He felt a flutter of anticipation and decided to open it immediately, without going inside. He sat on the bench beside the door and squinted in the bright sunshine, his thick Guernsey jumper keeping him warm against the unseasonal chill.

He peeled back the seal and reached inside to pull out the contents, a booklet bearing the imprint of Samuel French publishers, with a handwritten letter attached to it by a paperclip.

Dear Edwyn,
I trust you are well. I am in the midst of sorting through Auntie's belongings—a wearying task, though she kept everything spick and span, so it could be worse. I found this script in the top drawer of her bedside table. This must have been what she wanted to give you before she died. I'm so glad to have found it and hope it will mean something to you.
Kind regards
Doreen

He removed the paper clip and laid the letter on the bench beside him, revealing a battered copy of Agatha Christie's play *Black Coffee,* its covers worn and creased and in danger of coming away from the spine. On a yellow sticky secured just above the title, Ursula had written *"For Edwyn. The man in the photograph is David. This was his script—left behind in Cardiff."*

He opened the script to reveal two small black and white photographs lying together on the frontispiece, the top right-hand corner of which bore the name David Demery in faded pencil.

He peered at the first photograph, unable at first to make out what it was, until he realised it was a close up of his mother sitting on the grass outside Cadwallader Hall, a loose fitting dress not able to conceal her swollen belly. He looked more closely and saw that despite the advanced stage of her pregnancy, his mother's face looked thin and peaky, though she was smiling for the camera, the same wide smile she wore in Jim and Brenda's wedding photograph. He turned the photo over and on the back, in Lily's handwriting, was an address: c/o Mrs Hawkins, 9 Marine Terrace, Criccieth.

He ran his finger gently over her face, before laying the photo carefully aside and turning to the other. Frustratingly, this one was not a close up, taken from such a distance that the figures looked small and slightly out of focus, but he could make out what appeared to be a family group: a man and woman standing close together, with a small boy between them, clutching the legs of the woman, as if needing them to steady himself.

He held his breath. So this was his father, this tall man, standing erect and laughing at the camera, with a woman clutching her son with one hand and her flyaway hair with the other. For a moment he was confused. Who was this child? Was it him, Edwyn? Then his head cleared and he realised that David had been carrying this photograph around during the spring and summer of 1946, before he was born.

So who was the boy in the photo? And who was the woman?

He turned the photograph over, hoping that someone would have recorded the date and place it was taken, but the back was blank apart from what might have been a coffee stain.

He sighed in disappointment, but then a disquieting thought occurred and he felt his nails dig into the palm of his hand. He turned the photo over to study it once more and winced at the possibility that this was an earlier family concealed by David Demery while he was all the while preparing for life with a new one.

What happened to them, Edwyn wondered, realising that untold others might have loved David Demery and been part of his story. Was theirs a tale of hurt and dislocation, of neglect and desertion? He knew that before the war, a mere handful of stops on the railway line was another world entirely, where you could contract a bigamous marriage, raise an illegitimate baby, or simply shake off your family name and start again, one step ahead of the prying eyes of your native community.

But why would a man keep this reminder of a relationship that had failed or been forsaken unless he was struggling with complex and conflicting feelings? Was David's abandonment of Lily an inevitable consequence of a noble impulse to correct earlier mistakes; did he go back to this other family to mend the broken ties?

Edwyn's head spun from one unanswered question to another. He laid the photo alongside the one of his mother and flicked through the script, scanning the pencil markings in the margins, many indecipherable, others seeming to be prompts to remind him of stage moves and business with props.

He put the book aside and stared out to sea, watching the seagulls bob on the gently undulating waves. He shivered. It was still chilly. Time to go inside.

His desk was strewn with the papers he'd left there the night before and gleaming in the sunlight was the large magnifying glass that had been Jim's and was now an invaluable aid to his study of documents written in spindly hands and worn with age. He re-opened the script and took out the family photograph, holding it under the glass and peering at the man, trying to make out his features, trying to recognise himself within them. The face was too blurred to reveal anything as distinct as that, but there was something about the man's bearing that was somehow tantalisingly familiar.

Chapter 48

Falling into bed, bleary and light-headed after the drive from Myddleton, sleep eluded her until the first glimmers of light pierced the flimsy bedroom curtains. She got up late and spent what was left of the morning dozing in the conservatory, glad to feel the sun seeping into her bones. When at last she stirred herself to get on with the day, she could only drift around the house feeling restless and unable to settle, strangely disorientated, as if the place was no longer hers and she was a visitor trying to nest in an unfamiliar environment. To her dismay, she found herself hankering for the familiarity of Forester's Cottage and the rhythm of life she'd grown used to there.

Trying to busy herself, she went out to the hall to collect the post, which she'd simply kicked aside as she'd staggered wearily through the front door in the early hours. A cursory scan confirmed it was merely a jumble of fliers and free newspapers, plus a handful of bank statements and bills she felt too dispirited to open. She leafed idly through the fliers until one with bold gothic lettering caught her eye: *Annie's Emporium, A newly-established Antiques Centre in Richmond, attractively laid out in what was St Mary's Church with 60 different businesses housed under one roof. The Emporium offers a range of antique and contemporary items including Furniture, Jewellery, Silver, China, Glassware, Pictures, Mirrors, Coins, Carpets, Upholstery Fabrics and many other interesting pieces.*

She glanced down at the details and realised the church was only a short walk away and the Emporium was open on Sundays until four o'clock. She brightened, thinking this could be the ideal place in which to find unusual first night cards and the picture frames she needed for Michael and Charlotte.

She itched to get out of the house, but after weeks in the country it was strange to be jostled on streets that were crowded even on a Sunday. Weaving her way through tourists drawn to Ham House and Richmond Park, she was relieved when she turned into a quiet square, the far corner of which was dominated by the enormous church of St Mary. At first sight the building was ugly and grimy, but the inside was an unexpected contrast to the unprepossessing exterior, with high ceilings, pale grey stone arches and an exposed roof structure creating an impressive open space in which the piety of Victorian Christianity had given way to the bustle of twenty-first century commerce.

With a bewildering array of different stalls and shops laid out in 'streets,' Annie's Emporium reminded her of the indoor market in Oxford, as did the pervasive and enticing smell of frying bacon and brewing coffee from the café at the far end of the building. She decided to start at the left hand side and work her way systematically up and down the aisles. At a stationery stall at the back, she found some arty postcards depicting features of Victorian country houses and gardens that would make ideal first night cards, but she'd wandered all the walkways without finding the picture frames she needed.

She stopped at a stall near the entrance, her flagging attention grabbed by the flair of the display and the striking appearance of the young woman in charge. She was chatting to a man from the stall next door, so Anna could study her unnoticed. Petite, with cropped purple hair set off by ornate gold earrings, she was wearing tight Lycra trousers in contrasting shades of pink, a purple velvet waistcoat studded with sequins and, underneath, a low-cut top revealing a tanned cleavage.

The woman looked round and smiled as she moved back into position behind her counter.

'Need any help?' she asked.

Anna had spotted a range of handcrafted wooden picture frames, the wood distressed and stained in a variety of colours, each one highly individual.

'What size are those?' she asked pointing at two that were propped together on a cabinet behind the counter, one pale turquoise, the other Wedgewood blue.

'They're standard A4 size,' she said, handing one to Anna. 'Beautiful aren't they? The wood's reclaimed and recycled in South Africa.'

'They're perfect,' Anna murmured in delight. 'Just what I was looking for. I'll take them both please.'

'I'll do you the two for £40 then,' the woman said. 'Is that OK?'

Anna nodded and smiled as the woman began to wrap them in sheets of black tissue paper. While she waited, Anna worked her way slowly around the long, curved counter, browsing through the trays and glass-fronted cabinets, until she came to a small wicker basket, the edges of which were draped with an assortment of silk scarves. Her eye was caught by one with a beautiful pattern of light blue and burnt orange flowers and paisleys woven on a dark navy background.

She fingered the piece gently and unfolded it in order to see it in its full length. It was smooth and soft to the touch and she resisted the urge to hold it to her face. Although it was distinctive and unusual, she had a feeling she had seen one identical to it, but frowned in frustration as she tried to remember when and where.

The woman was reaching under the counter for a carrier bag and watched Anna as she carefully refolded the scarf and put it back in the basket.

'Stylish isn't it?' she said as she eased the parcel into the bag. 'It's an opera scarf—made in the early 1950s. A limited edition of an exclusive Italian range for men.'

Anna was surprised to learn that it was intended for a man—it had looked too exotic for most men's taste, she thought. She paid for her picture frames and made to leave, but as she moved towards the door she took one last look at the scarf.

She stepped out blinking into the sunshine and decided to walk back a different way, knowing that a maze of streets that led off the square would take her home by a more circuitous but quieter route, away from the tourists. She turned into the last street before her own, a narrow terrace with modest cottages on one side and a row of handsome Edwardian houses on the other. Mid way along the terrace, she stopped at a house whose woodwork was painted a vivid cobalt blue, its small front garden paved but given colour by a collection of pots and troughs full of late-flowering summer flowers. Beneath the shade of the curved bay window, pools of tiny blue flowers with yellow centres blooming above their hairy leaves and stems had burst through a thin strip of soil.

Forget-me-nots.

Her mind somersaulted and as she hurried homewards, one memory triggered another until she knew exactly where she had seen that opera scarf before.

Perhaps it was the dankness of the day that made the house feel so chill and desolate, but as she made her way through to the silent kitchen, Anna knew it was because Jim had gone. She dumped her bag on the table and sat down with a sigh. Looking round she could see that everything was as it had been left when Jim was in hospital—clean and tidy, but no longer a home despite the relics of more than half a lifetime spent there. It would take some sorting, she knew, but so far Edwyn had shown no inclination to tackle any of it, so she had steeled herself to make a start, if only to keep her promise to the old man.

'I'll not be going back, Anna,' he had wheezed, his head wedged at an awkward angle against the hard hospital pillow.

'Don't say that, Jim,' she'd whispered, squeezing the hand that lay limp on the pale blue bedspread.

Jim tried to shake his head in protest, but she could see that he was too weak to move, his strength seeming to drain away before her eyes.

'Edwyn?' he asked.

'He's on his way,' she said. 'He'll be here soon,' but she feared he would be too late, caught as he was in a blizzard in Boston and unable to get a flight out until the next day.

The old man closed his eyes and grimaced, but she felt his grip on her hand tighten.

'You can do what you like with all of it,' he whispered, 'but promise me you'll keep my boxes.'

His eyes were open now and there was a momentary flash of intensity in them.

'Edwyn must keep the boxes.'

'Of course,' she'd promised. 'We'll look after them.'

She knew that most of the boxes would be stacked in Jim's workroom in the garden, but there had always been a few in the sitting room and kitchen, too. She could carry half a dozen or so at a time, depending on their size and weight, but it took her several trips out to her car before they were all loaded. She stacked them carefully in the boot and thought what a pretty display they made.

When the boot was full, she went back into the house to take a last look round. She stood at the bottom of the stairs and looked up, guessing there might be boxes in the bedrooms, too. She hesitated, fearing her loss would be heightened in these most private rooms, and as she made her way up, the pungent smell of Jim's aftershave caught in her throat and brought tears swimming to her eyes. On the narrow landing she paused. The bathroom smelt damp and musty, its shelf of medication, mouthwash and shaving paraphernalia more poignant than she could bear. She opened the door of the small spare bedroom and counted six more boxes piled in a corner. She moved on to the room that had been Edwyn's and was struck for the first time how little of him was there—no evidence at all to suggest this had once been his hideaway.

The door to Jim's bedroom was ajar and the smell of stale aftershave was more cloying. Again she hesitated, feeling there was something not right about venturing into this intimate space, but told herself she had Jim's permission. The room was ship-shape and soulless, the walls and furnishings looking bleached and shabby. Anna shuddered and bit her lip, anxious to leave, but a concentration of colour on top of a chest of drawers caught her eye. Another of Jim's boxes, covered in a mass of tiny blue forget-me-nots, it was larger and sturdier than most that Jim made and though it was closed, a piece of dark blue silk was caught in the lid.

She eased the lid open to reveal a bright floral scarf with navy hems at each end. One of Brenda's she assumed that Jim had kept after her death and used to cover the documents that lay beneath it. She folded the scarf neatly and closed the lid, carrying its heavy weight with care out to her waiting car.

Chapter 49

The large box stood proud from the others and, as she lifted it, she saw that it was older and more battered than she'd remembered, some of the paint chipped and faded. One of Jim's earlier efforts, perhaps. She took it into the sitting room and placed it on the low table in front of the sofa. The lid opened easily to reveal the scarf lying neatly where she'd laid it on that gloomy day in January. She lifted it gently and turned it over in her hands. It was more worn than the one at the Emporium, the silk thinning in parts, but the colours retained their lustre. She folded it again and placed it across the arm of the sofa before leaning to see what was beneath it.

The box appeared to be full of letters and papers organised neatly in pale blue folders underneath a layer of soft white tissue paper, on top of which were two envelopes sitting side by side. Neither had stamps nor full addresses; one had been opened and was addressed to *Mr Jim Maxwell*, the other was still sealed and simply bore the words *To my son*. Puzzled by this, Anna slipped her hand into the opened envelope and drew out a single sheet of A4 paper folded in three. The letter had been typed and she turned it over to see a handwritten signature, which read *With best wishes, Colin Farrar*.

The name meant nothing to her, and with her curiosity aroused, she turned back to the front page to check for a date and an address. In the top right hand side of the sheet was an address in Cheshire and a phone number, and underneath, *7th December 2005*. Jim had been admitted to hospital on the 13th December, so, having read the letter, he must have put it with everything else into one of his old boxes for safe-keeping.

Dear Mr Maxwell,

I hope you will forgive this intrusion, but now that I have at last found you, I am duty-bound to send you the letters, photographs and other cherished tokens you will find in this package and ask you to give them, along with the letter addressed To my son, to the baby who was born to your sister-in-law, Lily.

Anna gasped out loud and held her breath.

I am that baby's half-brother, and his father, David Farrar, was mine also, and before he died a few weeks ago, I promised him that I would do everything I could to seek out his son. It was my father's dying wish that he be able to set out the truth of what happened on that fateful day in June 1946.

Anna clasped the letter to her chest, too stunned to do more than stare in astonishment at the contents of the box.

You may wonder why I did not write when my father was alive. He had been looking for the boy in secret for several years and at last, when he knew he was ill, he told me the story and asked me to help him. He knew that Lily had died, but had no idea where and in what name her baby had been registered. We searched for Lily's sister and brother-in-law—hoping you could help us —but we couldn't find you. A search for James Maxwell threw up simply too many possibilities to follow up. I promised my dad I'd go on looking and it was only after his death that I remembered him saying that Lily once told him that you had an unusual middle name - that you were named after two great explorers. James Cook was easy to work out, but I think I went through all the others before I got to Ferdinand Magellan!

The last sentence made Anna smile, but then the significance of the date on the letter struck her hard: Edwyn's father had died not long before Jim, and Jim had received the package—and the news—shortly before he himself was taken ill and while Edwyn was away on a lecture tour of New England.

Since I first learnt about him, I have wondered about my brother, about what sort of life he has had, if he is still alive even, if he ever searched for his biological father. Such a search, if he embarked on it, would I fear have been hard, for the same reason you have proved so hard to track down: the need to have a full and correct name! Though I believe my father truly loved Lily, he was not entirely straightforward with her, and he concealed the fact that Demery was a stage name, (chosen simply for its alliteration) and that there was a wife and son he had left who bore his real name of Farrar.

The enclosed scarf was my father's—after the summer of 1946, he always wore something to conceal the scars on his neck. This was his favourite. I thought my brother might like it.

I would be very grateful if you would let me know if you are able to contact Lily's son. I trust you know where he can be found at any rate.

I would very much like to meet him.
With best wishes
Colin Farrar

She was astonished at the unexpected revelations to which the scarf had led her and moved by the candour and sincerity of the letter, recognised the generous spirit required to write in such a way.

She placed both the letters on one side of the box and gently lifted the tissue paper, opening the folder on top to reveal the mementos stacked neatly beneath—the faded photographs, the large bundles of letters, one of which was secured by a pink satin ribbon. She could tell that everything had been stored and preserved with great care and she resolved not to pry or disarrange further. She replaced the tissue paper, the letters from father and son, and the folded scarf.

She closed the lid and stood up, leaving the box where it was on the low table in front of the sofa. She guessed its contents might provide Edwyn with the answers he craved and hoped that assimilating the "truth" of his story into the tapestry of his life might enable him to move on.

But she also recalled her conversation with Nicholas when he had asked: 'Why do we assume the truth will set us free?'

She sighed and shut the door behind her.

Chapter 50

From inside the small marquee that passed as makeshift dressing room, Anna could hear the orchestra beginning its ritual tuning, the plangent sound of the oboe piercing the still air and causing the audience to fall disconcertingly quiet. The day was fading, ready for Graham's dark-toned lighting to work wonders in creating oppressive shadows that would only fleetingly allow light to penetrate the darkness.

The marquee, though, was filled with light falling in bright shafts across mirrors in which were reflected the pale faces of the six singers making their last minute preparations to makeup and costume, testing their voices on scales and snippets of Britten. Anna was palpably nervous, fighting back emotions that threatened to spill over and overwhelm her. She could feel the hot colour creeping up from her chest, leaving her skin a mass of feverish-looking blotches, and was grateful for the demure high neckline of her grey travelling dress.

It was always like this, but tonight her personal anxiety combined with the turning of the interlocking screws in the claustrophobic opera had brought her to a state of high tension. She shuddered as a moth brushed against her cheek, its wings skimming her eyelid as it flew off into the night. Jane, patiently weaving her long hair into a neat chignon, placed her hands on Anna's shoulders and whispered quietly in her ear, 'breathe, Anna, breathe. You'll be fine.'

Anna put her hands on Jane's and smiled.

'I know,' she said. 'I will.'

She looked round and thought how gay the place looked, with cards stuck to mirrors and gifts and lucky charms cluttering the dressing table tops of the four women. Nicholas and Michael were cocooned in a corner together, a screen providing some privacy, but Anna had seen that Michael's table was a mess of chocolates wrappers and half-eaten cookies. He'd wandered over to talk to Charlotte and was comparing his blue frame with her turquoise, thrilled with Anna's gift of his costume design and wanting to show it off.

Patrick came and adjusted her hair. She nodded over towards the two young people.

'Thank you,' she said. 'It was so kind of you to let me have those costume designs for the kids. You can see they've gone down a treat.'

'You're welcome,' he said, with a laugh. 'I've got about half a dozen versions of them—it always takes me several attempts to get it right.'

He moved on, checking the others before wishing them well and leaving to take his seat alongside Jonathan amongst the audience, just as Sarah's voice was heard over the backstage tannoy giving them their five-minute call.

Anna closed her eyes and tried to shut out the people and sounds around her, recalling what Jonathan had said to her a short while ago. He had leant against her dressing table and clasped both her hands.

'I know this has been tough for you, Anna, but I want you to know that you are my perfect Governess—thank you! I know you will be simply compelling out there. You conjure up such an astonishing mixture of insecurity and manic determination—just what I wanted. So go for it and enjoy!'

As she recalled his words of encouragement, she willed them to sustain her courage and her confidence through the evening ahead. She smiled and breathed deeply. The earlier agitation had subsided, replaced by excited anticipation and inner calm. She leant over and pulled a card away from her mirror. It was a reproduction of an impressionist painting showing a young woman hurrying through a rain-washed Paris street, her face turned sideways under her windswept umbrella, her expression a mix of fragility and pluck. On the back, Mark had written:

Dear Anna, I thought you might be able to use some of this young woman's determination and resolve. She reminds me of you. Keep sailing through! love Mark xxx

She heard Sarah's voice calling for beginners and saw that Grace and Emma were waiting for them, torches in hand. Anna hung back, standing quiet and still, thinking that this extraordinary period in her life, this interlude so resonant with loss and the prospect of change, would soon be at an end, that she and the others would move on to their next adventures. She looked round to take in her colleagues and soak up the support of final hugs and kisses, whispered good wishes, and resolved to cherish and enjoy every fleeting moment of it.

At the end, when the lights lifted and they took their bows, she tried to recall and relive the performance in all its detail, but it was half-caught, half-remembered images that raced through her mind's eye, leaving her slightly dizzy: the ensemble playing with hauntingly eloquent assurance; Paul ratcheting up the tension in the early scenes before bringing the drama to the boil with an almost demonic intensity; lighting that lent Louise's glamorous Miss Jessel an unhealthy, gothic luminosity and Nicholas a pallor that was at once menacing yet seductive; lighting that caught exactly the unnerving *"is that a ghost or just a trick of the light?"* quality of Henry James's novella; Elspeth's desolate cry, *"Dear God, is there no end to his dreadful ways?"*; Charlotte achieving the extraordinary trick of combining childlike innocence with pure malevolence; Michael's quiet, sweet piping of *"Malo, malo"* making her spine tingle, her heart lurch at his whimpering shudders when she cradled him at the desperate denouement.

*

The marquee buzzed with well-wishers as the singers cast off their costumes and exchanged joshing banter and relieved compliments. Anna had changed into a low cut cream jersey dress she'd brought from Richmond for the occasion, but decided to leave her hair in the chignon, adding a sparkly comb for decoration. She was gathering her gifts together when Grace touched her arm and stopped her: 'There's someone asking if they can come in to say hello.' She paused and raised an eyebrow. 'A man.'

Anna looked at her quizzically. She'd had no guests in the audience that night so the identity of the visitor was a mystery.

She shrugged and said: 'Unless you think he's a stalker, let him come in.' She held out her arms. 'I'm decent.'

She turned away to touch up her lipstick and was surprised to see Mark's reflection in her mirror as he walked towards her.

She spun round in surprise and pleasure.

'I thought you were away!'

'I should be,' he said. 'But I couldn't miss your show, so I'm leaving at the crack of dawn tomorrow to join the others in time for an 11 o'clock start.'

She gasped and hugged him.

'Thank you', she cried. 'Thank you, too, for not telling me you were coming. I'd have been even more nervous if I'd known you were here.'

He laughed and held her away from him.

'No need for nerves—you were sensational.'

'Really?'

'Really. What an achievement by everyone,' he said. 'I was glad when the interval came so I could retreat to the bar for a much-needed drink. I was in a state of shock; it was as if we were in the opera, too, and it's not a comfortable opera to be in.'

'As I know too well,' she laughed, feeling impetuous.

'I know you have an early start,' she said, seizing him by the arm, 'but will you come to the party for a while and meet the others?'

The tall windows of the Orangery had been draped with blackout curtains and throughout the performance had stood in darkness, providing an eerie backdrop to the stage action. Inside, the long narrow space had been transformed from their functional rehearsal room into a glittering ballroom, with dozens of miniature Christmas trees bedecked with fairy lights lining the long frontage of windows, and tables draped with crisp white linen offering drinks and food.

Daniel made a generous and witty speech of thanks and congratulations and as she helped herself to some canapés from a passing waiter, Anna was struck by how much had changed since that night only a few weeks ago when they had gathered upstairs to meet Nicholas and read through the Henry James story. Was it possible, she wondered, that if Harri's right leg had remained intact, she would still be adrift in a sea of unknowing? At the very least, it was reasonable to ponder whether if that night of Nicholas's introduction had not been stormy and she caught out in the rain, she might never have had that chance conversation with Daniel that precipitated so many discoveries.

Anna introduced Mark to some of her colleagues and left him talking to Nicholas while she went off to get them both a drink. She was preparing to carry away two glasses of wine when Louise whispered loudly behind her: 'Where did you find *him*? She squealed in excitement. 'Don't tell me you've hired him for the night!'

Anna laughed and saw that Grace was listening, also agog to know more.

'It's my friend Mark—we were at university together— he lives in Oxford.'

Louise raised an eyebrow and shoved her gently.

'Good for you, my girl. You deserve some good times.'
She took a gulp of her wine. 'He looks very nice—I'm
going over to check him out.'

Anna laughed and handed her one of the glasses she
was holding.

'OK—take him this then.'

Grace shook her head and looked over at Mark with
mock concern as Louise sashayed towards him.

A strand of hair had come loose and Anna wound it
round her index finger, wondering whether to tell Grace
about her growing friendship with Mark and her delight
that he was here. What would she say? With all the
revelations about Edwyn, she had barely had time to
process what—if anything—was happening and
understand it. Perhaps it was nothing more than the sort of
brief encounter that happened only too often in her highly
charged, itinerant profession.

To her surprise, she realised that she hoped not. She
turned to Grace

'You know,' she said, 'I think I may be ready to move
on.'

Chapter 51

She hated the goodbyes that bookended every project, fervently believed the promises to keep in touch, and was thrilled whenever her path crossed again with good colleagues, but the goodbyes that followed the final performance at Myddelton felt more poignant than usual.

In particular, she was sad to relinquish the special relationship she'd developed with Michael, and realised what strong maternal feelings he'd aroused in her. She was still sitting at her dressing table gathering up her cards and makeup when he came and stood behind her. She looked at his solemn reflection in the mirror and turned round to stroke his cheek.

"Yes! The Child is an angel!" she sang quietly, smiling fondly at his dejected expression. As the shadows fell across his face, his dark eyes looked like black orbs and he looked younger than ever.

"A good young lady, I'll be bound, and a pretty one too," he sang back, and came round to lean against the table.

She laughed.

'Do you think you'll ever come back to Oxford?' he asked after a moment's silence.

'Of course I will,' she said. 'Why?'

'Will you come and see me? I've written down my address.'

He handed her a piece of paper and she was touched to see his lower lip was trembling.

'I'd love to,' she said, drawing him to her and putting her arm around his waist. 'You really have been my little angel. I'll miss you.'

He eased himself out of her embrace and she leant to find a handkerchief in her bag. At the same time, she rummaged for the little note pad and pencil she carried with her.

'Here's my address,' she said, writing it out in careful capitals, 'and my email. If you've time, perhaps you'd write to me with your news? I'd love to hear how you're getting on.'

He nodded and put the slip of paper in his pocket.

'I'll be back in December anyway,' she said. 'I'm singing *Messiah* at the Town Hall. I'll send you the date—perhaps your mum would bring you.'

He brightened and said he'd ask her.

'Is she waiting for you?' Anna asked.

'Yes,' he said. 'She's outside—I'd better go.'

Anna realised it was time to "hand" him back to his mother, that he had only been her boy on temporary loan, and as he walked away from her she felt a keen sense that she was yet again losing something special. He turned to wave one last time and she felt her eyes fill with tears, wishing she could warrant that he would forever stay safe and happy, his dreams intact.

The pale gravel was gleaming in the moonlight as they walked down the drive to take the long way round to Foresters Cottage, where Mark had left his car before the performance. He'd returned from his cricket tour a day earlier than expected—the last match abandoned due to storms that had swept the country—and had come to see the show again. Water still sat in puddles along the uneven path, the rain having stopped only a few hours earlier leaving the night air damp and humid.

Anna walked in silence, dreading the further goodbyes to be said at the end of this walk. They had joined Daniel and some of the others for a farewell drink in the upstairs drawing room and she'd been grateful for Mark's easy, unobtrusive companionship. They had sat on the window seat and she'd told him about her discoveries in Richmond; her anxiety about her meeting with Edwyn the following week and her apprehension about what further secrets might be revealed in the letter from his father.

As she heard herself recounting the story to Mark, trying to make it sound coherent, she realised that she had needed to hear it out loud as if that would help her comprehend it, too.

'It feels like a big moment,' she'd said. 'I feel a great sense of responsibly in having uncovered all this and being the one to reveal it to Edwyn. I don't know how he'll react. I just hope it doesn't make things worse for him.'

Mark nodded in understanding.

'But you can't conceal it from him, he has a right to know, will want to know, even if he won't be able to predict what impact it will have and how he'll feel afterwards.'

They had reached the turning space alongside the three cottages, the row in darkness save for the cosy glow from the table lamps she'd left on in her sitting room.

'I'll miss my little cottage,' she said. 'It's been a perfect haven.'

She reached into her bag to find the door key and in her head, heard Michael's voice asking her whether she would ever come back to Oxford and now she found herself willing Mark to ask her the same question.

They reached the gate and stopped, but after his earlier ease Mark was tongue-tied and awkward.

'Will you come to my *Messiah* in December?' she asked shyly, and held her breath as she waited for him to reply.

She saw him hesitate, but when he at last looked up, his face was alive with trepidation and hope.

'Do I have to wait that long?'

She felt her shoulders relax as he held her close, his nose nestling in her hair. They rocked gently together for a few moments, her forehead resting on his, and then she pulled away.

'No,' she said softly. 'You don't.'

Chapter 52

Edwyn manoeuvred the car into a narrow parking space and walked the short distance to the house. It had a blank, empty look, as if no one lived there any more, though he was on time and Anna had said she'd be waiting for him. He thought about using his key, but changed his mind and knocked instead. He swallowed hard, waiting for the sound of footsteps from within, for the moment when she would open the door and invite him to step in to what had been their home.

Just as the door swung open, he realised the extent of his nervousness, unsure of the reception he might receive and dreading a frosty, stilted encounter. But Anna's friendly demeanour as she welcomed him inside allayed those fears and he felt his breathing quieten. He was relieved to see that her face had lost the pinched, wintry paleness he remembered from the time of their parting, her skin glowing a pale honey colour as if she'd been sitting in the sun.

He followed her through to the kitchen and sat watching her while she made some tea and asked about his journey. It was all so natural and inconsequential he almost forgot the purpose of the visit, though he could not deny the sense that he was a visitor and she was in charge. Something about her email was suggestive of he knew not what, but she'd alluded to having news that she needed to tell him in person.

She handed him his tea and sat beside him at the kitchen table, both hands clasped around her mug.

'So, was it a success?' he asked at last. 'Were you pleased with how it went?'

She looked up at him and smiled.

'It was, yes,' she said. 'Every performance seemed to grow in intensity and the last one in particular was a cracker.'

'How was Nicholas?'

'Oh, horribly plausible and wonderfully sinister,' she laughed.

'I'm glad things are looking up for him,' Edwyn said. 'He had a rough time when his brother died.'

The mention of Nicholas brought his own troubles centre stage and Edwyn flushed with discomfort, hoping to avoid the subject for as long as possible. Seeing him colour, Anna pushed her tea away and bowed her head, her loose hair concealing her face from him. He feared she was upset and braced himself for what was to follow, but when she looked up he could see no sign of distress, but sensed that she, too, was steadying herself for something difficult.

'I know that Jim gave you a box of mementoes of Lily and told you the part of her story that he knew.'

He nodded, surprised that this was where she'd started and wondering where it was leading.

'Well, I remembered something about a box I found in Jim's bedroom.'

Edwyn stopped fiddling with his mug and looked up.

'It was the only box I found in that room and it caught my eye because it had an unusual silk scarf caught in the lid —vivid blues and oranges and very lovely—and I assumed that the papers it was covering belonged to Brenda.'

His eyes widened at the description of the scarf—he felt sure he had seen one like it, but not on Brenda. He fixed Anna with his full attention.

'Later on,' she was saying, 'I learnt that the scarf was one of a limited edition of men's opera scarves, so when I was here a couple of weeks ago, I went to look for the box in the hallway—it was the one that jutted out because it was bigger than the others.'

He nodded again, remembering the box and its flourish of forget-me-nots, but still thrown by the account of the scarf.

'I didn't look further than the papers immediately under the scarf,' she said. 'There's much more, the box is full—but what I found was staggering.' She paused. 'It seems that just before Jim was taken ill, he received a parcel from someone trying to contact *you*.'

Edwyn held his breath, feeling his heart thumping in his chest, a vein twitching in his forehead. Anna saw his look of expectancy and placed her hand gently on his.

'You should prepare yourself Edwyn.'

He could see that she was struggling to find the right way to tell him something delicate.

'What is it?' he asked, his voice sounding hoarse and faint.

'For many years,' she said slowly and deliberately, 'your father tried to find you, but he had too little to go on. The man who wrote to Jim is Colin, your father's eldest son, your half-brother. He pursued the search and at last found Jim, hoping that he would know where you were.'

In an instant Edwyn recalled the hazy family photograph that David Demery had kept in his script. He gasped, but then his face clouded.

'My father's dead then?' he said, flatly.

Anna squeezed his hand.

'He is, I'm afraid,' she said gently.

She put her free hand on his shoulder.

'Colin sounds very kind—I read his letter—and he seems happy to share his memories of your father.'

She stood up and offered him her hand.

'Come on—I'll show you.'

She left him alone in the sitting room, urging him to take all the time he needed, before closing the door quietly behind her. He sat on the sofa staring at the box and for a moment, did no more than run his hand across the highly-decorated box and contemplate what he might be about to discover.

At last, he opened the lid and lifted out the scarf. He unfolded it carefully and studied it closely, turning it over and over in his hands, tracing the pattern with his fingers until something clicked in his head like the shutter of a camera and out of nowhere, threw him a picture from the past. In that momentary flash of memory, he saw two men, father and son, walking through a busy graveyard on a chilly April day, and a bunch of trumpet-shaped lilies with creamy white blossoms and lush green foliage lying at his mother's grave on what would have been her 80th birthday.

He read Colin's letter first, then David's, and afterwards could take in only a small part of what else the box contained—letters, photographs, postcards and sketches that Lily had sent to David and which he had kept until he died. That knowledge was hugely comforting, though it could not assuage the pain of learning that a series of cruel misadventures had befallen his father at the very moment when he and Lily were on the brink of life together, a life that he, too, would have been part of.

He folded away Lily's last letter. In the exhausted elation following the birth of her son, she had written to ask David to collect them, her tender description of her baby's bright blue eyes and downy fair hair almost unbearably poignant to read. He sighed as he slid the letter back into its crumpled envelope. She had addressed it in her flowing script to the New Theatre in Cardiff, but this had been crossed out in thick black ink and the Prince of Wales Theatre had been scrawled above in large capitals.

He returned the letter to the pile and retied the pink satin ribbon to hold the bundle together. If only, he thought, as he put them back into the box, she had not made that mistake and the letter had reached David earlier, might he have avoided that fateful Sunday journey?

He began tidying the rest of the papers away, feeling he could read no more today, and wanting to share what he'd learnt with Anna, lingering for a while over a colour photograph, included in the letter from his father, on the back of which someone had written *"Woodlawn Cemetery, Easter Sunday 2004."*

Chapter 53

Despite her apparent composure, Anna was discomforted by Edwyn's presence and the feelings it aroused. Sitting in the conservatory trying to read, she found it hard to concentrate, unsettled by the thought of him poring over remnants of his father's life, hoping to find the pieces missing from the jigsaw of his own. Knowing what revelations lay in store for him, she felt an unexpected desire to protect him, to forget his desertion of her and lend him tenderness and compassion. At the same time, though, she was saddened at the sight of him—as if he was in some way changed, diminished. She could not escape the thought that something she had once held precious had been spoilt and lost.

She had given up on her book and laid it aside when Edwyn came through and handed her two envelopes, the one she'd seen addressed *To my son* and another, larger one addressed *To my brother*. She looked up in surprise. It was clear he wanted her to open them.

'Which one shall I read first?' she asked.

'The one from Colin,' he replied bleakly.

There was no letter to accompany the contents—perhaps Colin had thought they would speak for themselves: an obituary of David Farrar in a local Cheshire newspaper and the order of service for his funeral in November 2005 at the Church of St James and St Paul in Marton.

'Oh Edwyn,' she said softly.

She read the newspaper cutting and then opened the order of service, interested to see what words and music had been chosen to mark David Farrar's passing.

'Did you see this Edwyn?' she cried, pointing. 'The readings were all given by grandchildren. You have nephews and nieces as well—a real family.'

Anna looked up to see his reaction, but he had turned away and was standing looking through the open door of the conservatory to the small courtyard garden. She returned the papers to their envelope and picked up the letter from David Farrar. As she slid it out of its envelope, a photograph fell out onto her lap. She glanced at it quickly before turning it over to read the inscription on the back. Frowning, she turned it over again and studied it more carefully: an elderly man wearing a dark overcoat, with a striking flash of colours at his neck, was standing tall and erect in front of a black marble headstone against which a bunch of white lilies had been laid.

She looked up, wide-eyed, and whispered: 'Your father?'

Edwyn nodded and sat down on the small wicker sofa beside her.

'At my mother's grave, on the same day I visited, two years ago. I saw him and Colin as they were leaving— something about them caught my eye, the scarf I guess...'

She looked again at the photo and back at Edwyn, trying to gauge how he was feeling, but his expression was inscrutable. She picked up the envelope.

'May I read it?' she asked.

'Of course,' he said.

She opened out the letter, the handwriting clearly that of an elderly hand, spindly and spidery, in places hard to decipher.

I realise this letter will come as a shock to you, but I hope that the people who brought you up, and who you will have known as your mother and father, will at least have told you something about your birth and confessed that they adopted you. I know nothing about the life you have lived and I guess you know nothing about mine, but I have never stopped wondering about you, hoping you were well cared for as a child and are happy as an adult with a family of your own.

I know I can never make amends for the years of absence and silence, but I have always wanted the chance to tell you what happened and ask for your understanding. When my wife died in 2001, I felt free to look for you, and as I face my final illness, it grieves me to know that I will never find you. If you are reading this, it will mean that my first-born son, Colin, your half-brother, has found you for me.

My name is David Farrar and I was born in Macclesfield at the end of the First World War. I began a degree in English at Birmingham University, but the next war intervened and off I went to fight. I lasted until 1944 when I caught a bad bout of malaria and was discharged from the army on medical grounds. While I was in Burma I got a taste for the stage and once I was home and well again, I decided to pursue a career as an actor. I was always on the move from one theatre to the next and this was a problem for my wife. You see, I'd got married early on in the war and had a son, Colin, but I found it hard to settle back into family life, and the nomadic existence was a convenient escape. We drifted apart and I moved out. Not long afterwards, I met Lily, your mother, who was a dresser at a theatre I was performing at.

She was lovely. I've put together all the photographs I have of her and I hope you'll agree she was a bonny lass. She was always smiling, always cheerful, and she was very artistic, had a real talent for art and design. We became sweethearts, but because I was on the road so much of the time, we relied on our letters to keep in touch between the times when we could be together. We celebrated Armistice Day together and it was then that she told me she was pregnant. We made plans for the future, but she didn't want anyone else to know about the baby until after it was born and we were a proper family, all above board. She went off to a home for unmarried mothers in North Wales to have you before moving to rooms in Criccieth, where the landlady was a friend. We'd agreed that I would come and collect you both at the end of my summer tour in Swansea. But nothing went to plan: you arrived a couple of weeks early and though she wrote to tell me this as soon as she could, she sent it to the wrong theatre in Cardiff, so there was a delay before I got the letter and could set off to north Wales. I gave in my notice after the Saturday night show, went back my digs to pack and set off by train at first light the next day. It was quite a journey in those days –it probably still is—and there were only a few trains on a Sunday, but I hoped I could get to Criccieth by nightfall. The day was hot and the engine overheated so we were stuck outside Craven Arms for several hours while they tried to make it safe to go forward. I knew that if I missed my connection at Shrewsbury, there might not be another that day. The rest of the journey was stop-start all the way—we were even delayed at one point by a flock of geese on the tracks. When we did eventually get to Shrewsbury, my connecting train had long gone and there was no alternative, but to find a hotel and stay the night and start off again the next morning.

So many times since then I've said "if only." If only I'd gone straight to the Lion Hotel by the station and spent a quiet evening there. But I didn't. I was hot and tired and thirsty and there were some squaddies on the train heading back to barracks after a few days' leave who were looking forward to a last night of freedom and were going out for a few drinks. If only I'd kept my mouth shut, but as soon as I said I was off to collect my newborn son, they insisted on me joining them, "to wet the baby's head" they said. They dragged me off to some dive they frequented and began pouring drink down me. After a few, I stopped complaining and got into the swing of it, but by closing time I was drunk and had nowhere to stay. The landlord was a useless drunkard, but his wife was a decent sort. She took pity on me and said I could sleep on a settle in the bar—he wouldn't let me sleep upstairs—and the last thing I remember is her leaving me a pillow and some blankets and saying goodnight. The next thing I knew I was being dragged from under a burning beam and could smell that my hair was on fire.

I was in a burns hospital in Birmingham for three months. They thought I might lose my sight—I didn't thank God—but I had burns to my body, my scalp and my neck. Though I had a fractured skull and bad concussion, I did remember where I'd been going and why. So as soon as I could travel again, I went there, hoping to find some trace of Lily, some forwarding address, but by then the place had been sold and the new owners hadn't yet moved in, leaving only an elderly caretaker in temporary charge.

I knew that Lily had a sister and brother-in-law she might have turned to for help, but I didn't know where they lived. I was at a loss, a dead end.

It may be hard for you to imagine or believe my desolation, how helpless and hopeless I felt. There were times I thought I might go mad with the guilt, the grief, the not knowing, In the end it was my wife Molly who saved me. She took me back and cared for me, even when she must have guessed I wanted to be somewhere else with someone else. In time, we had another child, a daughter, also Molly, and as I could not be any sort of father to you, I resolved to be a good father to her and Colin.

I gave up any notion of the stage and trained as a teacher. And overall, we had a good life. But though time does heal, I never got over the loss of Lily and my son. I never forgave myself for leaving her to think I'd abandoned her to fend for herself, alone, with a child.

It was a bitter blow to learn that she died so soon after you were born, but I was glad to be able to visit her grave on Easter Sunday a couple of years ago, and lay some flowers there for her. It would have been her 80th birthday.

I have wondered what her death meant for you and hope that you found kind and loving people to bring you up as their own and give you a good start in life.

I've no idea what you look like, who you take after. I cannot call you by your name—I don't know it —but I have always thought of you as my boy, my son.

And I send you my love.

When she had finished reading, she let the letter slip onto her lap and sat in silence, finding it unbearably poignant to visualise that elderly man, on the brink of death, opening his heart, seeking forgiveness from a son who might never be found.

'Thank you,' Edwyn said at last.

She looked at him in puzzlement.

'Thank you for saving Jim's boxes. I'm sorry I was so ungracious about it at the time. If you hadn't looked after them, they might have gone with the house clearers and I would never have known all this.'

Anna smiled.

'Jim made me promise to keep them,' she said. 'I was simply doing what he asked.'

'I know,' he said, 'but you did more than that. You cared enough to want to find the truth, to connect some of the clues.'

He swallowed hard and she saw that he was struggling to hold himself together.

'I'm truly grateful to you,' he said at last, his voice sounding thick and unsteady.

She took his hand and squeezed it.

'How do you feel?'

He shook his head.

'I don't really know yet,' he said, 'but…'

She waited.

'It's heart-breaking to learn that all the time I was looking for him, he was still alive, and that for some of that time, he was looking for me, too.'

'I know,' she said. 'That is hard to bear, but do you take comfort from the fact that he didn't intend to desert you and Lily? That it was chance, or rather misfortune, that threw them apart?'

'Yes,' Edwyn said slowly. 'I think it does help to know that.'

He didn't sound fully convinced, and she sensed he was still trying to find solace in that knowledge, to ward off the disappointment that he had been found too late.

'Right now,' he said, 'I'm left with a profound sense of the random nature of life.'

Anna nodded in agreement.

'But the good thing is you have a brother and a sister,' she said, 'and the brother certainly seems keen to welcome you into his life. That must mean something.'

Edwyn looked surprised, as if he had not fully registered the significance of these siblings and their families or begun to imagine how they might help him achieve some sort of acceptance and connectedness.

'What will you do next?' she asked at last.

He shook his head again and she held her breath, wondering if these revelations would change the way he saw the future, whether he might no longer feel the need to be alone, removed from all vestiges of his former life.

'I don't know yet. I'll need some time to let all this sink in.'

'Will you stay in North Wales?'

He looked bemused, as if the question was incomprehensible, the answer obvious, and then he flushed, as if he sensed what she was really asking.

'There's no going back to my former life,' he said. 'It's where I was born and for now, it's where I feel some rootedness.'

Anna turned her head away and bit her lip, aware he was watching her.

'I'm not asking for a second chance,' he said at last.

She turned to face him again.

'I used to look at you and think how lucky I was to have you in my life,' she said sadly. 'Now I think I would always be wondering what secrets you're keeping from me that you think are best kept to yourself.'

He flinched and she knew she'd hit a nerve.

'You're right,' he said. 'I used my pain and confusion to withdraw, to pull away from you. I was frightened to talk about how I was feeling in case it exposed my fragility.'

'I feel our marriage was tested and found wanting. That's disappointing, it makes me sad.'

'It's easy to define a relationship by its end,' he replied with a hint of defiance, 'but it was good at the beginning wasn't it?'

'Yes, it was,' she said bitterly, 'but I still can't get over how quickly what we had fell apart.'

She was shocked at how harsh her words sounded, but before she could say sorry he put his head in his hands and began to weep. Horrified, she moved closer to him and put her arms around him, pulling him towards her.

'Oh Edwyn, I'm so sorry. Forgive me.'

He pulled away, struggling to control himself. His face was damp with tears and he fumbled in his pocket for a handkerchief and blew his nose. When he spoke again, his voice was thick with emotion.

'Anna, my darling girl, you have absolutely nothing to apologise for. It's all my fault—I think I must have faulty wiring—I've never really known what family love is, or how to go about it.'

The endearment—and the admission—had taken her off guard and she felt a catch in her throat. He turned to face her and she adjusted her position, allowing him to take hold of both her hands in his.

'The thing is, Anna,' he said. 'People can't give you what they don't have to give. And you deserve better.'

He squeezed her hands and smiled at her, reminding her of all the many smiles that had won her heart all those years ago. But she understood what he was saying and knew she had to accept that he was altered now and his detachment was final.

Chapter 54

They sat for seemingly ages in silence, huddled together on the sofa, holding hands, both clinging to some last moments of closeness, before Edwyn eased himself up and said he should make a move, insisting that he would drive back to North Wales that evening.

'It's too far to go today,' she said with concern. 'Why not stay here tonight and leave first thing tomorrow?'

'That's kind of you Anna, but I need to get away.'

'I understand,' she said, unsure whether she was relieved or disappointed, and realising their other decisions would have to wait for another day. 'But at least think of breaking your journey somewhere on route.'

She followed him as he went to collect the box of papers from the sitting room. She waited in the doorway as he opened the lid and placed the two envelopes in the folds of the scarf.

'You know,' he said, looking round at her. 'I recognise the name of that church, the one where David was buried.'

'Really?' she said with surprise.

'It was restored in the nineteenth century by William Butterfield, the architect of Myddleton.'

'Fancy that!'

'It's the oldest timber-framed church still in use in Europe.'

He brightened.

'Perhaps I'll head towards Marton and stay somewhere round there tonight. I could visit the grave in the morning.'

Anna stepped towards him and rubbed his arm affectionately.

'So much to take in,' she murmured.

Edwyn nodded.

'Not just for me either,' he said.

Anna looked quizzical.

'Well, Colin and Molly have had to come to terms with the fact their father had a secret in his past, another life, and a son to show for it.'

With the unwieldy box clutched under one arm and Anna edging past him to open the front door, the hallway was too small, and their nearness felt awkward and upsetting. As if he sensed this, Edwyn hurried out, only to stop on the doorstep, where he leaned towards her and kissed her lightly on the cheek. She held his shoulders gently, until he turned away and walked towards his car.

The house felt hollow and cheerless without him, as if it, too, knew that something had changed. She wandered listlessly from room to room, looking for distraction, hoping for consolation, finding none. She went at last to sit on her bed, the copy of *No Name* still there on the bedside table, now finished and waiting to be taken back to Edwyn's study. She gave a wry shrug, knowing that he did at last have a name he could call his own.

She looked at her watch: it was early, not yet five o'clock, and the summer's day was still young enough to enjoy. From somewhere within her, she felt a rush of energy, a desire to strike out and see where it would lead. She picked up the book and went next door to return it to Edwyn's large collection of Wilkie Collins novels. As she found its place on the bookshelf behind his desk, she replayed in her head what he'd said when he thanked her: that she had cared enough to search for the truth.

And she saw this now as her final gift of love for him; and hoped that freeing him to make of it what he might, would enable her to move on with her own life.

She made her way downstairs and stood for a moment undecided, her eyes dazzled by the sunlight streaming through the porthole window and dancing off the rainbow colours of Jim's boxes. She checked her watch again; he would not yet be home from work; might be busy that evening, with plans already made.

Should she call him first, she wondered, or simply take a chance and turn up unannounced? Sixty miles, not far to drive. She could be there in just over an hour.

As she grabbed her bag and her jacket, she blushed, thinking he might laugh and tease her, say that, like Bathsheba, she had at last come courting Mr Oak.